GOOD MORNING

MR. TAYLOR

The World is on Fire

Written By Nick Simoneschi

CHAPTER 1

The tranquility of Nick Taylor's den was obliterated in an instant as a deafening roar tore through the apartment, transforming his sanctuary into a hellscape of fire and fury. The blast sent a tremor through the building's very bones, and for a split second, the world hinged on the brink of chaos.

As the initial shockwave subsided, the air thickened with dust and the acrid tang of smoke, signaling destruction's aftermath. Nick's collection of antique maps, once meticulously framed and mounted on the walls, now lay in tatters amid a sea of broken glass that glittered like treacherous diamonds on the floor. The mahogany bookshelves, a testament to Nick's intellectual pursuits, were eviscerated, their contents—a melange of classic literature and espionage treatises—scattered and singed, the wisdom they held seeping away like blood from a wound.

The windows, which had offered panoramic views of the city's skyline, were now gaping maws; the curtains that had fluttered gently in the evening breeze just moments before were ablaze, their fabric curling and blackening as they succumbed to the flames. It was a cruel mockery of the domestic order Nick had so painstakingly cultivated since his retirement—a life far removed from the cloak-and-dagger existence of his past, yet still haunted by its specters.

Amidst the disarray, the elegant lines of his mid-century modern furniture were obscured by plaster and debris, the carefully chosen palette of neutral tones now marred by the brutal intrusion of violence. The air itself seemed to scream in silent agony, heavy with the stench of smoldering wood and the chemical bite of explosives—a scent all too familiar to a man who had spent years navigating the treacherous terrain of geopolitical intrigue.

Nick had always prided himself on being prepared for any eventuality, but no amount of training could have readied him for this moment of raw vulnerability within his own home. His personal oasis, once a bulwark against the outside world, was violated in the blink of an eye, leaving only ruin and the bitter taste of betrayal lingering amidst the swirling smoke.

The shock wave hit him like a freight train. Nick Taylor's instincts didn't falter; years of CIA fieldwork had honed his reflexes to near preternatural sharpness. His body moved before his mind fully processed the chaos—a dive to the floor, an arm flung protectively over his head, as if the sinew and bone could shield him from the devastation that rained down.

His apartment, once a meticulously arranged sanctuary with its sleek lines and thoughtfully curated collection of antiques, was now a battlefield. The explosion had torn through his fortress of solitude, obliterating the tranquility he had fostered in his retirement. In the split-second of respite, Nick's analytical gaze swept across the room. The remnants of his shattered life lay strewn about—books that chronicled history's greatest strategists, glass from what had been an impressive display of first edition novels—now shards beneath his palms, cutting into flesh that had already seen too many battles.

Then, gravity yanked at his core, sending him sprawling as the building trembled under the force of the blast. Years etched onto his visage were suddenly made manifest as he stumbled, a momentary lapse that betrayed the stoicism he wore like armor. Nick, the tall, grizzled veteran, who carried himself with the assurance of one who had navigated perilous geopolitical landscapes, fell hard against the cool, herringbone-patterned hardwood floor that had been warmed earlier by the late afternoon sun.

Disorientation clouded his vision, the room spinning—a carousel of fire-licked walls and upturned furniture. The air hummed with the deafening silence that follows catastrophe, punctuated only by the distant wail of alarms and the crackling of flames feasting upon his past. He lay there, dazed, amidst the ruins of his own making, the taste of dust and betrayal thick in his mouth.

Nick's world, once defined by the certainties of duty and allegiance, now lay as fragmented as the pieces of his blown-out windows. As consciousness threatened to flee, the indomitable will that had carried him through countless covert operations clawed its way back. He had to move, to think, to survive. This was no time for weakness—not when every second could mean the difference between life and death. With effort, he pushed away the fog encroaching upon his senses, his pulse a drumbeat calling him back to the fight.

It was a grotesque tableau set within the confines of what was once a haven of intellectual pursuit and physical well-being, now twisted into a grim landscape of destruction. Nick Taylor, survivor, would need every ounce of his formidable spirit to rise from the ashes of this onslaught. But first, he had to get off the ground.

Nick's narrowed gaze struggled to pierce through the billowing smoke as he fought to prop himself against the remnants of his shattered bookshelf. The once orderly collection of intelligence tomes and geopolitical treatises lay strewn across the floor, their pages fluttering in the harsh wind that now invaded the sanctum of his apartment. As if awakening from a nightmare, Nick's ears tuned into the pandemonium beyond his fractured walls.

Shouts ricocheted through the smog-laden air—a symphony of fear and confusion—as neighbors spilled out into the hallway, their voices climbing over one another in a desperate plea for comprehension. The elderly Mrs. Henley from next door was screeching for her missing cat, while Mr. Kowalski, the Polish war veteran, barked orders with a military sharpness dulled only by age. Young couples clutched each other, their eyes wide with the terror of the unexplained. Each individual, a story halted mid-sentence by the explosive intrusion.

Through the gaping wound where his window once stood, the unmistakable flash of emergency lights painted the night in urgent strokes of red and blue. Sirens wailed—a modern-day overture to disaster—as they cut through the city's cacophony, announcing the arrival of first responders trained for moments like these.

Paramedics burst into the scene like a well-orchestrated troop; their movements precise and deliberate amidst the chaos. They were clad in navy uniforms, badges of service shining amidst the debris. Their faces, etched with lines of concentration and purpose, remained stoic as they navigated the labyrinth of destruction Nick's home had become.

"Sir, can you hear me?" one of them asked, a young woman with determined eyes that belied her calm demeanor. Her partner, a broad-shouldered man with a buzz cut that spoke of military precision, scanned the room for dangers even as he knelt beside Nick.

"Stay still, we've got you," the man's voice was a low rumble, a grounding force in the disarray. They worked in tandem, assessing Nick's injuries with swift, practiced motions, the urgency of their task apparent in the quick exchange of medical jargon.

"Possible concussion, lacerations, need C-spine," the woman relayed to her team outside, her hands steady as she secured a cervical collar around Nick's neck.

"BP is dropping." Concern flickered in the man's eyes as he wrapped a blood pressure cuff around Nick's arm with an efficiency that came from years of saving lives in the golden hour.

As oxygen flowed through a mask placed carefully over his face, Nick's mind wrestled with fragments of memory—flashes of his training, his missions, the faces of those he trusted. He could not afford the luxury of yielding to pain or fear. Even now, as gentle yet firm hands immobilized him on a stretcher, his instincts screamed at him to rise, to evade, to counterattack.

But his body betrayed him, sinking further into the grasp of forced vulnerability as the paramedics whisked him away from the remnants of his battle-scarred refuge. The last thing Nick saw before succumbing to the darkness was the ceiling passing by in a blur—each crack and imperfection a testament to the fragility of life and the deceptive quietude of the night that had so violently been shattered.

CHAPTER 2

The wail of sirens pierced the night, a relentless cry that heralded urgency and dread. Red and blue lights strobed across the jagged remnants of Nick Taylor's apartment as the ambulance cut through the chaos of the city. With each sharp turn and sudden acceleration, the paramedics inside worked to maintain their balance and focus on their patient. Nick lay strapped to the gurney, his usually stoic face now etched with lines of pain and confusion, the graying tufts of his hair matted with blood.

Buildings, mere silhouettes against the dark sky, blurred past the vehicle's windows. The sprawling metropolis was a hive of life, but within the speeding ambulance, it felt like an isolated microcosm where every second counted and every decision could mean the difference between life and death.

Upon arrival at the hospital, the back doors of the ambulance burst open, and Nick was immediately engulfed in the fluorescent-lit frenzy of the emergency room. White-coated figures moved with a sense of purpose that betrayed no uncertainty. The sterile smell of antiseptic mingled with the metallic tang of blood, creating an atmosphere that was both clinical and charged with tension.

"Trauma team to bay three!" barked a nurse, her voice cutting through the din. She was a middle-aged woman with keen eyes that missed nothing— a seasoned veteran of countless crises, her demeanor unflappable despite the pressure.

Nick was wheeled rapidly down the hallway, the wheels of the gurney humming against the polished floor. The doctors and nurses surrounding him were a blur of motion, checking vitals, calling out observations, and preparing for immediate intervention. One doctor, a young man with intense brown eyes and a steady hand, inserted an IV line with practiced ease, his mind already cataloging the steps to stabilize his patient.

"Multiple contusions, probable internal injuries," he stated, his voice detached and analytical, yet betraying a hint of empathy. He was the type who thrived in the eye of the storm—intellectual, yet intuitively attuned to the human element of his work.

"Let's get a CT scan stat," commanded another, her authoritative tone slicing through the chatter. She was tall and athletic, the kind of person who ran marathons before sunrise—a force of nature in scrubs.

As they transferred Nick onto the ER bed, the overhead lights glared down unforgivingly, highlighting the severity of his injuries. His world had been reduced to this moment, to these faces marked by concentration and determination, to the hands that moved with swift precision to save what remained of his life.

The walls of the trauma room were lined with cabinets filled with medical instruments and supplies, everything meticulously organized to facilitate rapid access in moments just like this. Monitors beeped insistently as they tracked Nick's faltering vital signs, adding their electronic voice to the symphony of survival being orchestrated around him.

"Stay with us, Mr. Taylor," urged a nurse, her voice a blend of command and encouragement. It was clear she was accustomed to pushing through adversity, her spirit undiminished even amidst the stark realities of the ER.

In the chaos of the emergency room, action was currency, and hesitation was an unaffordable luxury. Here, in the midst of beeping machines and swirling white coats, Nick's fate hung suspended, a precarious balance of skill, knowledge, and the indomitable will to live.

CHAPTER 3

The steady beep of a heart monitor punctuated the tense silence in the ICU, where a small cluster of solemn-faced individuals stood by a bed. The figure on the bed lay motionless, his face ashen against the stark white of the hospital pillow. Nick Taylor, once a bastion of strength and determination, was now enveloped in a cocoon of tubes and wires—a silent testament to the fragility of life.

"Coma," the doctor spoke, the word cutting through the heavy air like a scalpel—clinical, precise, irrefutable. Dressed in a white coat that bore the emblem of years of medical dedication, he addressed the figures whose eyes were all fixed on him, searching for a sliver of hope in his somber expression. "It's difficult to say when—or if—he'll wake up. The next 48 hours are critical."

A woman, her face lined with the subtle signs of a life spent deciphering the world's most guarded secrets, clasped her hands tightly. She was the embodiment of poise under pressure, yet the tremor in her fingers betrayed her inner turmoil. Standing beside her, a man whose posture spoke of military precision fought to maintain his composure, his jaw set in a hard line.

"Nick's strong," the woman murmured more to herself than the others, an attempt at summoning the positive thinking that had been a guiding principle in their clandestine operations.

Inside Nick's mind, the darkness was pierced by shards of light—fragmented memories flickering like old film reels. There was the scent of rain on cobblestones, a mosaic of faces he once knew, and the echo of a laugh that felt both foreign and achingly familiar. Images of narrow European alleyways, the burnished glow of a sunset over a desert landscape, and the adrenaline surge of a chase blurred together in a kaleidoscope of his past.

But it was the flash before the explosion that haunted the fringes of his consciousness—a blinding, searing moment that sought to claim everything he was and once had been. His thoughts clawed for clarity, desperate to reconstruct the narrative that led to this sterile room of hushed voices and beeping machinery.

"His vitals are stable for now," the doctor continued, his words underscored by the rhythmic hiss of the ventilator. "We've done all we can at this point. It's a waiting game."

As the group absorbed the gravity of the situation, they formed a silent pact, an unspoken agreement to stand vigil, to be the keepers of the flame for a man who had always carried the torch for them. In this sterile sanctuary of healing, surrounded by the hum of life-preserving devices, they waited—for a sign, for a miracle, for Nick Taylor to come back to them.

Nick's eyelids fluttered, the sterile light of the hospital room piercing through the darkness that had cradled him in its depths. His first breath was a gasping, ragged draw that clawed at his throat, each subsequent inhale an echo of pain. Awareness crept in slowly, a cruel and unwelcome intruder. The world swam into focus, a bleached palette of whites and blues framed by the stark geometry of ceiling tiles and medical equipment.

His body felt foreign, a leaden weight that refused to obey the commands of his mind. Panic rose as he tried to move, but his limbs betrayed him, bound by a paralysis that seemed more than physical. He struggled against the restraints of bandages and tubing, the beeping monitors crescendoing in response to his rising heartbeat.

"Mr. Taylor, try to remain still," came a voice, calm yet distant. "You're in a hospital. You've been in a coma."

The words carried a gravity he could not grasp, slipping through the cracks of his shattered memory like sand through desperate fingers. Nick's eyes darted around the room, searching for something—anything—that might anchor him to reality. But the faces that hovered within his field of vision belonged to strangers, their features etched with clinical concern rather than personal connection.

"Wha—" His voice was a croak, unfamiliar to his own ears. His thoughts raced, frantic for a foothold amidst the disarray. Yet there was nothing—no recollection of the life he'd lived, no identity to claim as his own. Only a profound sense of disorientation and loss, as if he were adrift in a sea of white coats and antiseptic scents without a compass or a destination.

"Your memory may return in time," one of the doctors offered, a touch of optimism threaded through her professional detachment. "For now, let's focus on your recovery."

Nick's gaze settled on the window, the view obscured by the gauzy curtain that did little to mask the silhouette of the city beyond. It was a skyline that should have stirred recognition, a landscape he had navigated with confidence and purpose, but now it was just a jigsaw missing too many pieces.

As the medical team bustled around him, their actions efficient and rehearsed, Nick lay back against the pillow, his mind a blank canvas smeared with the residue of fear and frustration. He was a ghost in his own life, haunting the corridors of a past that refused to reveal itself.

Nick staring at the ceiling, each square tile a reminder of the order and structure he desperately needed to reconstruct. The unknown loomed large, an abyss waiting to be filled with the fragments of a life blown apart. He would have to learn to navigate this new existence, to piece together the puzzle that was his identity, and to unearth the truth hidden in the shadow of the blast that had almost claimed him.

Amidst the steady hum of machinery and the soft whispers of attending nurses, a singular determination took root in the depths of Nick's being. He would remember. He would uncover the layers of deceit and betrayal that had led to this moment. And when he did, those responsible for the explosion that had wiped clean the slate of his life would have nowhere to hide.

CHAPTER 4

The glare of the mid-morning sun reflected off the sliding glass doors as Martin De Simone stepped into the antiseptic chill of St. Andrews Hospital. His eyes, accustomed to deciphering shadows for threats, quickly adjusted to the bleach-scented brightness. The walls were painted a muted beige, artwork depicting tranquil landscapes hung at precise intervals, and the floor bore the sheen of relentless polishing. Despite the calm colors, there was an undercurrent of urgency that pulsed through the corridors like an unseen heartbeat.

Martin's leather shoes clicked against the tile, his steps purposeful, betraying none of the apprehension that tightened the muscles beneath his tailored suit. He had worn a navy blazer, the fabric stretching slightly over his broad shoulders, a nod to both formality and freedom of movement should the need arise. His short, dark hair was neatly combed, though one could imagine it might seldom fall out of place, even in a scuffle.

The hospital staff weaved through the halls and waiting areas: nurses in scrubs patterned with cartoon characters aimed to comfort, doctors donning white coats that whispered authority, and orderlies maneuvering gurneys with practiced ease. Their faces were etched with focus, and their movements spoke of a choreography honed by countless life-and-death performances.

Martin, ever the observer, noted the slight tremble of a young nurse's hand as she administered an injection – the kind that spoke of either too much caffeine or too little sleep. An older doctor paused to adjust his glasses, eyes weary yet sharp behind the lenses, hinting at a mind that cataloged symptoms and conjured diagnoses with relentless precision.

As he passed the reception desk, the air buzzed with the low hum of hushed conversations and the tap-tap-tapping of keyboards. Martin offered a curt nod to the receptionist, her blonde hair pulled back in a bun so tight it seemed to pull the skin taut across her high cheekbones, a testament to the control she exerted over her little domain of clipboards and insurance forms.

He knew that beyond this façade of routine medical care, danger lurked in the sterile shadows. His friend, Nick, lay somewhere within these walls, and with every step, Martin reaffirmed his resolve to shield him from the peril that clawed at their heels. It was a familiar dance for Martin, this mingling of intellect and instinct, the two forces intertwining to form the unbreakable threads of his determination.

Today, within this citadel of healing, he wasn't just a visitor. He was a guardian, cloaked not in armor but in solemn conviction.

Martin's boots clicked a staccato rhythm on the polished hospital floor, echoing through the labyrinthine corridors that smelled of antiseptic and carried an undercurrent of barely suppressed urgency. His eyes navigated the signage with the precision of a trained operative, each turn he took calculated and swift. The bright fluorescent lighting above cast a clinical glow on the pale green walls, reflecting off the laminated notices about patient care and hygiene standards.

His hand brushed against the textured wallpaper as he moved, feeling the raised patterns beneath his fingertips—an unconscious tallying of distance to his destination. He passed by a nurses' station where charts were aligned with meticulous care, a stark contrast to the tumult churning in Martin's chest.

Turning another corner, he came upon a series of rooms, their doors slightly ajar, offering glimpses into the private battles fought within. A janitor pushed a cart laden with cleaning supplies, its wheels whispering secrets along the corridor.

Martin spared the man only a fleeting glance, his attention honed on the numbers ascending above each doorway.

Then, there it was: Room 1317. Nick's room. Martin exhaled a breath he hadn't realized he'd been holding, a silent prayer of thanks that he had arrived undetected. Through the small window on the door, he saw Nick lying propped up in bed, his face paler than usual but still possessing the resolute lines forged from years in the field.

Martin pushed the door open gently, the faint squeak of hinges sounding thunderous in his ears. He stepped inside, his gaze locked onto Nick's, conveying a wordless plea for trust. The room was adorned with the sterile touch of efficiency—beeping monitors, crisp white linens, and a single vase of flowers that seemed out of place amidst the machinery.

"Nick," Martin began, his voice low and steady, "we need to talk. It's important." The gravity of his tone was meant to bridge the gap between them, to stitch together comrade and confidant in the span of a heartbeat.

Despite the relief that washed over him at finding Nick unharmed, the weight of what they faced pressed down upon Martin like a tangible force. He stood at the foot of the bed, his posture rigid with the burden of protection, his eyes never leaving Nick's. The message was clear in his unwavering stare: he would go to any lengths to keep his friend safe. This was more than duty; this was the unspoken vow of soldiers who had weathered storms side by side.

This was a promise that he would guard Nick Taylor's life with his own.

Martin leaned forward, arms braced against the cool metal railing of Nick's hospital bed. His dark eyes scanned his friend's face for signs of understanding. "Someone put a target on your back, Nick," he said, the urgency of his message sharpening his features. "This isn't paranoia—it's intel."

Nick's reaction was muted, his mind still foggy from medication. He propped himself up slightly, squinting at Martin through weary eyes that struggled to focus. The graying hair around his temples seemed more pronounced in the bleak lighting of the room, and his athletic frame, though confined to the bed, tensed with an ingrained instinct to confront danger.

"Intel?" Nick's voice was gravelly, skepticism woven into the single word like thread through fabric. "You're saying this is real? Not just some drug-induced nightmare?"

"Real as it gets," Martin replied, his tone insistent yet laced with compassion. He reached out, placing a firm hand on Nick's shoulder. "I wouldn't be here if it wasn't. We've been through hell together. You think I'd drag you into another mess without damn good reason?"

The sterile glow from the overhead lights cast stark shadows across the room, creating a contrast that seemed to mirror the dichotomy in their situation—clarity versus uncertainty, safety versus peril. Martin watched as confusion played across Nick's face, the lines of strain deepening as he attempted to piece together the fragmented reality presented to him.

"Martin," Nick started, his skepticism yielding to the edge of concern, "if what you're saying is true, why am I still breathing? Why hit me now, after all these years out of the game?"

"Good questions," Martin conceded, his expression taut with thought. "Questions we need answers to. But right now, the priority is keeping you alive long enough to find them." His words were deliberate, each syllable underscored by the gravity of the situation.

Nick's gaze drifted towards the window where the first hints of dawn cast a soft light on the world outside. It seemed distant, untouchable—a normalcy that felt leagues away from the covert existence they once lived. Yet, as his mind cleared, the familiar stirrings of caution and resolve began to surface. Old habits, it seemed, died hard.

"Okay," Nick said at last, the skepticism in his voice receding like a tide going out. "Let's hear it then. What's the play, Martin?"

Martin's lips curved into a half-smile, relief mingling with determination. "First, we get you out of here. Then, we start connecting the dots."

A silent oath hung between them, as potent as any spoken vow. They were in this together now—against the looming shadow of an unseen enemy, ready to plunge once more into the clandestine world that never truly released its grip on them.

CHAPTER 5

Martin leaned forward in the sterile white chair of the hospital room, his dark eyes scanning Nick's face for signs of acceptance. "Elms," he began, his voice low and steady, a contrast to the beeping monitors and distant chatter of the medical ward. "There's a chalet there—secluded, off the beaten path. Belongs to an asset we used back in '06."

Nick's brow furrowed as he processed the information, the sterile scent of antiseptic pervading his senses. He was still dressed in the hospital gown, its papery texture a stark reminder of his vulnerability.

"Switzerland?" Nick questioned, his tone reflecting both surprise and a hint of admiration at Martin's acumen. "How do you plan to get me out of here without raising alarms?"

"Private transport. Ambulance on the outside, but armored to the teeth," Martin said, reaching into his jacket pocket to reveal a set of forged transit papers. "Driver's one of ours. Trustworthy."

"Armored ambulance to La Guardia" Nick mused, a ghost of a smile tugging at his lips despite the gravity of their situation. It was classic Martin, always two steps ahead, with a meticulous eye for detail that had saved their skins more than once.

"Private jet to Frankfurt, there we switch to a Eurocopter—waiting in a private hangar. It's been scrubbed clean, untraceable." Martin unfolded a detailed map of their route across Europe, spread it across the small over-bed table, and pointed to a series of checkpoints they'd clear. "We'll be ghosts."

"Resourceful as ever," Nick acknowledged, pushing himself up from the bed with a grimace. His athletic frame was leaner now, age and injury conspiring against him, but the determination in his eyes was undimmed.

"Always," Martin replied with a wry grin as he helped Nick into a set of civilian clothes—neutral colors, functional fabrics, and no labels. Dressed now, Nick looked less like a patient and more like the operative he once was.

With one last sweep of the room, ensuring nothing was left behind, Martin slipped a Beretta M9A3, silenced pistol into Nick's hand. The weapon was unassuming but deadly—a perfect embodiment of the man who now gripped it.

"Ready?" Martin asked, his gaze locking with Nick's. "Let's move," Nick responded, pocketing the firearm.

They exited the room, blending seamlessly with the flow of nurses and doctors. Martin, every bit the part of a concerned visitor, kept his posture relaxed yet alert. Nick, leaning slightly into the role of a convalescing man, followed suit.

Together, they navigated the labyrinth of hospital corridors until they reached the back service entrance where the ambulance awaited. Its engine hummed quietly, the driver—a woman with sharp features and hawk-like eyes—gave them a subtle nod.

"Nicole," Martin introduced briefly as they loaded Nick onto the stretcher. Her hands were steady, her movements efficient as she secured him in place.

"Nice to meet you," Nick grunted, playing his part as the rear doors shut, cloaking them in privacy.

The ambulance pulled away, its siren silent, lights dormant. From the outside, it was just another vehicle on the streets, but inside, every inch was engineered for survival and evasion.

"Next stop, Elms," Martin murmured, peering through the tinted windows at the cityscape sliding by. Nick closed his eyes, not in fear, but in preparation. The game was afoot again, and this time, the stakes were as personal as they got.

CHAPTER 6

Nick Taylor's consciousness swam back to him like a cautious fish approaching bait. He blinked open his eyes, immediately squinting against the soft glow of morning light that filtered through the room. Disoriented, he lifted his head from the pillow, taking in his surroundings with the meticulous caution of a man who had learned never to trust an unfamiliar ceiling.

He was lying on a luxurious king-sized bed, its linens crisp and cool against his skin. The chalet's bedroom exuded rustic elegance—exposed wooden beams above hinted at architectural tradition, while the contemporary art adorning the walls whispered modern sophistication. Nick noted the thick carpet beneath his bare feet as he swung them over the edge of the bed, its plushness a stark contrast to the cold, unforgiving floors of safe houses he'd known in the past.

Confusion knotted in his stomach. How did he get here? His last memory was the muted cadence of the ambulance's engine, Martin's silent profile set against the blur of the city. No sign of struggle, no memory of transition—just the sudden thrust from one reality into another.

Standing up, Nick moved toward the window, muscles tense, gaze sharp. He parted the heavy curtains, revealing a breathtaking view of the Swiss Alps. Their jagged peaks stood sentinel around the chalet, their presence a natural fortress. Here, amidst these titans of rock and ice, he found an unexpected sense of safety. Isolation played to his advantage; only those with intent and resources could find him in such seclusion.

The chalet itself was a blend of grandeur and fortress-like security. The furniture was opulent, yet not ostentatious, crafted from fine woods that held the warmth of the sun. Antiques were placed with careful consideration around the room, each piece telling a story of craftsmanship and time. The space was not just designed for comfort, but for defense—the windows, though generous in offering views of the outside world, were reinforced, a subtle reminder of the chalet's true purpose.

Despite the uncertainty that gnawed at him, Nick couldn't help but acknowledge the thoughtfulness behind the choice of this sanctuary. It spoke of Martin's understanding of both luxury and strategy—a place where one could rest and plan simultaneously. In the quietude of the chalet, away from prying eyes and ears, secrets could be kept, and strategies formed.

With a deep breath, Nick let his trained eyes sweep the room once more, cataloging potential threats or escape routes out of sheer habit. Assured of his immediate safety, he acknowledged the need to understand the full picture. Martin would have answers, and together, they would forge their next move.

For now, Nick allowed himself a moment to appreciate the silence, the peace that came with high-altitude solitude. There would be time enough for action, for the chessboard of espionage awaited no man. But in this brief interlude, Nick Taylor, retired CIA spy, found solace in a world away from cloak and dagger—at least until the game called him back to play.

CHAPTER 7

Nick's eyes found focus as the door to the chalet clicked open, and Martin De Simone stepped through—a solid presence against the backdrop of sleek wood and frosted glass. His friend wore a casual Armani V-neck sweater that did little to hide the physique of a man who had never truly left the rigor of agency life behind. Martin's dark hair was tousled from what Nick assumed was the crisp Alpine breeze, and his jaw set with a determination that had always been his most defining feature.

"Good to see you awake, brother," Martin said, his voice carrying the faintest trace of an Italian accent that tightened with concern. He approached the bed where Nick sat propped up against a mountain of pillows, their textures as rich and varied as the life he'd left behind.

"Martin..." Nick's voice was rough, not just from sleep but from a tangle of emotions he wasn't ready to unravel. The word was an anchor, something familiar in a sea of unsettling disorientation.

"Listen, Nick, I know this is hard to process," Martin began, settling into a chair beside the bed, his posture relaxed, yet alert—always the operative. "But we had to get you out of there. It's not safe for you in the hospital."

"Safe?" Nick echoed, his gaze sharpening as old instincts began to stir within him. "What aren't you telling me?"

"Someone wants you dead," Martin stated plainly, his eyes holding Nick's with unflinching honesty. "I don't have all the details yet, but I'm working on it. And until I do, this chalet—" he gestured to the luxurious expanse around them, "—is our fortress."

The room spoke of careful selection—the kind of place that would impress a diplomat or a visiting dignitary. The walls were adorned with antique ski equipment and black-and-white photographs of the mountains in times gone by, while the modern furniture gave a nod to comfort without sacrificing style. It was clear that Martin had chosen this location not just for its security features, but for the tranquility it offered—an acknowledgment of the toll their line of work took on the soul.

Nick absorbed the gravity of Martin's words, feeling the weight of their shared history settle around him like a cloak. "Why didn't I see this coming?"

"Because you're human, Nick." Martin's tone softened. "You've spent a lifetime looking over your shoulder, but you're allowed to let your guard down sometimes. That's what friends are for."

"Friends," Nick murmured. The concept felt strangely foreign after years of compartmentalizing every relationship. But here was Martin, the embodiment of loyalty and camaraderie, risking everything for him.

"Damn it, Martin. If they're after me, they'll come after you too," Nick said, the worry lines at his temples deepening.

"Let them try," Martin replied, a wry smile tugging at the corner of his mouth. "I've still got a few tricks up my sleeve. Besides, protecting each other is what we do. You would have done the same for me."

A silent agreement passed between them, as palpable as the chill that seeped in from the snow-covered pines outside. Nick nodded slowly, the skepticism that had clouded his thoughts beginning to dissipate. In its place grew a profound sense of gratitude, warming him against the alpine cold.

"Thank you," he said at last, his voice firmer now. "For getting me out, for...for being here."

"Always," Martin assured him, clapping a hand on Nick's shoulder with a familiarity that spoke of countless shared dangers and triumphs. "Now, let's focus on keeping you alive so you can thank me properly with a bottle of that scotch you keep hidden away."

"Deal," Nick agreed, a ghost of a smile crossing his features. Trust, once given, was unshakable between men like them. And as the light faded from the day, casting long shadows across the polished floors of the chalet, Nick Taylor knew that with Martin De Simone at his side, the game was far from over.

CHAPTER 8

The gentle crackle of the fireplace punctuated the silence, casting a warm glow over the two men sitting opposite each other. Nick Taylor lounged in an armchair that seemed to envelop his tall, athletic frame. The years had etched lines into his face, but they only served to enhance the sharpness of his gaze, reflecting a lifetime of strategic thinking and covert operations. His graying hair, once as dark as midnight, now bore witness to his experience and age. Yet, even in repose, he exuded an air of readiness, like a seasoned predator at ease but never truly off guard.

Martin De Simone sat across from him, his short dark hair and muscular build a testament to a disciplined regime that had not slackened with desk work or retirement. He wore a simple sweater and khakis, the kind of attire that would blend seamlessly into any European crowd. Intelligence sparkled in his eyes, a reminder that beneath his casual appearance lay a calculating mind, always working, always analyzing.

"Nick," Martin began, breaking the comfortable silence. "We can't stay in this chalet forever. We need to figure out who's behind this threat."

Nick nodded pensively, the ghost of a smile fading as his mind shifted gears. "I know. But we're flying blind here. Whoever's after me has resources and patience. We need a solid lead before we make a move."

"Agreed," Martin said, leaning forward, elbows on knees. His demeanor was earnest, his tone conveying the gravity of their situation. "But consider this: they tried to take you out in broad daylight, in a city swarming with witnesses. That's bold. Desperate, even. It suggests they might be closer to achieving their goal than we'd like."

"Which means time isn't on our side," Nick concluded, his analytical mind piecing together the implications. "We have to go on the offensive, smoke them out."

"Exactly." Martin's lips formed a thin line, a reflection of his deep-seated belief in justice and protecting those who no longer had the agency to protect themselves. "I've still got contacts that owe me favors—people who don't pop up on regular radars. We gather intelligence, find out what's changed in the game since you left."

"Contacts," Nick echoed thoughtfully. The firelight danced in his eyes as memories of old alliances and covert exchanges filtered through his consciousness. "We'll need to be cautious; trust is a luxury we can't afford right now."

"Of course," Martin affirmed, understanding all too well the high stakes of the espionage world they had once navigated daily. "But it's a start. And if there's anyone who can sift truth from deceit, it's you."

"Then it's settled." Nick stood, stretching his limbs, feeling the weight of the coming challenge settle upon his shoulders. "Tomorrow, we start making calls. Tonight, we rest and regroup. After all," he added, a playful edge returning to his voice, "you still owe me that bottle of scotch."

"Deal," Martin replied, standing to match his friend's height. "But first, let's secure this place for the night. We've managed to dodge their sights so far, but I'm not taking any chances."

"Neither am I," Nick agreed.

As the last light of day faded beyond the snow-lined windows of the secluded chalet, the two men set about reinforcing their sanctuary. They moved with methodical precision, checking locks, setting subtle alarms—a dance they had performed countless times in countless locales around the world. Outside, the pristine Swiss landscape offered a stark contrast to the intricate web of treachery they were about to unravel. Inside, the fire continued to crackle, its warmth a silent promise that as long as they stood together, the embers of their resolve would never grow cold.

CHAPTER 9

Martin De Simone's flight touched down at JFK International with the evening sky painted in hues of deep orange and fading blue. His jaw was set, a physical manifestation of the resolve boiling inside him as he made his way through the bustling terminal. He was dressed in a stark black suit that hinted at his past life — a life where covert operations and clandestine meetings were commonplace. With every step, his polished shoes clicked against the gleaming floor, echoing the rhythm of his racing heart.

Exiting the airport, Martin navigated the New York City traffic, his mind replaying the events that led to this moment. Nick Taylor, his comrade-in-arms, had been targeted, and there was no line Martin wouldn't cross to uncover the perpetrators. Like a sentinel, the city's high rises loomed over him, their glass facades reflecting the twilight as he passed by, each one a witness to countless stories unfolding within their walls.

Once settled in the backseat of a taxi, Martin placed a secure call to Michael Freeman. The phone rang twice before Michael answered with an urgency matching Martin's own. "Michael, it's Martin. I need eyes on Nick's place, now," Martin said, cutting straight to the chase.

"Martin," Michael acknowledged, his voice grave, hinting at the weight he carried as a committed field office of the FBI in New York. "I'm on it. How soon can you get here?" "Twenty minutes," Martin replied tersely as the taxi weaved through the snarl of traffic. "Make it fifteen," Michael shot back. There was no room for pleasantries when lives hung in the balance.

Martin arrived at the FBI's New York field office, a formidable structure of concrete and steel that stood as a bulwark against the chaos of crime. Inside, Michael greeted him with a firm handshake — the kind shared between men who understood the stakes.

"Let's get to work," Michael said, his athletic frame moving with purpose toward the bank of monitors in the surveillance room. A former military man decorated for demonstrate excellence and courage in Afghanistan and Iraq War, his movements exuded discipline and precision.

"Footage is cued up," Michael announced, pointing at the screens where grainy images flickered to life.

Together, they scrutinized the CCT footage, Michael's keen eyes missing nothing as he controlled the playback. "There," Martin pointed, "pause it." On the screen, a suspicious figure lingered outside Nick's apartment, carrying what looked like heavy bags.

"Explosives," Martin murmured, his analytical mind piecing together the puzzle. The footage was a treasure trove of leads, and his friend's expertise was the key to unlocking them.

"Analysis confirmed it was RDX," Michael added, referencing the powerful explosive material used in the bombing. He studied Martin's face, seeing the determination etched onto his features. "Listen, Martin, I'm pulling in my best team. We'll catch this bastard."

"Thanks, Michael," Martin said, clapping a hand on his friend's shoulder. "I knew I could count on you."
"Always," Michael replied with a tight smile. "Now let's go over this frame by frame."

The two men leaned closer to the screens, their shadows merging into one as the night deepened outside. They embarked on the painstaking task of dissecting every second, every pixel, that might hold a clue. As they worked, a silent vow hung in the air around them — a promise to bring justice for Nick, whatever the cost.

CHAPTER 10

The moon hung low in the sky, casting a pale glow over the desolate street as Martin De Simone slipped from the shadows of an alleyway. He moved with a deliberate grace that belied his muscular build, every sinew and tendon honed from years of disciplined training. His attire was nondescript: dark jeans, a fitted black sweater that hugged his torso, and sturdy boots—chosen for utility rather than fashion. The infrared camera hung securely around his neck, its lens cap reflecting the muted light like the eye of some nocturnal creature.

As he approached the site of the bomb attack, the once vibrant street now felt like an urban mausoleum. Windows of neighbouring buildings gazed down upon him, empty sockets devoid of life. The air held the acrid tang of burnt materials, a scent that Martin had come to recognize in his years of service.

With each step closer to the building's entrance, Martin's training kicked in. His pace slowed to a measured tread, movements deliberate and quiet. He was a Specter amidst the wreckage, a ghost navigating a world turned upside down by treachery.

Martin's gaze swept the perimeter of Nick's apartment building, a gutted shell of its former self. Scaffolding clung to its sides like the exoskeleton of a great metallic insect, eerily silent in the night. The air was thick with the acrid scent of char and decay—a stark reminder of the violence that had torn through the structure's heart.

He paused, his sharp intellect mapping out his entry. The main entrance was a gaping maw, flanked by police tape fluttering lazily in the breeze. Too obvious. Martin's eyes traced the fire escape, a zigzagging promise of clandestine ingress. He approached it, every step measured, his keen ears picking up the distant murmur of the city's nightlife, punctuated by the occasional siren—a lullaby for the sleepless.

With practiced ease, Martin ascended the metal stairs, his hands finding purchase on cold steel, his movements quiet as a whisper. At each landing, he paused, surveying the darkness for any sign of movement or threat. But there was only silence, the kind that presses against the eardrums and heightens the senses.

Reaching the floor of Nick's apartment, Martin crouched low, his infrared camera now cradled in his hands like a sacred artifact. He removed the lens cap, and the world transformed before him into shades of heat and shadow. He scanned the corridor, the camera's display painting a surreal landscape of what once was—now only outlines and empty spaces where life had thrived.

He navigated the debris of one of the apartments of the Nick's floor, his steps silent amidst the rubble. Martin moved with precision, a tactician waging a silent war against the clock. He was driven not just by duty, but by a deep-seated need to protect, to serve as guardian to those like Nick, who had been caught in the crossfire of a hidden battle.

With the building's interior mapped out in his mind, Martin continued his surreptitious advance, ever vigilant, ever determined in direction of the supposed Nick's apartment. The night shielded him for now, but he was under no illusions—the true test of wits and wills had only just begun.

CHAPTER 11

Martin's boots crunched softly over the debris as he maneuvered through the desolate remains of the Nick's apartment building. The stillness was pervasive, a haunting contrast to the chaos that had ripped through these walls. He could feel the pulse in his temples, each heartbeat a reminder of the stakes at play.

The infrared camera in his hand cut through the darkness, revealing the aftermath in stark thermal contrasts. Martin paused before the remnants of a couch, its form distorted by the blast, now just a carbonized husk. He took a photo, the camera's soft click punctuating the silence. It wasn't just a piece of furniture—it was a marker, a potential indicator of the bomb's cruel epicentre.

As he moved, his eyes swept over a once familiar setting turned alien by violence. The kitchen lay exposed, appliances eviscerated by the explosive's fury. The fridge door hung askew, its insides gutted, and what remained of the stove was twisted metal and ash. Martin documented it all, capturing the ruin in meticulous frames. Each image held the latent promise of revelation—of fingerprints left by an unseen adversary in the shrapnel and scorched earth.

With every step, Martin threaded through the narrative of destruction, piecing together the story told by the ruins. His focus never wavered; this was where intellect met instinct, where years of training and an intimate knowledge of espionage converged on a singular goal: justice for a friend, for all those threatened by the unseen hand that had dealt this blow.

He operated with a precision born from a career in the shadows, his mind cataloguing details with the efficiency of a seasoned analyst. Later, when he would pore over these images, searching for the invisible signatures left by the bomb maker, this night's work would prove crucial. But for now, he was the silent witness to the aftermath, the bearer of truths yet to be uncovered.

And so Martin continued, his actions a quiet testament to the resilience of those who stand against the darkness, a chronicler of the evidence that would soon illuminate the path toward retribution.

With each methodical movement, he extracted fragments of carbonized wood, their blackened edges crumbling slightly under his firm yet gentle touch. His fingers, clad in tactical gloves, worked with practiced care as he selected pieces that bore the telltale signs of an intense heat far beyond any accidental house fire.

He placed each sample into small, meticulously labelled containers—evidence bags designed to preserve the integrity of their contents against contamination. These fragments, mute witnesses to the violent event that had claimed this corner of the building, now rested in Martin's hands, carrying with them the secrets of their own undoing. They were keys waiting to unlock the identity of a compound that had wrought such havoc.

The air around him was thick with the residue of destruction, a pungent mix of scorched materials and the stale aftermath of extinguished flames. He could feel the weight of the silence pressing against his ears, a silence that spoke volumes to a man accustomed to listening for the nuances of danger.

Martin's pulse thrummed in his temples, a metronome ticking down with each passing second. Time was running fast. He knew that somewhere out there, the clock was running on the perpetrator's next move, each tick bringing potential disaster one step closer.

As he moved, his eyes never ceased scanning his surroundings—the skeletal frames of furniture, the jagged outlines of broken windows. Every shadow could be a hiding place, every sound a signal. Martin's experience as a field operative had honed his senses to a razor's edge, and now they sliced through the stillness, searching for the faintest hint of a threat.

His mind danced between the immediate task at hand and the larger picture it painted—a web of intrigue that spanned continents and whispered of conspiracies nestled within the highest echelons of power. Yet even as his thoughts flitted from micro to macro, Martin's actions remained precise and undistracted. Each sample secured was another step toward unravelling the plot that had endangered his friend Nick, and by extension, countless others.

With the samples safely stowed away, Martin took a moment to observe the twisted metal and fractured walls surrounding him. This was no mere crime scene; it was a battleground in a war fought in the shadows, where civilians became collateral damage in the games of espionage and political machinations.

Yet amid the desolation, Martin's resolve hardened. This was why he had chosen this path, why he bore the burdens that came with it. For truth. For justice. For the assurance that those who wielded chaos as a weapon would not do so with impunity.

CHAPTER 12

Martin moved finally through the gutted Nick's apartment with a precision that mirrored his days in the field, every step measured and silent. He paused to photograph a shattered mirror, its silvered glass reflecting the chaos of the room. The once luxurious living space had been reduced to a war zone of ash and broken dreams. Plush furniture was now just a memory beneath the soot; elegant wallpaper peeled away to reveal the raw vulnerability of exposed brick.

His eyes, sharp as a hawk's, scanned for anything out of place—a wire, a fragment that didn't belong. He took samples meticulously, knowing each fiber could tell a story of who had brought devastation upon his friend Nick, a man whose life had been dedicated to navigating and neutralizing such threats.

The desolation around him was palpable, a stark reminder of the fine line between civilization and chaos. Yet Martin's focus never wavered from his mission. The apartment's interior design, once a tapestry of modern elegance and comfort, lay in tatters—artworks slashed by shrapnel, furniture gutted by force. Amidst it all, Martin stood as an anchor of resolve, his intellect cataloging the scene, his physicality a testament to years of disciplined training.

He navigated the remnants of Nick's life, past a toppled floor lamp whose sleek design spoke of late nights and the soft illumination of intimate conversations. Its metallic frame, twisted and jagged, reflected the harsh reality of their profession—a world where light and dark collided with violent finality.

"Nick would've seen this coming," Martin muttered under his breath, a mix of respect and regret lacing his words. His friend's instincts were honed to near perfection, yet even the best were not invincible when it came to the shadowy world they lived in.

There was a coldness to the air, the sort that sunk into your bones, as if the building itself was mourning its marred beauty. Martin shivered, not from the chill, but from a realization—someone had planned this with chilling efficiency. This was no random act of terror; it bore the hallmark of professional wrath, the kind that was bought at a high price or commanded by power.

He continued to document everything—the way the light from his flashlight cast elongated shadows over the fallen beams, the eerie silence that swallowed the sound of his footsteps, the bitter scent of destruction that lingered in the air.

As he slipped through the remains of the kitchen, where once laughter and camaraderie filled the air, Martin couldn't shake the thought that this bomb wasn't just an attack—it was a statement. A declaration that someone, somewhere, wanted to send a message of fear and control. The sophistication and scale suggested a perpetrator beyond a simple mercenary or lone wolf. This was the work of a formidable entity, one with resources and reach.

The apartment seemed to watch him as he moved, its opulence scarred by violence. As he stepped over the threshold for the last time, Martin felt the gravity of what lay ahead. There were layers to this intrigue that would test his mettle and loyalty, but he was ready. For Nick, for justice, for a semblance of peace in a world teetering on the brink of unseen wars, he would wade through the murk of lies and danger.

"Yes! An act of war," he whispered to the darkness, feeling the weight of the phrase. It was more than just a figure of speech; it was a call to arms, a siren in the night beckoning him back into the fray.

Finally, Martin began the delicate process of exiting without a trace. He treads backwards through his own steps, ensuring nothing was disturbed. It was second nature, a dance of discretion learned from years in covert service where the difference between life and death often lay in the smallest detail.

With a final glance at the charred remains of Nick's sanctuary, Martin melted into the New York night, a ghost among the millions, carrying with him the first pieces of a puzzle that threatened to engulf them all in its complexity and peril.

CHAPTER 13

Martin's hand grazed the cold, jagged edge of the doorframe as he slipped out of the fractured building. The night air embraced him with a brisk chill, a stark contrast to the acrid scent of charred remnants that clung to his clothes. He had done everything with meticulous precision, from gathering the blackened samples to documenting the scene through the unblinking eye of his infrared camera. Now, with vials of potential evidence secure in the inner lining of his jacket, Martin made haste along the deserted alleyway.

The city loomed around him, skyscrapers piercing the heavens, their countless windows reflecting the moonlight like facets of a giant, indifferent gemstone. Martin moved with purpose, his well-worn boots making soft sounds against the pavement, blending into the hum of the metropolis. Each step carried the weight of responsibility; the debris-laden room he left behind was more than a crime scene—it was a chessboard of geopolitical machinations.

As Martin navigated his way through the streets of New York, the subtle play of shadow and light painted an abstract mural on the time-weathered brick walls. His journey back to his safe haven—a nondescript apartment tucked away in one of the quieter boroughs—gave him precious moments to reflect.

He thought of Nick, whose once vibrant life had been reduced to this chaos. The bomb—the malicious herald of an enemy unseen—had not discriminated. It had torn through steel and flesh with equal ferocity, leaving scars on both the physical and the psychological landscape. Martin felt the burden of unravelling this twisted narrative, where each clue could be a lifeline or a further plunge into the abyss.

His safe haven came into view, a modest structure sandwiched between aging edifices that whispered tales of a bygone era. The façade was unassuming, almost forgettable, which was precisely the point. Inside, Martin's quarters were a testament to functional minimalism. A single antique desk of dark mahogany stood against the wall, its surface clean except for a strategically placed vintage lamp that cast a warm glow across the grain. Bookshelves lined another wall, filled with an eclectic mix of literature and non-fiction, each volume meticulously arranged.

Martin secured the door behind him and immediately set about analysing the implications of what he'd found. The samples—small pieces of a larger, sinister puzzle—held the potential to unlock the identity of those who sought to tip the balance of power through fear and destruction. His mind teemed with theories, each more unsettling than the last.

"Who stands to gain from this turmoil?" he pondered aloud, his words dissipating into the stillness of the room. It was a question that echoed in the silent chambers of his consciousness, demanding an answer that would surely come at a great cost.

The room seemed to shrink around him, the walls inching closer as the magnitude of his task settled upon his shoulders. Yet, within Martin burned an unwavering resolve. He knew that the path ahead was fraught with peril, but he welcomed the challenge with a steely determination. For within the intricate web of deception and violence lay the truth—and for that, Martin De Simone would move heaven and earth.

CHAPTER 14

Martin's fingers danced across the keyboard with a practiced ease, each keystroke an orchestrated part of the urgent symphony playing out in the dimly lit confines of his study. The room was a testament to his years of service—a shrine to the pursuit of truth—with every antique and artifact telling a tale of past missions and bygone eras. Oak panels adorned the walls, the wood's dark patina speaking of age and the quiet dignity of craftsmanship from another time.

He paused, glancing at the brass-framed clock that commanded attention from its perch above the fireplace. Time was slipping away, just as the culprits he hunted were trying to do under the shroud of chaos they had unleashed upon the city.

"Michael, it's Martin," he spoke into the secure line, his tone carrying both the weight of his findings and the urgency that underscored their mission. "I've got something. Images and samples—evidence we need to move forward."

On the other end of the line, Michael Freeman's voice was a calm and reassuring contrast to the tempest of thoughts churning in Martin's mind.

"Good work, Martin. Get everything to me. We'll analyse the materials immediately."

"Every detail could be critical," Martin pressed, his gaze flitting over the plethora of photos and the sealed containers housing the remnants of destruction. "We're dealing with an adept enemy. Every piece helps to complete the puzzle."

"Understood. I'm sending a secure courier. Keep everything on lockdown until they arrive," Michael instructed, the unspoken gravity of the situation hanging between them.

"Will do," Martin confirmed before ending the call. His reflection stared back at him from the black screen of his encrypted device—a mirror image of the dedication that had defined his career.

As the night get darker, Martin stood, stretching his muscular frame which was beginning to feel the strain of relentless vigilance. He walked over to the window, gazing out at the sprawling cityscape below. The glow of streetlights mingled with the stars above, a canopy of light against the night's canvas.

His determination did not falter; it was the bedrock upon which he built his resolve. There was no room for doubt, only the methodical process of elimination and discovery. The next steps were already forming in his strategic mind, each one calculated and precise.

The truth behind the attack on Nick remained veiled in shadow, but Martin De Simone was no stranger to the darkness. He would delve into its depths, armed with intellect and unwavering purpose, to bring the light of justice to those who skulked within it.

Martin's thoughts shifted gears, turning towards the next steps that lay ahead. He knew that the evidence he'd collected was just a part of the puzzle. There were still players in the shadows, moves to predict, strategies to formulate. Each piece of intel, each analyzed sample, was a step towards peeling back the layers of obfuscation. One question start to bit his mind: where is the 18 Century Nick's Clock Watch?

With a final glance at the orderly room that served as his sanctuary and command center, Martin turned off the vintage lamp, allowing the shadows to reclaim their territory. Tomorrow, he would continue the hunt. Tonight, he allowed himself a moment to breathe, acknowledging the small victory in obtaining the evidence they so desperately needed.

CHAPTER 15

The alpine sun filtered through the gauzy curtains, casting a warm glow over the rustic interior of Nick's room. As the door creaked open, Dr. Emma Stein stepped inside, her presence as comforting as the morning rays. In her hands was a tray laden with the promise of a fresh start—a hearty breakfast of scrambled eggs, wholegrain toast, and freshly squeezed orange juice, its citrus scent mingling with the crisp mountain air.

"Good morning, Nick," she greeted him, her voice carrying the melody of optimism. A smile unfurled across her face, bright as the daffodils that dotted the chalet's garden outside. Her long brown hair was pulled back into a practical ponytail, revealing the sharp intelligence in her piercing blue eyes.

Nick shifted beneath the soft linen sheets, his tall frame an outline of determination against the plump pillows. The gray streaks in his hair caught the sunlight, telling tales of wisdom earned and battles fought. He returned her smile, albeit with a hint of effort—as if each facial muscle was relearning its purpose.

"Morning, Emma," he replied. His voice, once commanding in briefing rooms, now held a softer timbre within these four walls adorned with local timber and stone accents.

"How did you sleep?" Emma inquired, setting the tray on the bedside table crafted from aged pine, its knots and grains a silent testament to the resilience of nature.

"Like a rock, surprisingly," Nick said, sitting up to allow the weight of his body to ground him in the present. "No dreams, no shadows from the past... just rest."

Emma nodded, taking note of his response. Her patient's sleep patterns were as much a part of the recovery process as the therapy itself. She perched on the edge of the bed, her posture relaxed yet attentive. "That's good to hear. A solid night's sleep is crucial for your recovery."

As Nick tucked into the simple, nourishing meal, Emma observed him with clinical precision masked by casual interest. Each movement he made, each bite he took, was a sign of progress, a step towards regaining the autonomy that his condition had stolen from him.

"Ready to get moving after breakfast? I have organized a full checkup and rehab plan!" she said, already anticipating the regimen she had tailored for him.

"Perfect! Let's do it," he said, pushing the plate away with a newfound vigor. The food had refueled his body, but it was the prospect of reclaiming his strength that truly nourished his spirit.

They moved to a spacious area of the room where the plush carpet gave way to smooth, polished wood floors. Emma guided Nick through a series of exercises designed to rebuild his muscular memory. Standing beside him, she demonstrated each movement with the grace of a dancer and the precision of a scientist.

"Start with shoulder rotations—nice and easy," she instructed, rotating her own shoulders to emphasize the motion. Nick mimicked her, feeling the stretch pull at muscles that hadn't been used earnestly in far too long.

"Good. Now let's try some lunges," Emma continued, her tone encouraging. Nick followed suit, bending his knee and extending his leg with a focus that seemed to defy the blank spaces in his mind. Each lunge was a silent battle against the frustration gnawing at the edges of his consciousness—the frustration of not remembering.

"Remember, it's about coordination and control," she reminded him, her words a gentle anchor as he navigated the uncharted waters of his physical rehabilitation.

"Coordination and control," Nick echoed, the mantra seeping into his movements. His legs shook slightly with the strain, a testament to the effort he exerted with each deliberate step. Sweat beaded on his forehead, but his gaze remained sharp, locked onto the path of recovery he was carving out with every flex and extension.

"Excellent work, Nick," Emma praised, her affirmation genuine and heartfelt. "We're rebuilding you, piece by piece. Muscle by muscle."

Nick exhaled deeply, his chest rising and falling with a rhythm that echoed the resolve etched into the lines of his face. He knew the journey ahead was steep, but he also knew that the will to ascend was woven into the very fabric of his being. Emma watched with pride, recognizing the unwavering spirit of the man who once treaded in the shadows for his country. Now, he stood in the light of a new day, ready to confront the mysteries of his own past.

CHAPTER 16

Nick slumped on the edge of his bed, his lean muscles still quivering from the morning's exertions. The room was bathed in the soft glow of dawn filtering through the sheer curtains, casting a tranquil ambiance over the chalet's intricately carved wooden interior. Dr. Emma Stein, her long blonde hair tied back and eyes reflecting determination, set aside the tray from which he had barely eaten and replaced it with an assortment of cognitive exercise tools.

"Let's begin with something simple," she said, her voice steady, a calm counterpoint to the turmoil in Nick's mind. She laid out a series of black and white flashcards, each bearing a stark image: a tree, a car, a gun.

"Tree," Nick stated plainly, recognizing the silhouette at first glance. "Good. And this?" Emma asked, flipping to the next card.

"Car," he responded, a trace of impatience threading his tone. He felt the weight of expectation—his own more than hers—to remember.

"Gun," he added quickly as the final card was revealed, but the word triggered nothing more than a faint throbbing at the base of his skull.

"Excellent," Emma encouraged. "Now, let's try associating words. I say 'night,' you say..."

"Dark," Nick shot back immediately. The word association game continued, a rapid-fire exchange that seemed to dance around the edges of his consciousness, never quite piercing through to the memories locked within.

"Espionage," Emma said, and for a moment, Nick's eyes flickered with a spark of recognition before fading into confusion.

"Secrets," he answered hesitantly, a frown creasing his forehead.

"Relax, Nick," Dr. Stein reassured him gently, noting his clenched fists. "This isn't about getting every answer right. It's about awakening your mind."

She moved on to visual memory exercises, presenting complex geometric patterns for him to replicate. With each shape he drew, his hand wavered less, his lines became surer, yet the frustration mounted. He could feel his pulse in his temples, a silent drumbeat urging him to remember.

"Enough!" Nick's outburst filled the room as he pushed away from the table. His chair skidded across the polished wooden floor with a screech that echoed off the alpine-themed tapestries adorning the walls.

"Nick," Emma said, standing and placing a comforting hand on his shoulder. "It's okay. This is a process, and these moments of doubt are part of healing."

He looked up at her, his sharp gaze clouded with the vulnerability of a man grappling with the unknown. "What if I never remember? What if who I was... is gone forever?"

"Your past doesn't define you, Nick." Her blue eyes held his steadily. "Even now, you're showing the resilience and commitment that speak volumes about who you are. Be patient with yourself."

Her words were like salve to his raw nerves. He nodded, taking a deep breath, finding solace in her unwavering support. They both knew the road to recovery would be long and fraught with shadows, but in the quiet assurance of her presence, Nick found the strength to face the uncertain path ahead.

CHAPTER 17

Nick followed Dr. Stein out onto the veranda, the morning chill nipping at his bare arms. He took a deep breath, and the crisp Alpine air filled his lungs with an invigorating purity that seemed to wash away some of the frustration lingering from the earlier therapy session. Emma handed him a light jacket, its fabric soft but sturdy between his fingers—a tactile reminder of the care she took in every detail.

"Come on," she encouraged with a smile that seemed to pull at the corners of her eyes, "the mountains are waiting."

They stepped off the veranda and onto a gravel path winding through the lush verdure surrounding the chalet. Nick's gaze swept across the panorama—the imposing peaks stood like silent sentinels, their snow-capped summits piercing the clear azure sky. Below, a tapestry of pines and firs spread out, interspersed with the fiery reds and golds of autumnal foliage. A gentle breeze whispered through the trees, carrying with it the distant murmur of a brook. The serenity of the landscape seeped into Nick's consciousness, its tranquility a stark contrast to the turmoil within his mind.

"Beautiful, isn't it?" Emma mused, walking beside him. Her hair caught the sunlight, casting warm glints that danced around her face.

"Stunning," he admitted, his voice a low rumble, as much to himself as to her. For a moment, he allowed himself to simply be present, engulfed by the natural splendor without the pressure to remember.

As they ambled down the path, Emma initiated a new line of conversation, her tone casual yet probing. "Nick, back when things were... normal for you, what did you enjoy doing? Any hobbies or passions?"

He frowned slightly, the question nudging at the empty spaces in his memory. "I'm not sure." His words were hesitant. "I think I liked to read... maybe thrillers or historical novels?"

"Sounds about right for a man of action like you." She glanced at him, her expression encouraging. "Anything else? Sports, perhaps?"

"Maybe something outdoors... climbing or hiking?" He tried to grasp at the fragments that skittered just out of reach, elusive shadows in the recesses of his mind.

"Given where you find yourself now, that wouldn't surprise me," she chuckled softly, her laugh a subtle melody against the backdrop of rustling leaves.

A grimace crossed Nick's rugged features, his hands clenching into fists at his sides. "It's like trying to catch smoke with my bare hands," he confessed, his voice tinged with exasperation.

"Hey," Emma stopped, turning to face him, her hand coming to rest lightly on his arm. "It's okay, Nick. These things take time. And sometimes, when we stop chasing so hard, the memories come to us on their own."

He met her gaze, the blue of her eyes reminding him of the skies above—limitless and full of possibility. There was a steadfastness in her that grounded him, even as everything else felt adrift.

"Let's keep walking," she suggested with a gentle nudge. "The best we can do is to live in the here and now while the past sorts itself out."

And so they continued, side by side, with the mountain air as their companion and the promise of tomorrow carried on the wind.

CHAPTER 18

The morning's alpine glow filtered through the sheer curtains, casting a warm golden hue across the spacious room. Nick sat at a polished oak table, the grains of the wood swirling beneath his fingertips. He was dressed in a soft cotton shirt that clung to his athletic frame, evidence of a life spent in pursuit of physical excellence. Dr. Emma Stein entered, her long brown hair pulled back into a practical ponytail, a photo album tucked under her arm.

"Good morning, Nick," she said, her voice a blend of professional warmth and genuine care. She set the album down before him with the reverence usually reserved for ancient texts. "I thought we could try something a little different today."

Nick glanced up at her, apprehension and curiosity competing in his sharp gaze. "What's this?" he asked, running a hand through his graying hair, a habit that spoke to his underlying frustration.

"Memories," Emma replied, flipping the cover open to reveal the first glossy page. "Your memories, specifically."

Each photo was a meticulously captured slice of life, vibrant and frozen in time. Nick leaned forward, his fingers hovering over images of himself in various locales—cobblestoned streets in Europe, sun-drenched deserts in the Middle East, and bustling markets in Asia. The photos were like windows into a world he could not enter, each one framed by notes and annotations in Emma's neat handwriting.

"Here," she pointed to a picture of him standing atop a mountain, the azure sky a striking contrast to the snowy peaks below. "You led an expedition here once, part of a covert operation in the Andes."

Nick absorbed the details—the way the wind tousled his younger self's hair, the determined set of his jaw. "It looks familiar... but it's like looking at someone else's life," he muttered, a twinge of sadness in his eyes.

"Let's keep going," Emma encouraged, her blue eyes reflecting patience and understanding. "Tell me if anything stands out to you."

They moved through the album methodically, Emma providing context where she could, her voice a soothing accompaniment to the visual journey. Then, as they neared the end of the album, Nick paused. His breath hitched, fingers trembling as they traced the outline of a face—a woman with blonde hair and an enigmatic smile, her arm linked with his.

"Her..." Nick whispered, his heart racing. "I know her."

"Who is she?" Emma leaned in closer, her pulse quickening with shared anticipation.

"Katya," the name rolled off his tongue, a key unlocking a door long sealed. "She was... is important. I can feel it."

"Excellent, Nick!" Emma beamed, her elation palpable. "This is a breakthrough. Do you remember anything else about her?"

"Bits and pieces... flashes." He struggled to articulate the sudden flood of emotions and fragmented memories. "Laughter, danger, a partnership."

"Take your time," she soothed, placing a comforting hand on his shoulder. Her touch was light, yet it anchored him to the moment, to the rush of connections being remade within the depths of his mind.

"Thank you, Emma," Nick said, offering her a grateful look. His eyes, still fixed on Katya's image, held a new light, a spark reignited.

"Today is just the beginning," Emma reassured him, her words a balm to his weary soul. "Together, we'll uncover the rest."

As they closed the album, the chalet seemed to hum with newfound energy, its antique furnishings and elegant decor bearing witness to the rekindling of a formidable agent's identity. With each memory that surfaced, Nick Taylor was becoming whole again, piecing together the puzzle of his remarkable past under the watchful, hopeful gaze of Dr. Emma Stein.

Nick's muscles tensed as the first chords of a classic rock anthem reverberated through the room. Dr. Emma Stein watched him carefully from across the chalet's plush, cream-colored divan, gauging his reaction to the music therapy session she'd devised. The sun spilled in through floor-to-ceiling windows, casting a warm glow on the rustic hardwood floors and Nick's rugged features.

"Remember this one?" Emma asked, her voice a gentle nudge as Led Zeppelin's "Stairway to Heaven" filled the space with nostalgia.

Nick closed his eyes, letting the melody wash over him. His foot began to tap unconsciously, fingers drumming along on the armrest of the leather chair that cradled his healing frame. A shadow of a smile played on his lips; the song was a familiar friend, a comrade from days gone by.

"Concert in Munich... undercover..." he murmured, his voice trailing off as he sifted through the haze of his memory. Each note seemed to pulse with the rhythm of secrets and shadows, the lifeblood of his former existence.

"Music often unlocks doors in our minds that we thought were closed forever," Emma said, observing him with her piercing blue eyes. She wore a simple navy blouse paired with black slacks, an ensemble that complemented her professional yet empathic approach to Nick's recovery.

"Tell me about your career, Nick," she encouraged as the track transitioned into a softer ballad. "What do you remember about being a spy?"

He opened his eyes, focusing on her inquisitive gaze. "It was more than just espionage," he started, his voice gaining confidence. "It was about protecting ideals, safeguarding truths hidden just beneath the surface."

"Like a guardian of the unseen world," Emma remarked, encapsulating his thoughts.

"Exactly." Nick leaned forward, animated by the topic. "I had to be quick on my feet, always thinking three steps ahead." He gestured with his hands, as if conducting an invisible orchestra of past exploits.

"Languages, surveillance techniques, hand-to-hand combat..." He listed the skills like medals earned in a clandestine war. "Each mission was a chess game, every move critical."

"Your dedication is still evident," Emma smiled, her admiration genuine. "That sense of duty doesn't fade, even when memories do."

"Part of me feels lost without it," Nick confessed, a crease forming between his brows. "The thrill of the chase, the adrenaline of a narrow escape..."

"Those experiences shaped you, but they aren't the sum total of who you are," Emma reassured him, her words wrapping around him like a comforting blanket.

"Who I am..." Nick echoed, the concept seeming both foreign and familiar. "I need to find that man again."

"And you will," Emma affirmed. "Piece by piece, we'll rebuild the mosaic of your extraordinary life."

"Thank you, Emma. For all of this," he gestured to the chalet—the embodiment of tranquility and rehabilitation—with a sweep of his hand.

"Part of the healing process is embracing the journey back to yourself," she replied, rising to change the record. "Let's see what other memories we can stir up."

As the strains of another classic hit began to play, it seemed to Nick that the majestic Alpine scenery outside, the elegance of the antique-filled chalet, and the determined compassion of Dr. Emma Stein were all conspirators in his quest to reclaim his identity. Each note of the music, each tale of his past whispered by the walls, brought him closer to the man he once was—a man he was slowly, but surely, remembering.

CHAPTER 19

Nick was methodically tracing the grain of the aged oak table when Dr. Stein set a leather-bound journal before him. The soft morning light filtered through the sheer curtains, casting a warm glow on its embossed cover.

"Writing can be a powerful tool for recovery," Emma said, her voice as gentle as the Alpine breeze. "It allows you to externalize your thoughts, memories, or dreams."

Nick lifted his gaze from the table to meet her piercing blue eyes; they held a spark of unwavering belief in him. He took the journal in his hands, feeling the weight of it—both physical and symbolic. The leather was supple, warmed quickly by his touch, and the pages were pristine, waiting to be filled with the fragments of his past and the inklings of his future.

"Thank you," Nick replied, his voice steady, but touched with an undercurrent of emotion. This journal represented a new starting point, a tangible connection to the self he was struggling to rediscover.

He opened it to the first page, the paper crisp against his fingers. With a pen poised, he hesitated only for a moment before starting to write. The words began as a trickle—a recounting of the melodies that had stirred faint echoes of memory, the discussions of espionage that tantalized his dormant knowledge.

As he wrote, his commitment to the task solidified. Each word was a step toward clarity, each sentence a bridge between the man he was and the man he longed to become again. It was more than a journal; it was a beacon guiding him through the fog that shrouded his memories.

That night, in the tranquility of his room, where shadows danced along the walls from the flickering fireplace, Nick fell into a deep slumber. His mind, perhaps spurred on by the day's reflections, conjured a vivid dream.

He was navigating a labyrinth of narrow streets in a city aglow with the golden hues of sunset. The sights and sounds were acutely familiar—the hum of conversation in a foreign tongue, the scent of spices in the air, the weight of a concealed weapon against his side. A face flashed before his eyes, a visage etched with the lines of experience and adorned with a knowing smile.

Nick awoke with a start, his heart racing, the remnants of the dream clinging to his consciousness like a lifeline thrown into tumultuous waters. He scrambled for the journal on his bedside table, the urgency to document the dream driving his movements. As he scribbled down every detail, a sense of exhilaration coursed through him—this was no mere figment of sleep; it was a clue, a key that could unlock the doors guarding his elusive past.

"Emma," he whispered to himself, a smile touching the corners of his mouth. "We've got something real here."

His determination was ironclad. With this significant clue cradled in the pages of his journal, Nick knew the path to uncovering his identity lay open before him. And with the break of dawn painting the sky in shades of promise, he felt the shackles of uncertainty begin to loosen.

"Piece by piece," he murmured, echoing Emma's earlier reassurance. The journey back to himself was fraught with shadows and whispers of who he once was, but the hope kindled within him was now a blazing fire. He would follow the trail of breadcrumbs left by his own subconscious, no matter where it led. After all, he was Nick Taylor—resilient, resourceful, and ready to reclaim the life he'd lost.

CHAPTER 20

Nick's fingers traced the rough edges of the wooden box, its surface worn by time and memories it safeguarded. Dr. Stein placed the container gently on his lap, her piercing blue eyes observing him with a mix of professional curiosity and personal concern. The chalet's morning light spilled through the windows, casting a warm glow on the antique oak interior and highlighting the precision of its Swiss design.

"Inside this box are pieces of your past, Nick," Emma said softly, her voice a comforting melody against the backdrop of the Alpine serenity outside. "Take your time."

He nodded, the lines of his square jaw tightening as he prepared himself for what might come. With a steadiness that belied the turmoil within, Nick lifted the lid. The first item he saw was a gleaming CIA badge, its gold eagle emblem catching the sunbeam and throwing specks of light across the room. He picked it up, thumb brushing over the engraved name—his name: Nicholas Taylor. His heart thrummed in his chest, a silent echo of a life once lived in the shadows.

Beside the badge lay a photograph, edges fraying, the image a frozen moment in time. It was a team photo; he recognized the setting immediately—a nondescript safe house where strategies were whispered, and lives hung in balance. The figures were shoulder to shoulder, camaraderie etched into their stances. A tall man stood out, his own younger self, with hair less gray and eyes full of secrets. Surrounding him were faces that tugged at the corners of his mind, tempting him with familiarity yet remaining just beyond his grasp.

"Your team," Emma prompted, studying his face for signs of recognition. "Feels like I should know them," Nick murmured, frustration lacing his tone.

"Give it time," she replied, her hand finding its way to his arm, a reassuring pressure. "Memory needs patience."

As he sifted through more items—a well-worn leather wallet, a Swiss watch with an inscription, a map with routes marked in red ink—each piece beckoned to a different part of his psyche, a puzzle waiting to be solved. He could almost feel the adrenaline of past chases coursing through him, the weight of responsibility and the thrill of espionage clinging to these relics.

"Who was I, Emma?" he asked, not looking up from the box. "You were...are...a man of action and integrity," she answered. "You dedicated your life to protecting others."

His gaze finally met hers, and she saw the determination that had always been his hallmark. The artifacts of his former life had kindled something within him, a spark of the agent he used to be. Although the memories remained elusive, the feelings they evoked were undeniable.

"Let's keep digging, then," he said with a resolute nod, his positive thinking unshaken despite the long road ahead. "Piece by piece," Emma echoed, her smile warm and encouraging.

As he replaced the items carefully, reverently, he felt an ember of hope ignite. He would reclaim his past, one memory at a time, with the relentless tenacity that had defined his career—and with Emma, his steadfast guide, beside him every step of the way.

CHAPTER 21

In the meantime, in Los Angeles the sun dipped below the horizon, casting shadows across the skyline of Los Angeles. Martin De Simone and Michael Freeman stood in a dimly lit room, huddled over a table strewn with photographs, reports, and evidence bags. The hum of traffic outside the window was barely audible as they focused on the task at hand.

"Look at this," Michael said, pointing to a photograph taken at the crime scene of Robert Shain's murder. "The precision with which his body is positioned... It's almost artistic."

Martin nodded, his eyes scanning the image intently. "You're right. And it's the same with Diego Alvarez 's attack. Both crime scenes are meticulously staged, but with no witnesses or surveillance footage. This guy knows what he's doing."

"Patterns and similarities?" Michael asked, sifting through the papers on the table.

"Both Shain and Diego were involved in high-profile matters in connection with organized crime, especially with South America in the field of narcotics" Martin replied, rubbing his chin thoughtfully. "It seems like someone wants to send a message."

"Or eliminate potential threats," Michael added.

"Either way, we need to find out who's behind this," Martin said, determination etching his features.

The next day, Martin and Michael visited the murder scene of Robert Shain, a luxurious penthouse apartment overlooking the city. The place had already been swept by forensics, but the duo hoped to catch something that others might have missed.

As they entered the living room, Martin couldn't help but notice the opulence that surrounded them. Designer furniture, tasteful artwork, and state-of-the-art gadgets adorned every corner. This was a man who enjoyed the finer things in life.

"Quite a view," Michael commented, stepping onto the balcony and gazing at the city below.

"Shain certainly knew how to live," Martin agreed, his eyes wandering over the interior design. It was a blend of modern minimalism and classic elegance, with subtle hints of Shain's personality shining through. A small collection of antique books rested on a shelf near the fireplace, indicating an intellectual side to the businessman.

"Let's focus on the crime scene," Michael said, pulling Martin from his thoughts.

"Right," Martin replied, stepping over to where Shain's body had been found. He crouched down, examining the intricate pattern of blood spatter on the floor. "This was no ordinary hit. The killer took their time."

"Almost like they were enjoying it," Michael added, a shiver racing down his spine at the thought.

"Could be our link to the Medellin Cartel," Martin mused, his mind already working through the possibilities. "They're known for their brutal methods."

"True," Michael conceded. "But we'll need more evidence to make that connection."

As they continued to comb through the apartment, Martin couldn't shake the feeling that they were missing something crucial. Whoever had done this was skilled, leaving no trace behind. But in the world of espionage and political intrigue, there was always a clue waiting to be uncovered.

"Let's keep digging," Martin said, his resolve unwavering. "We'll find the truth, no matter what it takes."

CHAPTER 22

The sun starts dipping below the horizon, casting long shadows over the city as Martin and Michael stood outside the upscale office building where Robert Shain had conducted his business. The towering glass structure loomed above them, reflecting the dying light in a vibrant display of oranges and purples.

"Let's split up," Martin suggested, his eyes scanning the entrance for any signs of security. "You contact the forensic team, see if they've found anything useful. I'll start talking to Shain's colleagues. We need to cover as much ground as possible."

"Agreed," Michael replied, pulling out his phone to make the call. He stepped away, his voice barely audible over the bustling sounds of the city.

Martin took a deep breath, steeling himself for what lay ahead. He knew that to get the truth, he'd have to navigate a minefield of personal connections and red herrings. With each interview, he would have to read between the lines, looking for the subtle clues that could lead him to Shain's killer.

He entered the building, immediately struck by the opulence of the marble-lined lobby. A massive chandelier hung from the ceiling, casting warm light on the polished floor below. People milled about, dressed in the finest suits and designer clothing – a testament to the wealth and influence that surrounded Robert Shain.

Excuse me," Martin said, approaching the receptionist who sat behind an enormous marble of Carrara desk, her fingers tapping away at a sleek computer keyboard. Her perfectly styled blonde hair framed a face that was both professional and alluring, drawing Martin's gaze like a moth to a flame.

"Can I help you?" she asked, her voice sultry yet efficient. "Martin De Simone," he introduced himself, flashing his CIA credentials. "I'm here to speak with some of Mr. Shain's associates regarding his recent murder."

"Of course," she replied, her eyes widening slightly at the mention of Shain's death. "I'll let them know you're here."

As Martin waited, he studied the surroundings, taking note of the tasteful art pieces and expensive furnishings that adorned the space. It was clear that no expense had been spared in cultivating an atmosphere of success and prestige.

"Mr. De Simone," a tall, distinguished man called out, extending a hand as he approached. "I'm Thomas Whitaker, Robert's business partner. I understand you have some questions?"

"Thank you for your time, Mr. Whitaker," Martin said, shaking the man's hand firmly. "I'd like to start by asking about any threats or enemies that Robert may have had."

"Enemies?" Whitaker frowned, his brow furrowing in thought. "Robert was a shrewd businessman, but he always played fair. As far as I know, he didn't have any enemies who would want him dead."

"Could there be any connections to the Medellin Cartel?" Martin asked, gauging the man's reaction.

"Medellin Cartel?" Whitaker scoffed, clearly taken aback. "That seems unlikely. We dealt with high-end private and institutional clients, Mr. De Simone. Our business was legitimate."

"Right," Martin replied, his mind racing as he considered other avenues of inquiry. He continued speaking with Whitaker and several others throughout the evening, searching for the elusive clue that would bring him closer to solving the murder.

Meanwhile, outside the building, Michael paced impatiently while on the phone with the FBI's forensic team. The news wasn't promising – no DNA or fingerprints had been found at the crime scene, leaving them with little to go on.

"Keep searching," Michael urged, frustration evident in his voice. "There has to be something we're missing."

As darkness enveloped the city, Martin and Michael reconvened, each feeling the weight of their seemingly fruitless efforts. Shain's murder had left an indelible mark on the community, and until they could uncover the truth, justice would remain elusive.

CHAPTER 23

As the first light of dawn crept over the jagged Swiss mountain peaks, it found Nick deep in the rhythm of his training regimen. The chalet's private gym, an elegant meld of rustic wood and cutting-edge technology, housed an array of equipment that now bore the brunt of his determination. His tall, athletic frame, shadowed by silver streaks at the temples, maneuvered through the space with purpose.

The weightlifting section of the program saw him engaging in deadlifts, where he hoisted the barbell stacked with plates, the metal clinking a harmonious symphony to his resolve. Each lift was a silent roar, muscles tensing and releasing with controlled power, veins standing in relief against his weathered skin. Dr. Emma Stein had tailored this routine not just for strength but for the reclamation of agility lost to time and injury.

Nick Taylor's every muscle burned as he pushed his body to the limit on the treadmill. Sweat beaded down his rugged, tanned face, and his heart hammered in his chest like a jackhammer. His graying hair was plastered to his head, a testament to the intensity of his workout. The state-of-the-art gym in the secret facility owned by Emma Stein, ex-

CIA operative, where he was recovering from his injuries pulsated with the thudding beat of the techno music he'd selected, the soundtrack to his drive. He was in his 50s now, but for a man who had left the life of a spy years ago, he was far from out of shape.

Dr. Emma Stein, a brain specialist and coma expert in her late 30s, entered the training area clad in her lab coat over a casual blouse and slacks, her long brown hair pulled up in a messy bun. Her piercing blue eyes sparkled with a mix of admiration and concern as she observed Nick's relentless routine. "Nick, you're pushing yourself too hard again," she said, her voice cutting through the music. He didn't acknowledge her, instead, dialing up the speed on the treadmill.

"Nick," she repeated, louder this time, "your body needs time to heal."

Finally, he relented, slowing the machine to a stop. He wiped the sweat from his forehead with a towel before turning to face her. "I don't have time to spare, Doc. The longer I'm here, the further ahead they get." Nick's sharp gaze betrayed the gears turning in his head, the determination in his hazel eyes.

Transitioning to martial arts, Nick's movements became a dance of precision and fluidity. His fists cut through the air, striking imaginary foes with the echo of a past laden with covert operations and clandestine encounters. He practiced katas, a series of defensive and offensive maneuvers that his muscle memory recalled with more fluency than his conscious mind could grasp at times.

His psychological fortitude mirrored his physical prowess; he was the embodiment of positive thinking, channeling every setback into fuel for progress. Sweat glistened on his brow as he moved onto endurance drills, his feet pounding against the treadmill's belt with the relentlessness of a man chased by ghosts. The panoramic windows offered a view of the pristine Swiss environment, an unforgiving terrain that mirrored the harsh landscapes he once navigated with stealth and vigilance.

This was no ordinary workout; it was a reclaiming of self, a methodical reconstruction of the agent he once was. With each passing day, Dr. Stein's program shepherded him closer to the apex of his former capabilities, ensuring that when the time came, Nick Taylor would be ready to face whatever shadows lurked in the corners of his storied past.

In the tranquility of the chalet, amidst antique furnishings that whispered tales of forgotten eras, and under the watchful gaze of the eternal mountains, Nick was slowly, but surely, becoming the spy he needed to be once again.

"Extend your reach, Nick. Focus on your target," Dr. Stein's voice cut through the silence, clear and authoritative yet laced with an undercurrent of encouragement. She stood by the sidelines, her form outlined by the natural light spilling in, giving her long brown hair a halo-like glow. Her piercing blue eyes never wavered from his movements, taking note of every shift in muscle and sinew.

He nodded without diverting his gaze from the invisible adversary before him, grateful for her presence. Emma had become more than a doctor; she was his anchor in these tumultuous seas of recovery, her expertise in neurological rehabilitation matched only by her unwavering support.

Moving on to grappling dummies, Nick grappled with the lifeless opponent, twisting and turning in a dance of controlled aggression. His movements were fluid, but there was an edge of strain in his expression. He was not just relearning; he was redefining himself, each maneuver bringing him closer to the operative he once was.

But as he transitioned into a complex takedown technique, his muscles seized with tension, and his balance faltered. The dummy slipped from his grasp, tumbling clumsily to the mat. Frustration flashed across Nick's features, a storm brewing behind the steely resolve in his eyes. It was a stark reminder that while his mind was willing, his body was still catching up.

"Patience, Nick," Dr. Stein said, stepping forward. Her voice was calm, a soothing balm to his chafed pride. "You're rebuilding connections that were dormant. It takes time."

He exhaled sharply, running a hand through his damp, graying hair as he straightened up. Emma approached with a sports bottle, her practical attire of a fleece-lined jacket and rugged trousers marking her respect for the alpine environment.

"Remember, it's about progress, not perfection," she continued, handing him the bottle. Nick accepted it with a nod, the cool liquid a welcome reprieve.

"Perfection was my baseline, Emma," Nick grunted between sips, the weight of his past excellence a heavy yoke around his neck.

"Was and will be again. But you've got to give yourself the chance to get there," she insisted, her gaze never wavering. "Now, reset. You know this move. Envision it, then execute."

Nick closed his eyes for a moment, summoning the image of the technique, recalling the days when such moves were second nature. With renewed focus, he faced the dummy once more. His movements were slower this time, deliberate. Muscle and memory aligned, and the takedown was seamless.

A small smile creased Dr. Stein's lips as she watched Nick rise from the mat, the slightest nod acknowledging his victory over the momentary setback.

"Better," she affirmed, pride evident in her tone. "Much better."

Nick met her gaze, the frustration ebbing away, replaced by the steady flame of determination. Here in the heart of the Swiss Alps, amidst the silent wisdom of centuries-old pine and stone, he found not only the relentless drive to reclaim his former prowess but also the patience to endure the journey.

"Let's go again," he said, his voice now steady with conviction.

"Again," Dr. Stein echoed, ready to guide him through every step, every misstep, until the echoes of his past became the triumphs of his future.

CHAPTER 24

Nick pivoted on the ball of his foot, the soft thud of his sneakers against the tatami mat a subtle undercurrent to the rhythm of exertion echoing through the chalet's training room. Dr. Emma Stein's eyes tracked his movements with clinical precision, her arms folded across the chest of her fitted, navy-blue tracksuit that hugged her athletic frame. The room's spacious interior, accented with sleek lines and modern décor, was a testament to Swiss minimalism—a sanctuary designed for the singular purpose of transformation.

In the mirrored reflection, Nick could see the lines of age etched into his weathered face, but as he faced his opponent—a sparring partner with padded gloves—he felt the years strip away. His gray-flecked hair was matted with sweat, and his muscles tensed, coiled springs ready to unleash controlled aggression honed from decades in the field.

"Remember to breathe, Nick," Dr. Stein reminded him, her voice a steady beacon amidst the storm of combat. "Let your instincts guide you."

Nick nodded tersely, his focus narrowing to the man before him whose own stance was a blend of wariness and challenge. Then, like a viper striking, Nick lunged forward with preternatural swiftness, his fist cutting through the air aiming for his opponent's defense.

As their dance of feints and jabs unfolded, Nick's mind was in the moment, yet somewhere deeper, a memory stirred—like the flicker of a shadow darting at the edge of his vision. It was a whisper of gunfire and the metallic taste of adrenaline; a time when each calculated move meant life or death in clandestine alleys and backroom dealings where the currency was secrets and silence.

The memory surged as he parried a blow, the familiarity of the motion unearthing fragments of his past. He saw himself—years younger, sharper edges, and eyes alight with unwavering purpose—exchanging coded whispers with a contact in the rain-soaked streets of Berlin, the weight of a concealed weapon a comforting presence beneath his tailored suit.

"Good! That's it!" Dr. Stein's encouragement snapped him back to the present, but the ghost of the man he'd been clung to him, fueling his resolve. Each block and counterattack flowed from muscle memory, his body remembering a time when such actions were as natural as breathing.

"Focus, Nick," she called out again, but there was no need. The echo of his former life had sharpened his senses, and he moved with a grace that belied his age.

Finally, as the sparring session wound down, Nick executed a swift combination, driving his partner back with a series of precise strikes that culminated in a controlled takedown. Both men were panting, the energy in the room electric with the tangible display of skill and survival instinct.

As they separated, respect passing between them in the form of a nod, Dr. Stein stepped forward with a towel and a bottle of water, her analytical gaze missing nothing. "You're getting there, Nick. I can see the agent you were in every move you make."

Nick accepted the towel, wiping the sweat from his brow, the ghost of his past receding into the depths of his psyche, leaving behind a lingering sense of purpose. He was a man caught between worlds, but here, in this moment, he was one step closer to bridging the gap.

"Again tomorrow?" Dr. Stein asked, already knowing the answer.

"Tomorrow," Nick confirmed, his voice resolute, the reflection in the mirror now showing a man who understood the cost of what lay ahead—and was willing to pay it.

CHAPTER 25

In the meantime, in LA, a rare cold rain fell from the steel-gray sky as Michael pulled his coat tighter around him, shielding himself from the biting wind. He stood outside the courthouse where Diego Alvarez had narrowly escaped an assassination attempt just days before. The lawyer's involvement in high-profile cases against organized crime made him an ideal target for retaliation, and Michael couldn't shake the feeling that this attack was connected to Shain's murder.

"Martin, meet me at the courthouse," Michael said into his phone, his voice barely audible over the howling wind. "I think we need to take a closer look at the footage from the attack on Diego."

"Copy that," Martin replied sharply, determination etched into his every word. "I'm on my way."

As Michael waited, he studied the imposing neoclassical facade of the courthouse, its tall Corinthian columns standing as silent sentinels. The building's grandeur contrasted starkly with the seedy underbelly of crime that it sought to combat. Inside, the marbled halls were adorned with intricate frescoes depicting scenes of justice and virtue – a reminder of the ideals they all fought for.

When Martin arrived, they entered the courthouse's security office, greeted by the scent of stale coffee and the hum of electronics. The head of security, a burly man named Frank, escorted them to the bank of monitors displaying the CCTV footage from the day of the attack.

"Here's what we got," Frank said gruffly, rewinding the tape to show the moment Diego exited the courthouse, briefcase in hand. "Watch closely."

As the rain on the screen mirrored the weather outside, Michael leaned in, scrutinizing every detail. He noticed a black sedan parked across the street, its windows tinted, seemingly innocuous but out of place among the other vehicles. A figure in a dark coat and hat emerged from the shadows, approaching Diego at a brisk pace.

"Stop the tape," Michael instructed, his mind racing. "Zoom in on that man."

Frank obliged, and the figure's face came into focus – a cold, calculating stare masked by a half-smile. The man was unfamiliar to them, but there was no doubt he was the would-be assassin.

"Did you run facial recognition on him?" Martin asked, his gaze fixed on the screen.

"Of course," Frank replied, irritation creeping into his voice. "Nothing came up. He's a ghost."

"Damn," Martin muttered under his breath, frustration mounting. "We need to find out who this guy is and what his connection is to Shain's murder."

"Let's go over the footage again," Michael suggested, his eyes never leaving the screen. "There must be something we're missing. A clue, a pattern, anything."

For hours, they dissected the video, pausing and rewinding, searching for any detail that could bring them closer to the truth. Martin felt the weight of their responsibility growing heavier with each passing moment, a crushing pressure that threatened to consume him. But he knew that justice demanded nothing less than their unwavering commitment, and so they pressed on, driven by the knowledge that their efforts could make a difference in the fight against the darkness that lurked at the heart of their city.

CHAPTER 26

Martin stared at the intricate spiderweb of connections sprawled across the large whiteboard, the red strings tying together pieces of evidence from both crime scenes. His fingers drummed against the conference table in front of him as he tried to make sense of it all. Michael Freeman leaned against the wall nearby, his arms crossed over his chest and his eyes squinting as he scrutinized their progress.

"Alright," Martin said, taking a deep breath. "Let's go through this one more time. What do we know for sure?"

"Both Robert Shain and Diego Alvarez had ties to situations involving the drug business in South America," Michael replied, ticking off each point on his fingers. "Both victims were attacked in secluded areas with no witnesses or security footage. And both attacks were carried out with military precision."

"Right," Martin nodded, rubbing his temples. "And none of our leads have panned out so far. I think it's time we try something different.

Let's run that facial recognition software again, but this time, let's expand the search parameters to include operatives and affiliate in international databases."

"Good idea," Michael agreed, pulling up the program on his computer.

As the software scanned through countless images, Martin found himself pacing around the room, his mind racing with possibilities. Each connection seemed to only raise more questions, and he couldn't help but feel like they were missing a crucial piece of the puzzle.

"Wait, hold on," Michael exclaimed suddenly, leaning in closer to the screen. "We've got a match!"

"Who is it?" Martin asked, rushing to his side.

"Alexey Zaprinski," Michael answered, pulling up a file on the man. "Ex-KGB assassin. He's been off the grid for years, but his MO matches the attacks on Robertn Shain and Diego Alvarez perfectly. Cold, calculated, efficient... this guy is as dangerous as they come."

"Damn," Martin muttered, studying Zaprinski's icy green eyes and short-cropped blonde hair. "We've found our ghost."

"Looks like he's been working as a freelance killer for various criminal organizations since the fall of the Soviet Union," Michael continued, scrolling through the file."But what's his connection between this 3 attacks?".

"Money, power, revenge... who knows?" Martin pondered aloud, his thoughts spinning. "But one thing's for sure – we need to find this guy before he strikes again."

"Agreed," Michael said, closing the file and looking over at Martin with determination in his eyes. "Let's bring this bastard to justice."

As they set off to track down Alexey Zaprinski, Martin couldn't help but feel a renewed sense of purpose. The stakes were higher than ever, and the weight of their responsibility weighed heavily on his shoulders. But with each step closer to the truth, he knew that they were making a difference, fighting against the darkness that threatened to consume them all.

CHAPTER 27

Martin stared at the collection of photographs and documents scattered across the table, his brow furrowing in concentration as he tried to piece together the puzzle that was Alexey Zaprinski. Michael leaned against a nearby wall, flipping through a thick dossier on the ex-KGB assassin.

"His record is extensive," Michael said, pausing on a page detailing one of Zaprinski's early assignments in Eastern Europe. "He was involved in several high-profile hits during the Cold War – politicians, businessmen, even other spies. "

"Always someone standing in the way of power," Martin mused, noting the calculated brutality evident in each photograph. He could see it now: the sharp angles of Zaprinski's face, the cold efficiency in his steely green eyes. This man was a living weapon, forged in the fires of political intrigue and honed to a lethal edge by decades of experience.

"Looks like he's been freelancing for various criminal organizations since the Soviet Union fell," Michael continued, turning the page to reveal a list of known associates. "Russian mobsters, Chinese triads, even some Middle Eastern extremists.

Seems like he'll work for anyone who can meet his price."

"Which brings us back to the Medellin Cartel," Martin said, his jaw tightening in determination. "I've got a few contacts in the intelligence community who might be able to help us track him down. We need to find out what he's up to in Moscow and why he's targeting Shain and Michael. And what is the connection with Nick?"

"Good idea," Michael agreed, setting the dossier aside and reaching for his phone. "I'll get in touch with my people at the FBI, see if they have any leads on Zaprinski."

As the two men split up to make their calls, Martin could feel a sense of urgency building within him. Time was running out, and they needed to uncover the truth before more lives were lost. He dialed the number for one of his old contacts at MI6, hoping that their past collaborations would be enough to secure some much-needed information.

"Edward, it's Martin De Simone," he said when the call connected, his voice firm but friendly. "I need your help with something."

"Martin, my old friend!" Edward Smith replied, his British accent as crisp and polished as Martin remembered. "What can I do for you?"

"Have you heard anything about a former KGB assassin named Alexey Zaprinski?" Martin asked, cutting straight to the chase. "He's popped up in relation to a case I'm working on, and I need to know what he's been up to lately."

"Zaprinski, you say?" Edward mused, the sound of papers rustling in the background. "Haven't heard that name in years, but I'll see what I can find for you. Give me a few hours, and I'll call you back."

"Thanks, Edward. I owe you one," Martin said, hanging up the phone and turning to Michael, who had just finished his own call. "What did your people say?"

"Nothing concrete yet," Michael admitted, frustration in his eyes. "But they're going to dig deeper and get back to me as soon as they have something."

"Good. We'll wait to hear from them and then figure out our next move," Martin decided, running a hand through his short, dark hair. As they sat in silence, waiting for the crucial pieces of information that could lead them to Zaprinski, Martin couldn't help but think about the lives that hung in the balance. They needed to act fast and bring this deadly game to an end before more innocent people were caught in the crossfire.

CHAPTER 28

The sun dipped below the horizon, casting a fiery glow across the room as Martin and Michael sat at a table covered in files, photographs, and notes. Martin rubbed his temples, trying to make sense of the complex web of information they had gathered so far.

"Robert Shain was heavily involved in high-stakes litigation against organized crime," Martin mused aloud, scanning through one of the many case files. "Diego Alavarez was no different. Both men put their lives on the line for justice."

"Right," Michael agreed, leaning back in his chair, the weight of their responsibility evident in the furrow of his brow. "But what do they have in common that would make the Medellin Cartel want them dead?"

"Shain's company had a history of aggressive legal action against cartels, particularly the Medellin," Martin explained, tapping a finger on a news article detailing one such lawsuit. "Diego Alvarez, on the other hand, made a name for himself defending whistleblowers and witnesses in cases against the cartel."

"Could it be as simple as revenge?" Michael questioned, his dark eyes searching for answers in the scattered evidence before them.

"Maybe," Martin conceded, though the doubt in his voice was clear. "But there must be something more – a bigger reason for the cartel to hire someone like Zaprinski."

"Let's go through it again," Michael suggested, determination etched on his serious face. "Maybe we're missing something."

For hours, they dissected every detail, analyzing each piece of the puzzle. All the while, the golden light faded from the room, replaced by the soft glow of a desk lamp.

"Wait a minute," Martin said suddenly, his gaze locked on a document. "Shain's company was co-operating with NSA and was about to unveil a new technology to trace illegal funds – something that could cripple the financial operations of the cartels."

"Michael was working on a high-profile case that could expose a major political figure with ties to organized crime – someone with the power to protect the cartel. The CIA file of Alavarez is not full readable. Something unusual. This level is only the

President," Martin added, his voice tense with excitement.

"Could these be the reasons why they were targeted?" Martin wondered aloud, as realization dawned on him. "Was it not just about revenge, but also about protecting their criminal operations?"

"Seems plausible," Michael said with a slow nod. "We need to present this to Nick right away and figure out our next move."

CHAPTER 29

In the meantime, in the Swiss Alps, Nick's fists sliced through the air, carving out precision and power with each strike. Sweat streamed down the contours of his face, catching the light that poured in from the windows of the chalet's state-of-the-art gym. His graying hair was a wild contrast to the discipline etched into every sinew of his body—a body that had once navigated the clandestine corners of the world with lethal poise.

The room—sleek and utilitarian—was a far cry from the opulent grandeur typical of Swiss chalets. Surrounded by walls adorned with mirrors reflecting his relentless pursuit, Nick was oblivious to the mountain vistas beyond. His gaze was inward, fixed on an invisible adversary. The thud of his gloves against the leather bag resonated like a metronome measuring his resurgence, each punch a testament to the strength regained, speed sharpened, and agility honed since his retirement.

In between sets, he paused, his chest heaving as he took in the quiet hum of the high-altitude retreat. It was here, amidst the tactile beauty of polished wood and the scent of pine disinfectant, that Nick reacquainted himself with the man he used to be. Not just an agent, but a guardian of secrets, a protector of innocents—a role now beckoning him back from the shadows.

He bent forward to touch his toes, a simple move that once would have been effortless. Now, it was a measure of progress, a stretch that didn't strain as much as the week before. A twinge in his hamstring was a stark reminder of the bullet wound he'd sustained in Berlin, a physical scar that mirrored the mental ones he carried. As he straightened, Nick's reflection caught his eye; a momentary glimpse of the operative who'd played chess with international conspiracies, who'd danced dangerously close to the precipice of espionage, seduction, and betrayal.

"Protect," he muttered to himself, the word a silent vow reverberating through the expanse of his mind. Protect what? He mused over the question as he transitioned into a kata, his movements a fluid narrative of attack and defense. Was it the nation he served, or the people he loved? Or perhaps it was the very essence of truth he fought to uncover, the hidden threads of political intrigue he aimed to unravel.

As the session progressed, Nick's body remembered more of its old rhythm. Muscle memory kicked in, and with each pivot and kick, he moved closer to the ghost of the agent he once was, each step a defiant march against time and atrophy. He was rebuilding himself, piece by piece, not just for the sake of nostalgia, but because the world hadn't changed as much as he had. Shadows still crept, and threats loomed—threats he knew how to confront, if only he could fully reclaim the mantle he had once worn with such ease.

"Never easy, is it?" he whispered to his own image, a thin smile breaking across his features. But there was a gleam in his eye that spoke of a fire reignited, a passion unquenched by years or wounds. In this sanctuary of solitude, Nick Taylor was becoming whole again—not just for himself, but for a cause greater than any one man.

And when the day's regimen ended, he stood silently, acknowledging his reflection one last time before the Alpine sun dipped behind the peaks. Tomorrow, he knew, would bring new challenges, but also, new triumphs. For now, he allowed himself the smallest of satisfactions: he was ready, and the world outside these walls needed to prepare for the return of Nick Taylor, the spy reborn.

CHAPTER 30

Nick's fists pummeled the heavy bag with a rhythm that echoed through the high-ceilinged room of the chalet, each strike a testament to his growing strength. Droplets of sweat flung from his brow, catching the golden rays of afternoon light that filtered through the expansive windows. The space around him was a blend of rustic charm and modern luxury, wooden beams intersecting with sleek, state-of-the-art exercise equipment.

"Rotate your hips more on the cross," Dr Emma Stein advised, her voice calm yet assertive over the thud of leather on leather. She stood at the edge of Nick's peripheral vision, her long brown hair tied back in a ponytail that swayed with the subtle movements of her head as she observed his technique. "You've got the power, Nick. Channel it."

He adjusted his stance, feeling the alignment of muscle and intent as he followed her guidance. Each corrected motion was a piece of the intricate puzzle of combat, slots falling into place under her expert eye. His gray T-shirt, darkened by exertion, clung to his sculpted torso—a canvas of physical progress.

"Good," she nodded, her piercing blue eyes scanning for any inefficiency, any hint of the old injuries that once threatened to confine him to a life of inactivity. "Remember, it's not just about hitting hard; it's about hitting smart."

Nick paused, lowering his hands and turning to face her fully. Her presence was both commanding and nurturing, an embodiment of intellect and empathy. The soft glow of the sunset bathed her features, highlighting the faint lines of concentration that framed her eyes—those of a woman who had seen the struggles of recovery up close, yet never wavered in her belief of resurgence.

"Thanks, Emma," he said, his voice rough with fatigue but edged with respect. "I wouldn't be here without you."

She offered a modest smile, walking over to hand him a towel. "Your determination is what's driving this, Nick. I'm just steering you clear of the pitfalls."

He wiped his face, feeling the coarseness of the fabric against his skin, and the underlying tenderness of muscles pushed to their limits. In the reflection of the mirror-clad wall, he could see both of them—the soldier and the healer—and the silent promise they shared: to restore what had been lost.

"Let's call it a day," she suggested, glancing at the antique clock that hung above the stone fireplace. Its steady ticking was a comforting reminder of time's passage, of moments lived and those yet to come. "Rest is as crucial as the training itself."

"Agreed." He tossed the towel aside and stretched his arms above his head, feeling the satisfying pull along his limbs. In this haven nestled amidst the majesty of the Alps, with its crisp air and tranquil beauty, there was a profound sense of purpose burgeoning within him.

As he walked toward the exit, the plush carpet beneath his feet muffled his steps. The room's warmth was a stark contrast to the chill that awaited outside, where twilight embraced the world in hues of purples and blues. But within him, a fire raged, stoked by every drop of sweat and every moment of pain endured.

"See you tomorrow, Emma," he called over his shoulder, his voice steady and sure.

"Tomorrow, Nick," she replied, her tone imbued with the certainty of a mentor who had witnessed the birth of countless dawns.

With his back to the setting sun, Nick Taylor crossed the threshold of the chalet. The night was approaching, yes, but so too was the dawn of a new day—a day for which he was increasingly ready. His mind sharpened by adversity, his body honed by discipline, he faced the encroaching darkness not with trepidation, but with the confidence of a man reborn, ready to reclaim his place in a game that had no rules, only survivors.

CHAPTER 31

The cold Alpine air bit at Nick's skin as he stood on the balcony, looking out over a landscape that merged natural beauty with human ambition. The angular modernity of the chalet contrasted sharply with the timeless majesty of the snow-covered mountains. Inside, the décor was a blend of rustic charm and high-tech efficiency, a reflection of Dr. Stein's philosophy that progress should never overshadow heritage.

Nick leaned on the carved wooden railing, his eyes scanning the horizon where the last rays of sun kissed the peaks. His mind raced faster than his pulse after a high-intensity workout. He knew the road ahead was fraught with more than just physical challenges; it was lined with the ghosts of his past operations, each waiting to test his resolve.

"Answers are out there, in the shadows," he murmured to himself, feeling the weight of the silence around him. The serenity of the Alps was deceptive—the perfect backdrop for the mental chess game he was about to re-enter.

As darkness enveloped the valley, Nick's keen gaze detected a flicker of light—a signal? It was too consistent for a star, too solitary for an aircraft. A coded message from an old contact? A trap set by an adversary? His instincts, sharpened by years in the field, buzzed with alertness.

"Justice isn't served on a silver platter," he thought, acknowledging the web of international conspiracy that lay ahead. He turned back inside, letting the heavy door close with a soft thud behind him. As he made his way through the chalet, his footsteps were quiet but deliberate, echoing the calculated nature of his next moves.

Reaching his room, Nick flipped open the laptop that had been meticulously cleaned of any digital footprints. He began to draft an encrypted message, reaching out to a network that operated in the deepest shadows of global espionage. The glow of the screen lit his determined face, revealing a man who was both hunter and hunted in this high-stakes game.

Suddenly, the laptop pinged—an incoming communication. Nick tensed, his fingers poised above the keyboard. The message decrypted slowly, its contents materializing one character at a time. The words that appeared sent a jolt through his system, electrifying the night's calm:

"Phoenix rises at dawn. The eagle watches." Nick's breath hitched. Phoenix—his old operative code name, known only to a select few.

And the eagle? That could only mean...

A sharp crack outside shattered the silence, and Nick instinctively dived for cover. The window exploded inward, showering the room with shards of glass. An icy gust swept through the opening, carrying with it the promise of a storm.

As he crawled to safety, his body honed by relentless training, Nick Taylor knew that the game had just begun. Whoever had sent the message was making their move, and his journey for answers would be more perilous than he'd anticipated.

CHAPTER 32

Together, Martin and Michael compiled all the evidence, carefully organizing the information into a comprehensive report. As they worked, Martin's thoughts drifted to their goal: apprehending Zaprinski and uncovering the truth behind the attacks. The stakes were higher than ever, and innocent lives hung in the balance. They couldn't afford to fail.

"Alright," Martin said finally, as he saved the last file onto a flash drive. "Let's get this to Nick and see if we can put an end to this deadly game once and for all."

Martin's phone vibrated violently against the cold, polished surface of his desk. The dim light from the screen cast an eerie glow across the documents strewn about, a stark contrast to the blackness that enveloped the room. With a furrowed brow and a mild annoyance tugging at the corners of his mouth, he reached for the device. His heart skipped a beat as he recognized the name flashing on the screen: Diego Alvarez.

"Martin," Diego's voice trembled through the line, barely audible over the faint beeping of hospital machines in the background. "I don't feel safe here.

Someone tried to kill me, and I can't shake the feeling that they're still after me."

"Diego, we're doing everything we can to find out who's behind this," Martin reassured him, his eyes scanning the darkened room as if searching for any potential threats lurking in the shadows. "We've got a lead, but we need more time."

"Time is something I might not have, Martin," Diego insisted, desperation seeping into his tone. "Please, you have to get me out of here."

"Alright, let me make some calls," Martin replied, his mind racing with the implications of Diego's request. He knew full well that extracting Diego from the hospital would be risky, but the alternative seemed even more dangerous.

"Thank you, Martin," Diego whispered before hanging up.

Wasting no time, Martin dialed Nick's number, pacing back and forth across the room as he waited for his former CIA colleague to answer.

"Nick, it's Martin. Diego just called – he believes his life is in imminent danger and wants us to get him out of the hospital immediately," Martin explained, struggling to keep his voice steady as the gravity of the situation settled upon him.

"Christ," Nick muttered, the sound of rustling papers in the background suggesting he was already formulating a plan. "Alright, we'll need to act fast. I'll arrange for a private jet to fly him to Switzerland. It's one of the few places we can guarantee his safety."

"Switzerland? Are you sure?" Martin questioned, his concern mounting.

"Positive," Nick replied firmly. "Now get over to that hospital and make sure Diego is ready to leave at a moment's notice. We can't afford any delays."

"Understood," Martin said, his resolve solidifying as he ended the call and grabbed his jacket. The weight of responsibility pressed down on him as he raced out the door; extracting Diego from the hospital would be no easy feat, but he had no choice. He couldn't let another innocent life be claimed by this deadly game of international intrigue.

CHAPTER 33

The sun dipped below the horizon, casting an eerie glow over the sterile white walls of the hospital as Martin and Michael approached Diego's room. They could feel the tension in the air, a palpable sense of urgency that hung heavy like the impending darkness.

"Remember, we need to be discreet," Martin whispered to Michael, his eyes scanning the hallway for any sign of danger. "The last thing we need is to draw attention."

Michael nodded; his jaw set with determination. As they entered Diego's room, they found him sitting on the edge of his bed, his face pale and gaunt but filled with steely resolve.

"Are you ready?" Martin asked quietly, knowing that the time for hesitation had long since passed.

Diego nodded, his eyes flicking nervously toward the door. "Let's get out of here."

As they moved through the dimly lit corridors, Martin couldn't help but marvel at the contrast between the hospital's pristine exterior and the tumultuous emotions roiling within its walls. It was a reminder that appearances could be deceiving – a lesson he'd learned all too well throughout his years as a spy.

"Keep close," Martin whispered, guiding Diego and Michael through a service exit that led to the parking lot. The sleek black SUV they'd used to arrive sat waiting, its engine idling softly in the darkened lot.

"Get in," Michael ordered, his voice steady despite the adrenaline coursing through his veins. He slid into the driver's seat, gripping the wheel with white-knuckled intensity as Martin helped Diego into the backseat before climbing in himself.

"LA Airport," Martin said tersely, feeling the weight of their task bearing down on them. "And step on it."

As the car sped through the deserted streets of Los Angeles, Diego leaned against the window, staring out at the city that had become a prison to him. "Thank you," he murmured, his voice barely audible over the roar of the engine. "I know this isn't easy for any of us."

"Save your thanks for when we're safely in Switzerland," Martin replied, his gaze fixed on the rearview mirror, ever vigilant for signs of pursuit.

"Switzerland?" Diego questioned, his eyebrows raised. "Why there?"

"Nick's arranged everything," Martin explained, his tone reassuring despite the nagging doubts that plagued him. "It's one of the few places we can guarantee your safety."

"Nick..." Diego murmured, a smile ghosting across his lips. "I always knew I could count on him."

The SUV roared to a stop at a private hangar on the outskirts of LA Airport, where a sleek jet awaited them. As they boarded, Martin felt a flicker of hope – perhaps they'd managed to pull off this daring escape without a hitch.

Hours later, as the jet touched down at Emmen, a secret military airport in central Switzerland, Martin allowed himself a small sigh of relief. They'd done it – they'd managed to extract Diego from the heart of danger. But there was no time to celebrate; they still had work to do.

As they disembarked, the crisp Alpine air hit their faces like a slap, a stark contrast to the stifling heat of Los Angeles. The night was alive with the sounds of crickets and rustling leaves, offering a serene backdrop to their harrowing journey.

"Come on," Martin urged, leading the way to a waiting car that would take them to the chalet in Elms where Nick was holed up. He could sense the stress radiating from his old friend even before they entered the cozy wooden building, its warm glow providing a welcome sanctuary from the darkness outside.

CHAPTER 34

Finally, they are all reunite. The Chalet in Elms was a fortress in its own right. Hidden within a thicket of ancient pines, its timbered façade and stone foundation spoke of timeless strength. Inside, the warmth of a crackling fire and the rich scent of aged wood welcomed them. Antiques adorned the rooms, each piece meticulously curated—a physical manifestation of Nick Taylor's appreciation for history and craftsmanship.

Nick, tall and broad-shouldered, his graying hair a badge of his years in service, stood before the hearth as they entered. His piercing gaze sized up the situation in an instant. With firm handshakes and subtle nods, they gathered around a hefty oak table, its surface scarred from years of use.

"Zaprinski," Martin began, his voice low and steady, "He's our ghost from the past. An ex-KGB assassin turned freelance. We've spotted him in the footage from both crime scenes."

Michael produced a tablet, displaying high-resolution images of a man with a cold, expressionless visage—an artist of death. "Facial recognition pegged him. No question about it."

Nick's sharp gaze intensified. "And the clock watch in my apartment... gone. Zaprinski knows its worth." He leaned forward, hands pressed firmly against the table. "It contained a microchip detailing the Cartel's entire financial network. Names, transactions, distribution chains—worldwide."

Diego interjected, his voice a whisper but carrying weight. "Shain and I were working on something big. NSA-grade tech designed to track financial movements covertly and globally. If we'd succeeded..."

"Then you'd have put a stranglehold on their operations," Martin finished for him. Their gazes locked, and in that exchange, they understood the gravity of what they held—the keys to dismantling a global criminal empire.

As the fire crackled and cast shadows across the room, the pieces of the puzzle lay bare before them. They could see the outline of the conspiracy, the tendrils of intrigue that tied the Cartel to the bloodshed. And now, ensconced within the walls of the Chalet, they plotted their next move against a backdrop of political chessboards and unseen threats, armed with information as lethal as any weapon.

They knew the road ahead would be fraught with peril, but within the safety of the chalet's embrace, they felt the stirrings of a plan taking shape—one that promised justice and retribution.

The embers of the dying fire cast a warm, amber glow over the room as Martin rose from his chair. He could see the silhouettes of his companions outlined against the rustic elegance of the chalet's decor, each figure etched with the weariness of their day's triumphs and trials. Michael leaned back in his seat, arms crossed over his chest, his sharp black eyes reflecting a mind that was always analysing, always calculating. His lean figure was relaxed, yet there remained an air of readiness about him, as if he could spring into action at any moment.

Nick stood by the window, his tall, athletic frame a pillar of strength against the backdrop of the Swiss Alps' eternal majesty outside. The moonlight streaming in highlighted the silver in his once-dark hair, a testament to battles fought and wisdom gained. His gaze lingered on the snow-capped peaks, the rugged lines of his face softening for a moment in contemplation.

Diego, still bearing the pallor of convalescence, had found solace in an oversized armchair, its plush upholstery enveloping his slender form like a protective cocoon. The golden threads woven into the fabric shimmered in the firelight—a stark contrast to the simplicity of his hospital gown and the vulnerability it implied.

"Time to turn in," Martin announced, his voice carrying an undercurrent of fatigue that mirrored the collective exhaustion of the group.

"Indeed," Nick agreed, turning from the window. "We've earned our rest tonight."

As they made their way through the chalet, Martin noted the harmony between the building's ancient timbers and modern comforts. The wooden beams, sturdy and aged, told stories of a time long past while supporting the weight of the latest technological advancements discreetly integrated into the structure. The walls were adorned with antique tapestries, their intricate patterns whispering tales of intrigue and history, now silent witnesses to the unfolding drama of their present endeavor.

Their footsteps were muffled by the thick, hand-woven rugs that lined the corridors, leading them to individual chambers designed with an understated opulence. Each room was a sanctuary, appointed with luxurious linens atop beds carved from rich mahogany, and en-suite bathrooms boasting gleaming fixtures that reflected the soft light from oil lamps perched on marble countertops.

Martin entered his room, where floor-to-ceiling windows offered a panoramic view of the night sky, the constellations a map of endless possibilities. He paused to draw the heavy velvet curtains, appreciating the sumptuous texture between his fingers—a subtle reminder of the life he'd left behind for clandestine operations and covert meetings.

Before retiring, he took a moment to reflect on the day's success. They had connected critical dots in a puzzle that spanned continents and cut deep into the shadowy world of espionage. Their collective efforts had yielded a breakthrough that promised hope in what had seemed an impenetrable darkness.

Lying down on the bed, Martin allowed himself a rare smile. There was a certain poetry to their current state—hidden away in a fortress of tranquillity, they were on the verge of exposing turmoil that churned beneath the surface of global corruption.

"Goodnight, my friends," he whispered to the absent figures, the words a silent vow to uphold the trust they placed in each other. With the strategic groundwork laid and the intelligence gathered securely within their minds, sleep came easily. It embraced them like the mountain's calm, and in those quiet hours, the agents found respite, their spirits buoyed by the promise of justice soon to be served.

Outside, nature continued her endless symphony—the rustling leaves and distant calls of nocturnal creatures a lullaby for the weary warriors. And as the night deepened, so did their conviction that, come morning, they would rise again to challenge the chaos that threatened the world's order. Tonight, however, accomplishment cradled them to sleep.

CHAPTER 35

The alpine sun filtered through the gauzy curtains, casting a warm glow over the rustic interior of Nick's and his friend's room. As the door creaked open, Dr. Emma Stein stepped inside, her presence as comforting as the morning rays.

"Good morning, Nick, Martin, Michael and Diego " she greeted them, her voice carrying the melody of optimism. A smile unfurled across her face, bright as the daffodils that dotted the chalet's garden outside. Her long brown hair was pulled back into a practical ponytail, revealing the sharp intelligence in her piercing blue eyes.

"Let's get to work," Martin said, standing up with a renewed sense of determination. "There's no time to waste. But first a big cup of black coffee". The group agree to wake up and start some extra analysis to get ready to find Zaprinski.

Together, they delved deeper into the day, their minds sharp and focused, knowing that each piece of the puzzle brought them closer to unveiling the truth. And somewhere in the intricate dance of light and shadow, in the interplay of intellect and intuition, Martin and Michael found solace in the knowledge that they were not just chasing a ghost—they were hunting down a spectre of a bygone era, determined to bring him to justice.

"Alexey Zaprinski," Martin read aloud, his tone laced with a mixture of triumph and trepidation. The profile that filled the screen showed a man in his 40s, his short-cropped blonde hair stark against the pallor of his skin, his steely green eyes devoid of warmth. The former KGB operative exuded danger, each line on his face etched with the history of a life spent in the shadows.

"Damn," Michael uttered under his breath. "An ex-KGB killer. That explains the efficiency."

"Explains why we're playing catch-up, too," Martin said, his thoughts already racing ahead. "He's been off-grid for years, but now he resurfaces for this? There's a bigger game at play."

"Agreed," Michael nodded. "We need to find out who's pulling his strings before he cuts them—and us—clean off."

Martin's fingers danced across the keyboard, each keystroke slicing through layers of encrypted databases like a scalpel. The glow from the monitor cast harsh shadows over his stern features—an angular jaw set in determination, eyes that had seen too much and yet missed nothing. Despite the late hour, Martin's posture remained impeccable, a testament to years of military discipline; his dark hair, though short, showed no sign of disarray.

"Look at this," Michael said, voice low but laced with urgency as he peered over a stack of scattered files, each one a breadcrumb leading back to Alexey Zaprinski's past. His lean frame was hunched in concentration, the overhead light glinting off his black hair.

On the screen, a dossier expanded, revealing a timeline of Zaprinski's assignments—shadows within shadows. There were grainy photographs of a younger Zaprinski, his wiry build deceptive of the lethality it contained. A paper trail of destruction followed him like a morbid résumé, listing associations with organizations whose names were spoken only in whispers.

"Here," Martin pointed to an operation in Chechnya, "he worked with the Vory. And this," his finger moved to another file, "ties him to the Bratva in Brighton Beach."

Michael leaned closer, the scent of black coffee on his breath mixing with the sterile air of the office. "The Cartel must've offered him something substantial to get him out of retirement. Or someone did."

"Or both," Martin mused. He reached for his phone, its sleek surface cold against his warm palm. He dialed with precision, each number connecting them to resources most would kill to access.

"Viktor, it's Martin De Simone," he spoke into the receiver, his voice carrying the weight of old camaraderie and unspoken debts. "We need everything you have on Zaprinski—current location, activities... Anything Moscow can provide."

The room filled with the tinny echo of a response, a voice distorted by distance and secure lines. Martin listened intently, his gaze never leaving the screen, while Michael scribbled notes onto a legal pad, the pen scratching in harmony with the distant voice.

"Spotted at the Bolshoi last month," Martin relayed, "seems our ghost enjoys the ballet."

"Or meeting someone who does," Michael interjected, his mind already profiling the kind of contacts Zaprinski would keep.

"Thanks, Viktor. Keep us updated." Martin ended the call and placed the phone back on the desk with a soft clack.

"From the looks of it, Zaprinski's been active in Moscow's underbelly," Martin summarized, "mixing with the same ilk he used to run with. It's not random; it's strategic."

"Let's compile everything we have," Michael suggested, "connections, sightings, patterns. We'll find the thread that leads to Zaprinski—and to whoever's behind this."

They worked in silence, the hum of the computer a steady heartbeat in the room.. As dawn threatened to break, the two men sat amongst the evidence of their quarry, a mosaic of violence and betrayal laid bare before them. Yet amidst the darkness, there was a glimmer of hope—a belief that justice, though elusive, was within their grasp.

"Let's lay it all out for Nick," Martin decided, standing up and stretching his back.

"Agreed," Michael said, closing the file with a snap. "We'll show him the web we've uncovered: the transactions, the shell companies, the dead ends that suddenly make sense when you see them from above."

"Then we strategize," Martin added, his mind already formulating plans to corner Zaprinski. "Nick's experience will be invaluable. We'll need his insight to trap a ghost."

"Especially one as elusive as Zaprinski," Michael remarked, standing up to stretch his lean frame.

Together, they gathered the evidence: photographs, financial records, transcripts of intercepted communications. Each document was meticulously organized, forming a tapestry of intrigue and malice. They placed the collected intelligence into a secure briefcase, its contents a narrative of treachery that only they could read.

"Ready to bring down a kingpin?" Martin asked, a wry smile flashing across his face as he hoisted the briefcase.

"Let's do it," Michael replied, his own smile mirroring Martin's determination.

With their findings in tow, they exited the study, the door clicking shut behind them like the final note of a symphony. The sun was peeking over the horizon, igniting the sky with the promise of a new day and the hope that justice would soon be served.

CHAPTER 36

Nick Taylor's eyes scanned the interior of the sleek Gulfstream as he boarded, the hum of anticipation buzzing louder than the aircraft's engines. His athletic frame maneuvered easily down the aisle, a testament to years of maintaining CIA physical standards even into his fifties. The fine lines etched around his eyes spoke of a life scrutinizing details others often missed. Graying hair, once jet black, now served as a distinguished crown, adding an air of seasoned wisdom to his sharp gaze.

Martin De Simone followed close behind, his muscular build hinting at strength not only physical but of character. There was an ever-present readiness in Martin's stance, a sense that he could spring into action without a moment's hesitation. His short, dark hair was impeccably groomed, and his deep-set eyes reflected a mind always in motion, analyzing, planning.

"Feels like old times, doesn't it?" Martin remarked, a wry smile tugging at his lips as they took their seats, the leather upholstery hugging their forms like a bespoke suit. The cabin whispered of affluence, from the polished mahogany panels to the subtle golden accents that adorned the fixtures. It was a far cry from the sterile government transports they were used to, yet there was no room for complacency; every luxury here served as a reminder of the stakes at play.

"Old times," Nick mused. "But with higher stakes."

"Except this time, we're not the ones being pursued," Michael added, adjusting the strap of the bag slung over his shoulder. His voice carried an undercurrent of excitement, betraying his anticipation for the mission ahead.

The plane taxied onto the runway, the engines' roar crescendoing until they were airborne, leaving Switzerland and its glittering Alps a receding memory. Their destination: Istanbul and after Moscow, where Alexey Zaprinski, the enigma wrapped in a riddle, awaited them.

As the flight progressed towards Istanbul, where they would connect to Moscow, it became a delicate ballet of sky and machine. The tranquility of cruising altitude was intermittently shattered by pockets of turbulence that rattled the plane, causing a symphony of gasps.

They landed in Istanbul amid a throng of international travelers, the airport a vibrant tapestry of cultures and intentions. Here, they transitioned to their connecting commercial flight, the bustle of the terminal a stark contrast to the remote airstrip in Emmen from which they had departed hours earlier. The layover was brief, a mere interlude in their quest, and soon they were lifting off again, this time bound for the heart of Russia.

The final leg of the journey unfolded under the cloak of night, the world outside their windows an abyss dotted with the occasional flicker of distant lights. Inside the cabin, whispers of conversation and the soft clicks of keyboards provided a steady soundtrack. Nick reviewed the mission details in his mind. There is a detail that make the difference: the microchip hidden in his clock watch of 18 Century was stolen and it was in the wrong hands.

Mid-flight, the jet hit a pocket of turbulence, jostling the passengers within. Nick's hand instinctively went to the armrest, his grip firm and steady—a trait honed through years of navigating far more treacherous situations than an air current.

As the landscape beneath them became a patchwork quilt of greens and browns, Nick's thoughts wandered to Alexey Zaprinski. His adversary's image was etched in his mind: the cold, calculating gaze of a seasoned killer. Nick knew the man's type well—intellectual yet lethal, a chess player who thought several moves ahead.

"Steady as we go," Nick murmured, his voice a calm anchor amidst the shuddering cabin. He caught Martin's nod, an unspoken understanding between men who had faced down death together and walked away.

"Keep focused," Nick reminded himself and his companions. "We're not here to make friends."

As the plane began its descent, the landscape gave way to the sprawling metropolis of Moscow, a city of contrasts and concealed truths. Nick felt the familiar thrill of the hunt surge within him—a feeling he'd known countless times, yet it never grew old.

"Ready for what's next?" Martin asked, catching Nick's eye.

"Always," Nick replied, his gaze unwavering. It was a simple affirmation, but it held the weight of their shared history and the unspoken promise of loyalty that would see them through the trials ahead.

CHAPTER 37

The jet wheels kissed the icy tarmac with a hiss, a sharp contrast to the gentle hum that had cradled Nick's thoughts during the flight. Moscow unfurled beneath them like a vast tapestry of steel and snow, the city streets a labyrinthine dance of chaos and methodical precision. A bitter cold welcomed them as they descended the plane's steps, the kind of chill that bit at exposed skin and promised a harsh winter.

"Welcome to the Russian bear's den," Michael muttered, pulling his coat tighter around him.

"Let's just hope we don't end up its dinner," Martin shot back, the breath misting from his mouth forming transient clouds in the frigid air.

Their private Maybach was a sleek black vessel amidst a sea of bustling traffic, tinted windows offering an illusion of solitude in the crowded metropolis. As they slid into the leather seats, the warmth inside offered a brief respite from the biting wind outside. The cityscape flew by in a blur, the vibrant life of Moscow pulsing like the heartbeat of some great beast—unseen but ever-present.

Hotel Lotte, in Noviskiy Boulevard, rose before them, an edifice of luxury and refinement standing guard against the stark Moscow skyline. Its lobby was a haven of opulence, marble floors gleaming under the chandeliers' soft glow, while antique furnishings whispered tales of a grandiose past.

"Mr. Komutov will see you now," the receptionist informed them with a practiced smile. Sergey Komutov was an enigma wrapped in a conundrum—a former KGB agent turned officially mathematician and chess master. His hair, though thinning, seemed an afterthought compared to the intensity that burned in his analytical gaze. It was the look of a man who had dissected the world into equations and strategies, each move calculated with precision.

"Nick, isn't it?" Sergey's voice was soft yet carried an undercurrent of iron. "I've been expecting you."

"Thank you for agreeing to meet with us," Nick replied, extending a hand that Sergey shook with a firm grip.

"Of course," Sergey said, releasing Nick's hand. "When it comes to Zaprinski, my interest is... piqued."

His reputation preceded him—a man who could unravel the most intricate puzzles with the same ease he dominated the chessboard. Though his suit bore no trace of ostentation, it hung on his lean frame with an understated elegance that spoke of meticulous care.

"Shall we get down to business then?" Sergey motioned towards a secluded corner of the lobby, where the din of the hotel seemed to fade into a distant murmur.

"Lead the way," Nick said, exchanging a knowing glance with his companions. They followed Sergey, their footsteps echoing softly on the marble floor, every sense attuned to the game of espionage that lay ahead.

CHAPTER 38

The private room on the first floor of Hotel Lotte was a study in opulence—a blend of modern luxury and classic Russian elegance. Heavy drapes, edged with gold thread, muffled the clamor of Moscow's winter evening, while a grand chandelier cast a warm glow over the polished mahogany table that anchored the space.

Nick Taylor surveyed the room, his sharp gaze taking in the details: the ornate carvings on the furniture, the rich texture of the leather chairs, the subtle scent of aged wood mingled with the faint aroma of high-quality vodka. It was the perfect backdrop for clandestine meetings where fates could be decided over a handshake or a whispered revelation.

Martin De Simone stood rigid by the window, his stocky frame outlined against the frost-laden glass, dark hair cropped short in a no-nonsense style. His hands, calloused from years of service, rested lightly on the back of a chair—a silent testament to his readiness to leap into action if needed.

Michael leaned against a sideboard, his relaxed posture belying the alertness that flickered in his eyes. The lamplight played across his weathered features, casting shadows that hinted at the many secrets etched into his soul.

Sergey Komutov sat across from them, an island of calm in the undercurrent of tension. His thinning hair was brushed back meticulously, and his suit, though devoid of embellishment, whispered of tailored precision. He folded his hands on the table, his analytical gaze scrutinizing each man in turn as if they were pieces on a chessboard, each move revealing their motives and intentions.

"Zaprinski is a ghost," Sergey began, his voice resonating with the quiet confidence of a man accustomed to unraveling mysteries. "Finding him...it's a perilous endeavor."

Nick nodded, acknowledging the gravity of their task. "We know the risks," he said, his voice a low rumble of conviction. "But this goes beyond personal vendettas. It's about justice—about stopping a killer before he strikes again."

"Justice," Sergey echoed, weighing the word as if it were a riddle to be solved. "A noble pursuit. But nobility can be a costly affair."

"Cost is no object when lives are on the line," Martin interjected, his tone edged with the steel of unwavering principle.

"Indeed," Sergey conceded, a hint of respect surfacing in his otherwise impassive demeanor. "You have the resolve. But do you possess the information? Zaprinski's location remains a cipher within a labyrinth."

Nick leaned forward, the ambient light catching the silver threads in his graying hair. "We're close," he assured, his blue eyes steady. "We've been tracking his movements, piecing together his network. What we need is the final piece—the exact location."

"Patience," Sergey advised, the ghost of a smile touching his lips. "This game is played in careful stages. When the time is right, when the board is set, I will provide you with the coordinates."

"Time isn't a luxury we have," Nick argued, his determination unyielding as the frozen ground outside. "Every minute we wait, Zaprinski becomes harder to find, and more people are at risk."

"Let's see" Sergey said, recognizing the unshakable commitment in the faces before him.

CHAPTER 39

Nick paced the length of the dimly lit private hotel room, his footsteps muted against the plush carpet. His graying hair seemed almost silver in the low light, and his tall, athletic frame cast a long shadow across the floor. He halted abruptly, turning to face Sergey, who sat with the poise of a chess grandmaster, his thinning hair a stark contrast to his otherwise meticulous appearance.

"I must admit, your visit has me...intrigued," Sergey said, steepling his fingers together. "It is not often I receive guests of your stature in Moscow."

"Desperate times call for unlikely alliances," Nick replied evenly.

Sergey raised an eyebrow. "Yes, I have heard of your reputation, Mr. Taylor. A formidable spy in your time." His glance shifted to Martin and Michael in turn. "And agents De Simone and Freeman, of course. Legends, even in my circles."
"You're too kind," Martin said wryly.

"You need to give us the location of this criminal, Sergey," Nick pressed on.

"I will do my best. But tell me...why seek him out? He is dangerous." Sergey's gaze was penetrating.

Nick hesitated. How much to reveal? He opted for a version of the truth. "Let's just say he has information we urgently need. Information that poses a global security threat if it falls into the wrong hands."

Sergey considered this, then gave a brisk nod. "Very well. I will help, but we must be discreet. Many eyes in this city."

Nick felt a wave of relief. "Good. We'll provide any resources you need."

The men discussed logistics, poring over maps and making notes. Nick observed Sergey's keen intellect as he pointed out potential locations and surveillance blind spots. The man certainly knew this city inside and out.

With the first part of the discussion with Sergey, Nick felt the stirrings of hope. Perhaps this unlikely alliance would lead them to Zaprinski after all. " Now is the time to cut the deal with this guy" was thinking Nick.

Sergey leaned back in his chair, gazing at Nick with a hint of skepticism. "You seem certain we will find this Zaprinski. But Russia is large, and Moscow has many shadows to hide in."

Nick nodded. "I know it's a long shot. But we must try. Zaprinski has intel that could undermine national security if it gets out. He steal a microchip from my house with details about Medellin Cartel "

"Da, you said as much earlier," Sergey replied. "But what is this intel exactly? And why involve yourself in such danger?"

Nick hesitated. He needed Sergey's help, but how much to reveal?

"Let's just say Zaprinski was hired for a job, one with big implications," Nick said carefully. "We need to find who hired him and why. Lives are at stake. He attempted my life and kill few people in US".

Sergey narrowed his eyes, considering this. After a moment, he shook his head.

"A noble cause, perhaps, but foolish. Zaprinski is not so easy to find, nor convince to talk."

Nick leaned forward, holding Sergey's gaze. "Which is why I need you. Your skills, your resources. With them, we have a chance."

Sergey looked skeptical. "Even if we find him, it is madness to confront Zaprinski directly. He is dangerous."

"I know," Nick said. "But we'll take precautions. We just need to get him alone, someplace secure. We'll go in prepared."

Martin chimed in. "Nick's right. Zaprinski has information we desperately need. We're willing to take the risk."

"Kidnapping Zaprinski is a high stakes move," Sergey said, his analytical gaze scrutinizing Nick. "It's not just about locating him. Can you handle what comes after? The repercussions will be severe."

Martin interjected, his muscular build tense with restrained energy. "We've faced worse odds before. Our record should speak for itself."

"Records are history," Sergey retorted, folding his hands on the table. "This is now, and Zaprinski is no trivial opponent. He's a specter in the shadows, a ghost that doesn't want to be found."

"Which is why we need someone like you",

Michael said, his voice steady, revealing none of the adrenaline coursing through his veins. And he concluded "This guy is criminal hired by the most dangerous criminal organization of South America, The Medellin Cartel!'

Nick met Sergey's steady stare with one of equal conviction. "Sergey, I've been in this game long enough to know when to take a risk. We get one shot at this. Kidnapping Zaprinski, interrogating him—it's our best chance to prevent further bloodshed."

"Your confidence is admirable," Sergey said dryly. "But confidence alone doesn't dismantle a man like Zaprinski."

"True," Nick conceded. "But experience does." He leaned in closer, the lines of his face etched with the hard-earned wisdom of past covert operations. "I've been where you are, weighed down by doubts. But I've also been on the other side, where action clears the fog of hesitation. Trust me when I say we can do this, and we can do it right."

Sergey studied him for a moment longer, then exhaled slowly, as if releasing the weight of his skepticism. "You have a reputation, Nick Taylor. As a skilled operative. As someone who sees things through."

"Reputations are built on actions," Nick replied. "Let us prove ours."

Sergey frowned, glancing between them. Finally, he sighed.

"You are serious about this, I see. Reckless, but courageous." He paused. "Very well. I will help you find Zaprinski. But extraction, that is your affair."

Nick felt a rush of gratitude. "Thank you, Sergey. We won't forget this."

He extended his hand, and after a moment Sergey shook it firmly. An unspoken pact made.

Nick sat back, pleased with their progress. "Once we grab Zaprinski, we'll take him someplace secure for questioning. Any ideas?"

Sergey thought for a moment. "I have a safehouse we can use. Out of the way, no connection to me. It should suffice." "Perfect," Nick said. He felt the thrill of the hunt taking hold, that addictive mix of fear and purpose that had drawn him back to this life again and again.

"Very well," Sergey acquiesced, the glint in his eyes betraying a hint of respect. "I will help you find Zaprinski. But remember," he warned with his strong Russian accent, his voice lowering to a near whisper, "the game we're playing has no rules and no mercy. One misstep and we could all be pawns sacrificed in a much larger strategy."

"Understood," Nick acknowledged, a grim smile touching his lips. "We play to win, Sergey. Always."

Come what may, they would be ready. Zaprinski was the key, and failure was not an option. The game was on.

CHAPTER 40

After a short break, all the Group met again in the strategic room on the first floor, a strategic command center temporarily fashioned with the urgency of their mission. Martin De Simone with Michael was cross-referencing maps of Moscow with an intensity that mirrored his years of military precision. Sergey Komutov, their newfound ally, hunched over a chessboard in the corner of the room, his thinning hair and analytical gaze fixed on the pieces as if they were operatives in the field.

"Chess is like warfare," Sergey commented without lifting his eyes, moving a bishop with calculated assurance. "Every piece has its role, its strength. Together, they form a strategy." He finally looked up at Nick and Martin, a wry smile cutting across his solemn features. "And our objective is clear—Zaprinski."

"Exactly," Nick agreed, clapping a hand on Sergey's shoulder. The cold Russian air had left a rosy hue on Nick's weathered cheeks, but his grey eyes were sharp, reflecting a mind that never stopped strategizing. "You're the eyes, Sergey. Your knowledge of Moscow, your network—it's our edge."

"And you," Sergey pointed to Martin, "the muscle?"

"More than that," Martin interjected before Nick could answer, his muscular frame straightening. "I'm the contingency. The fail-safe for when things don't go by the playbook—which they rarely do."

"Speaking of playbooks," Nick said, redirecting the conversation as he unfolded a large map of Moscow on the wooden table. The creases were sharp, mirroring the lines of determination etched into his face. "We've got leads to follow, contacts to meet. Zaprinski's a ghost, but ghosts leave trails."

Sergey joined them at the table, his attention shifting from the game of chess to the real-life game unfolding. "This area," he pointed to a dense cluster of buildings on the map, "is where Zaprinski might hide. It's perfect for someone who doesn't want to be found."

"Then we start there," Nick decided, his fingers tracing the streets that snaked around the district like veins. "We need equipment. Discreet comms, surveillance gear. Nothing that screams foreign operatives."

"Local tech," Michael suggested, running a hand through his short dark hair. "Can't risk imports. They'll be flagged."

"Leave that to me," Sergey assured, standing tall despite his lean frame. "I have contacts. We will blend in like shadows at dusk."

"Good," Nick nodded, folding the map with precision and slipping it into a leather satchel that rested against the leg of the table. His movements were swift, betraying years of training where every second counted. "Remember, Zaprinski is no amateur. We can't afford to underestimate him."

"Nor will we," Martin added, checking the chamber of a handgun with a click that resonated in the silence of the room. "But he hasn't faced us yet."

"Let's keep it that way until we have him where we want him," Nick said, locking eyes with both men. "No surprises. We work as one unit, each piece supporting the other."

"Da," Sergey replied with a nod, the word hanging in the air like a vow.

"Tonight, we prepare," Nick stated, the energy in the room coalescing into a tangible force of readiness. "Tomorrow, we hunt."

The group men stood in unison; their alliance cemented by the shared objective that brought them together—the capture of Alexey Zaprinski. Each carried the weight of their past, their skills honed by years of clandestine service. Together, they formed more than a team; they were a living strategy set into motion, ready to face the labyrinthine streets of Moscow and the specter that haunted them.

CHAPTER 41

The day had dawned gray, the sky a heavy canvas of clouds that seemed to press upon the sprawling city below. The streets of Moscow were alive with the pulse of the masses—people wrapped in thick winter coats moving like blood through the veins of the metropolis. Nick Taylor's breath materialized before him in fleeting clouds as he walked in the direction of the Smoleskaya Metro station close to the Ministry of Foreign Affairs with purposeful strides, flanked by Martin and Sergey Komutov.

Sergey, despite his intellectual demeanor, moved with an athlete's grace—a testament to a lifetime spent evading surveillance and playing the most dangerous game of chess. His attire was understated, yet meticulously chosen for mobility and nondescript appearance, the mark of a man who understood the subtleties of blending in.

Nick's sharp gaze swept over the surroundings, instinctively cataloging potential threats, escape routes, and watchful eyes that lingered too long. Every passerby was a possible informant, every window a vantage point. They conversed in hushed tones, their words barely breaching the muffling effect of the dense, cold air.

"Keep your phone secure," Nick reminded Sergey, whose thinning hair did little to conceal the earpiece that provided a direct line of communication with Michael back to their temporary headquarters at the Hotel Lotte. "We're not the only ones hunting today."

"Understood." Sergey's analytical eyes flickered with the thrill of the chase, a spark that belied his otherwise calm exterior.

"Zaprinski was last spotted here," Sergey said, circling an area on the map. "An industrial district on the outskirts of Moscow. He is known to frequent the warehouses there."

"Let's enter the metro and get there to make a first tour of recognition" say Nick to Sergey.

Nick studied the map, considering entry points and escape routes. "Tight quarters for an extraction. We'll need to draw him out into the open."

"I have contacts keeping an eye out for him," Sergey said. "With some luck, we may get advance warning before he arrives."

Martin nodded. "Good. The more prep time the better. We should stock up on supplies too - weapons, restraints, comms equipment."

As they wove through the labyrinth of the Moscow Metro, a message blinked into life on Sergey's encrypted device: coordinates and a timestamp. Zaprinski's location was now 100% known, and with it, a surge of adrenaline flooded their veins. The time for action was imminent. Sergey decide to go finally to the safe house where pick up the weapons.

Nick, Martin, and Komutov entered the apartment building, their footsteps echoing in the dingy hallway. Komutov led them to a door marked 9C and gave a specific knock - two quick raps, a pause, then three more.

The door opened a crack, revealing a sliver of a man's unshaven face. He and Komutov exchanged brief words in rapid Russian before the door swung open.

"Come in, quickly, this is our safe house" the man urged in accented English, ushering them inside.

The apartment was sparse - just a table, a sofa, and a few chairs. The man - Yuri, as Komutov called him - disappeared into the back room and returned with a black duffel bag.

"Untraceable, as requested," Yuri said, unzipping the bag to reveal handguns, ammo cartridges, and other supplies.

Komutov inspected the weapons, then passed them to Nick and Martin. "Clean, reliable. Thank you to bring also these special grenades set device shock – shock RGS -50 useful for the assault to Zaprinski. Good work, Yuri."

Yuri nodded. "I have served you well in the past, Komutov. I expect appropriate compensation?" "Of course. The usual arrangements."

Satisfied, Yuri withdrew to let them examine the weapons. Nick checked the clip on a Glock 19, feeling the familiar heft of it. He was happy to find a new beretta among the best 9mm pistols on market. Beretta is obligatory choice for those as Nick with a military background. Glock is the most used pistol in the world.

"This will do nicely," he said. "What's our next move?". " Let's go back to the Hotel and have a nice dinner" say Sergey and " please take all material. We are ready for combat!'.

CHAPTER 42

Returning to the opulence of the Hotel Lotte felt like stepping from one world into another. Its interior was an ode to luxury and history, with grandiose chandeliers casting golden light across polished marble floors, and walls adorned with antique tapestries whispering tales of a bygone era.

They made their way to the Italian Restaurant of the Hotel Lotte on the first floor. They found a nice table and they sat ready to order some special recommended dish. The waiter arrives with a nice complementary plate of olives, some bred and fragrant olive oil from Sicily. He took the orders from Nick and his friends: Carpaccio, salade, "Pizza Napoletan" and Spaghetti "aglio, olio and peperoncino".

Nick Taylor's gaze drifted from the intricately painted ceramic plate, a vivid portrayal of the Amalfi coast, back to the conversation at hand. The Italian restaurant in the hotel Lotte was aglow with warm light, casting deep shadows over the antique mahogany paneling that lined the walls. In the meantime, Martin De Simone, his old comrade-in-arms, was outlining their next strategic step, his fingers drumming on the tablecloth woven with threads of gold and crimson.

"Everything looks clear," Martin observed " Now we have the location and digital screens displaying 3D layouts of Zaprinski's dwelling—a fortress masquerading as a residence". His senses equally attuned to the undercurrents of danger that might lurk within even the most serene settings. They plotted, strategized, and equipped themselves mentally and physically for the task ahead.

"Nick, we need to consider the possibility that they've already infiltrated the local networks," Martin's voice was barely above a whisper, but it carried the weight of years spent navigating the treacherous waters of international espionage.

Nick nodded, the muscles in his jaw working thoughtfully. He was a man sculpted by discipline—a runner's lean physique, eyes that missed nothing, and a mind always mapping out the chessboard of high stakes intrigue. His silver-flecked hair, once jet black, betrayed only the passage of time, not a diminishment of his sharp faculties.

As Martin continued to expound on their leads, Nick's sharp gaze swept across the Restaurant. It settled on a group of individuals who had just entered the restaurant. They were an incongruous sight amidst the opulence of the surroundings: three figures draped in dark attire that seemed to swallow the soft lighting. Their movements were too deliberate, too synchronized for casual diners.

"Excuse me for a second," Nick murmured, his attention locked onto the newcomers.

Martin paused, following Nick's line of sight. A seasoned operative himself, he immediately picked up on the subtle cues of tension emanating from the trio. "Trouble?"

"Potentially," Nick replied, taking in every detail. The men wore tailored suits that did little to conceal the athletic builds underneath, their posture too rigid for comfort. One had a hairline that receded more than it framed his face, eyes darting like a cornered animal. Another was broader, his hands large and seemingly restless at his sides, while the third was taller, angular features set in a mask of stoic indifference.

Their eyes skimmed the room, never quite settling, yet absorbing everything. It was a dance Nick knew all too well—the quiet calculation of risks, angles, and exits.

"Stay alert," Nick said quietly, his voice a low hum beneath the ambient melody of clinking glasses and subdued conversation. "I don't like the look of this."

"Neither do I," Martin agreed, turning back to the others at the table. Each one of them—a mosaic of expertise and unwavering loyalty, bound together by past missions and shared secrets—nodded in silent understanding. Their jovial dinner had taken an unexpected turn; the flavors of Tuscany on their tongues now mixed with the metallic taste of impending danger.

CHAPTER 43

The air in the Italian restaurant was laced with the aromas of garlic and simmering tomatoes, a rustic charm hanging over the dimly lit room adorned with antique wall sconces and tables draped in white linen. It was a place that whispered of old-world elegance, where time seemed content to dawdle amidst the clatter of fine China and the soft murmur of diners.

Nick Taylor's sharp gaze, however, was not on the Baroque-inspired paintings adorning the walls, nor the vintage Chianti bottles that lined the wooden racks. His attention was riveted to the reflection on his wine glass, which provided a distorted view of the restaurant's entrance. The three individuals who had entered earlier were now seated, but their presence cast an invisible net of tension that slowly enveloped the room.

Other patrons, a blend of intellectuals with their measured discourse and well-heeled tourists basking in the novelty of authentic Italian cuisine within the hotel Lotte, began to sense the disquiet. A woman in a silk dress paused mid-gesture, her fingers laden with rings catching the light as she turned to glance at the stoic trio. A writer, judging by the moleskin notebook peeking from his coat pocket, frowned slightly, his intuition nudging him away from his solitude and into the collective unease.

Nick's friends, all of whom wore the quiet confidence of military men accustomed to life's sharper edges, exchanged terse nods. Their laughter had ebbed, replaced by the silent language of vigilance.

Then, without warning, chaos erupted.

The tallest among the newcomers, his angular features betraying nothing, stood abruptly. His hand moved with lethal grace beneath his jacket, producing a weapon with the cold gleam of purpose. The sound of gunfire tore through the harmony of the restaurant, shattering the tranquility as easily as it did the heirloom mirrors along the walls.

Panic ensued as the other two assailants joined their companions, their movements synchronized and deadly. Bullets sliced through the air, embedding themselves in antique woodwork and puncturing the upholstery of chairs that moments before cradled unsuspecting guests.

Nick's instincts roared to life, adrenaline sharpening his senses as he assessed the situation with the clarity of a man who had stared down death more times than he cared to count. The restaurant had transformed into a battlefield, the scent of basil and oregano now tainted with the acrid stench of gunpowder.

As screams and the cacophony of overturned tables filled the space, Nick's mind was already racing through potential strategies, his body poised to act. He knew that survival hinged on the next few seconds—seconds that would demand every ounce of his experience, skill, and unyielding resolve.

The attackers, faces impassive behind the violence they wielded, had made one critical error: they hadn't counted on facing adversaries like Nick Taylor and his comrades, men forged in the crucible of covert operations and unspoken oaths. And as the echo of gunfire melded with the screams of terror, Nick was ready to remind them of that oversight.

Glass shattered and the staccato rhythm of gunfire reverberated off the restaurant's aged terracotta tiles, interspersed with the screams of patrons caught in a maelstrom they could never have anticipated. The aroma of garlic and simmering tomato sauce was violently usurped by the metallic tang of spilled blood and gun smoke. Women in elegant cocktail dresses and men in tailored suits clambered desperately under tables, their fine attire ill-suited for crawling on hands and knees across the cold marble floor, seeking any sanctuary from the hail of bullets.

Nick Taylor, his silver-flecked hair falling into his eyes as he ducked behind an overturned table, had already catalogued the exits, potential weapons, and cover points in a glance that lasted no more than a heartbeat. His dinner jacket was abandoned in favor of mobility, revealing a trim waist circled by a belt that, to the untrained eye, held nothing more than a leather pouch. To Nick, it was a lifeline—a hidden holster housing a compact Sig Sauer P365, which he now gripped firmly in his calloused hand.

Beside him, Sergey Komutov's intellectual facade crumbled away, revealing the steel core of a man who had once navigated the shadowy corridors of the Kremlin. His thinning hair was plastered against his forehead with sweat, but his blue eyes were sharp and calculating. In one fluid motion, Sergey slid a chair aside with his foot, using it as both shield and distraction as he calmly extracted a Glock 19 from the concealed compartment of his briefcase. With the precision of a grandmaster moving across a chessboard, he aimed and fired, each shot a deliberate move to counter the chaos.

"Stay low, use the environment," Nick barked out over the noise, his words clipped and resolute. They moved in tandem, synchronizing their breathing with the rhythm of their return fire. Each trigger pull was a symphony of resistance, a testament to their training and their refusal to be felled by faceless adversaries.

The attackers weaved between the columns that lined the restaurant, their ruthless efficiency marred only by the unexpected resilience of their targets. But even as they advanced, Nick and Sergey's counter-assault was a dance of survival—two steps forward, one step back, a continuous push against the tide of violence that sought to engulf them.

Their movements were a blurred harmony of experience and brutal instinctual response, honed through years of service to agencies that dealt in secrets and sacrifice. And now, that lifetime of allegiance to a greater cause culminated in a fight not just for justice, but for the very breaths they drew amid the shattered remains of what was meant to be a quiet evening meal.

The crescendo of gunfire would eventually ebb, but for Nick Taylor and Sergey Komutov, this battle was far from over—it was merely the opening gambit in a game played against an opponent who had yet to reveal their full hand.

CHAPTER 44

Nick's hand snaked out, seizing a heavy ceramic plate from the disarrayed table before him and hurling it with precision at the nearest assailant. The projectile served as both distraction and defense, buying precious seconds as he flipped the solid oak table onto its side, scattering silverware and half-empty wine glasses that spun like glittering rain in the strobe-light chaos.

"Martin, Sergey, flank!" he barked, his voice a razor-edged command amidst the pandemonium. His eyes, the color of storm clouds, narrowed as he assessed their makeshift fortress—a mosaic of overturned chairs and linen-draped barricades that transformed the upscale Italian eatery into a warzone.

Sergey, whose reflexes were as sharply tuned as the blade he kept in his boot, was already on the move. He slid across the polished terrazzo floor with the grace of an ice skater, using the decorative potted ficus as cover before launching himself over a banquette to take aim.

"Stay low," Nick warned through clenched teeth, the line of his jaw set in determination. Martin nodded, his own movements a testament to a youth spent more on rugby fields than in lecture halls, utilizing brute strength to tip a grand piano onto its side for additional cover.

The attackers, clad in nondescript dark attire that made them shadows against the restaurant's mahogany paneling, advanced with trained malevolence. Their steps were silent on the carpet, but the clinking of their ammunition belied their positions.

It was then, just as another volley of gunfire threatened to splinter their defenses, that an unexpected ally emerged. The security team, led by the burly form of Oleg Tiachenko, burst through the kitchen doors like a cavalry charge of old. Oleg, a bear of a man who had traded military fatigues for the crisp uniform of hotel security, barreled forward with a determined scowl etched into his weathered face.

"Cover!" Oleg shouted, his deep voice resonating above the fray. His team fanned out with practiced precision, their black tactical vests a stark contrast to the pristine white of the chef's aprons flapping forgotten on nearby hooks.

Nick felt a surge of relief, albeit short-lived, as he recognized Oleg's stance—the way the man's eyes darted strategically, scanning for threats, his handgun clutched with the expertise of someone who had seen more battles than boardrooms. It was clear that Oleg's past, much like Nick's, was painted in shades of duty and sacrifice.

The ensuing firefight was a ballet of bullets and bravery. Oleg and his team provided a much-needed buffer, their presence tipping the scales as they engaged the assailants with a ferocity born of protection—for their guests, their establishment, and perhaps something more personal: a shared understanding of combat's grim dance.

Under the cover of Oleg's men, Nick and his friends repositioned, using the towering centerpieces and ornate silver service trays as reflective shields to obscure their movements. Each maneuver carried the weight of countless similar encounters, each twist and turn a verse in the silent song of survival they all knew by heart.

Their combined efforts, a symphony of strategy and strength, slowly began to push back the darkness that had invaded the space. But even as the tide turned in their favor, Nick knew this battle was but a prelude. Whoever had sent these assailants had underestimated them—and that, he vowed silently, would be their enemy's gravest mistake.

The air in the Italian restaurant, once redolent with the mediterranean aroma of garlic and oregano, was now acrid with gunpowder. Nick Taylor's ears rang as another round of gunfire erupted, the symphony of chaos playing its discordant tune. He squinted through the haze, his vision marred by the smoky aftermath of discharged weapons. A fine rain of plaster and glass fell from above, dusting his once-pristine navy blazer as he crouched behind an overturned mahogany table.

"Left flank!" Nick mouthed to Martin, who nodded tersely in understanding. The former CIA spy's hand signals were crisp, honed by years of necessity where silence was survival. They moved in unison, a dance they had performed in countless clandestine stages across the world. The clink of shell casings on the tiled floor punctuated their steps, as bullets whizzed past, embedding themselves into the ornate wall sconces and richly framed landscape paintings that adorned the walls.

Martin, ever the intellectual with a strategic mind honed at Langley, slid a magazine into his pistol with the mechanical precision of a chess grandmaster making a game-winning move. His eyes, sharp and calculating, caught those of Nick, conveying a wordless plan. In contrast, Sergey, whose muscular frame and judicious movements spoke of a history etched in military discipline, provided covering fire. Each shot was measured, efficient, betraying not a hint of the adrenaline that undoubtedly surged through his veins.

A bullet shattered a nearby wine decanter, its contents bleeding out onto the white linen like a slain soldier's tribute. The staccato rhythm of gunfire was momentarily drowned out by the high-pitched shattering of the restaurant's grand chandelier; it descended in a cascade of glittering terror, the light catching on its many facets before it crashed onto the floor below.

"Three o'clock," Nick communicated with a jerk of his head, alerting his team to the shifting positions of their assailants. Martin responded with a concise nod, his lean form darting behind a baroque statue that miraculously remained intact amidst the destruction.

Oleg Tiachenko, orchestrating the hotel security's response, provided a brief respite as his team unleashed a barrage of return fire. The former military man had transformed the entrance 's decorative elements into a fortress of defense, the plush velvet drapes now hanging in tatters but serving as momentary shields for his advancing men.

Nick's green eyes, reflecting years of experience and a steady calm that belied the maelstrom around him, flickered towards Sergey. With a sharp gesture, he signaled toward a vulnerable point in the attackers' formation. Understanding flashed between them, and without hesitation, they exploited the weakness.

Their attackers, faces obscured by the dim light and the tumult, moved with trained precision, but Nick and his companions knew the language of conflict better than most. Each response from Nick's team was a counterpoint, a parry to the thrusts aimed their way.

The dialogue of battle was terse, the exchange of gunfire a deadly conversation. But amidst the cacophony, there was clarity—a unity forged in the crucible of shared purpose and trust. As the last echo of gunfire faded, replaced by the distant wail of sirens and the ragged breaths of survivors, Nick surveyed the scene, his mind already piecing together their next move.

CHAPTER 45

Nick Taylor's hand was steady as he took aim, the pistol feeling like an extension of his will. His eyes, sharp as ever despite the years etched into the lines on his face, scanned the Italian restaurant turned battlefield. The antique chandeliers, once a testament to luxurious taste, now swung precariously, their crystals raining down like icy tears amidst the chaos.

Sergey pressed his back against a column of marbled alabaster. He gave a short nod, acknowledging Nick's signal, and they moved as one. Their bodies were adrenaline-fueled engines of survival, every muscle fiber and sinew working toward a singular goal: to live, to fight another day.

Around them, the air was thick with the scents of gunpowder and rich tomato sauce—a bizarre juxtaposition that would have seemed absurd under any other circumstance. The walls, adorned with oil paintings of the Capri and Amalfi landscape, were scarred by bullet holes, the tranquil scenes violently interrupted.

Martin ducked behind an overturned table. His breaths were measured, his movements deliberate. Together with Nick and Sergey, they formed a triangle of resistance, each covering the blind spots of the others, communicating through sharp glances and hand signals.

The attackers—three shadows dressed in tactical gear that melted into the darkened corners of the restaurant—had not anticipated such fierce opposition. They moved with the lethal grace of panthers, but this was not the jungle, and they were not the only predators here.

Nick could see it in their momentary hesitations, the split seconds when their choreographed assault faltered under the weight of unexpected resilience. Their plan had unraveled, thread by thread, with each determined stand taken by Nick and his companions.

Then came the turning point—the moment when the tide of battle shifted perceptibly. Oleg's security team, like a cavalry of old, burst through the entrance with the ferocity of those who fought to protect their own. The attackers' cold eyes betrayed a flicker of doubt as they realized their exit routes were cut off, their numbers dwindling.

"Fall back!" one of the attackers hissed to the others, the words barely audible over the din of conflict.

But it was too late for retreat. Nick, Martin, Sergey, and the hotel security, a relentless force, advanced. Bullets found their marks, and the attackers' movements grew erratic, desperate. Then, silence fell, punctuated only by the clatter of weapons hitting the floor.

Nick stood amidst the destruction, chest heaving, his friends beside him. Their faces were grim, smeared with soot and sweat, but their eyes burned with the unspoken knowledge that they had overcome. The three would-be assailants lay motionless, their threat extinguished by the very hands they had sought to make their victims.

For a moment, there was stillness—a collective inhale as the reality of survival settled on the shoulders of the living. But for Nick and his allies, there was no time for rest. This battle may have been won, but the war, the unseen enemy weaving its web of international conspiracy, was far from over.

The sirens wailed a requiem for the chaos that had just unfolded, their piercing cries slicing through the newfound silence of the restaurant. Nick Taylor's breaths came in ragged gasps as he leaned heavily against an overturned table, its white cloth stained with the evidence of survival. His once-pristine suit was marred by dust and debris, and his gray hair, which had always given him a distinguished look, now hung limply around a face etched with lines of fatigue and resolve.

He looked over at Sergey Komutov, who was methodically checking his weapon for any remaining ammunition. The ex-KGB agent's thinning hair seemed to stand on end, as if electrified by the adrenaline that still coursed through them both. His intellect, usually reserved for the chessboard or mathematical puzzles, had been replaced by a calculative coolness required for the grim task at hand.

The Italian restaurant, once brimming with the aroma of garlic and oregano, now bore the acrid smell of gunpowder. Splintered wood from antique chairs and tables lay scattered like the aftermath of a tempest, while velvet drapes were shredded by the ballet of bullets that had danced through the air moments before.

Outside the ravaged dining area, the Lotte Hotel's grandeur stood unblemished, its marble floors reflecting the flashing lights of police vehicles that converged on the scene. Uniformed officers and medical personnel flooded into the space, their movements swift and practiced. They took control with an efficiency that spoke volumes of their training, cordoning off areas and attending to the wounded with a precision that restored a semblance of order amidst the pandemonium.

In the lull that followed, Nick exchanged a knowing glance with Martin, whose once-charming features were now shadowed by the gravity of their ordeal. They were warriors in a different kind of battlefield, one where enemies wore no uniforms and allegiance shifted like sand. The local authorities, with their commendable response, had shown that not all battles were fought alone.

CHAPTER 46

As night draped its cloak over the city, Sergey quietly began to piece together the puzzle of their assailants. With meticulous care, he photographed the fallen attackers, their faces unknown but their intentions clear. He sent the images to FSB with a message devoid of emotion, a simple request for identification that belied the urgency of their situation.

Hours later, as the moon climbed high and the hotel returned to a cautious peace, Sergey's phone buzzed with the awaited confirmation. The three men were indeed professional killers, shadows or ghost who left no trace but the havoc they wrought. He relayed the information to Nick, who received it with a stony silence.

"Professional killers," Nick mused, his voice low. "Which means someone wanted us dead badly enough to hire the best. And they're still out there."

They stood side by side, two men carved from different stones but united by a common thread of duty and an unspoken bond that had been forged in the crucible of combat. It was clear to that the night's revelations were mere specks in a larger, darker tapestry. The dots remained unconnected, the image unclear, but the outline was slowly taking shape—a shape that promised more danger, more questions, and a relentless pursuit of the truth.

With dawn approaching, they prepared to delve deeper into the labyrinth of espionage and shadows, knowing that each step forward could be met with a bullet. But for Nick Taylor and Sergey Komutov, retreat was never an option. The game was afoot, and they were the players tasked with unravelling an enigma wrapped in an international conspiracy.

"North Korean assassins," Sergey stated, the words carrying a weight that felt almost physical. "It appears Somebody wants Us death. Zaprinski is not working alone!"

Nick's jaw set in determination, his gaze meeting those of his comrades. This new development only sharpened their resolve.

"Then our timeline just advanced," Nick said, a steely edge to his voice. "We move tonight. Discretion is paramount, but so is speed. Let's move before anyone else get to Zaprinski before we do."

"Agreed," Martin echoed, his hand subconsciously drifting to the firearm concealed beneath his jacket.

"Da," Sergey affirmed, his intellect already plotting the revised course of action.

Together, they stood—a group bound by loyalty, skill, and the urgent beat of a mission that brooked no delay. The hunt for Alexey Zaprinski was on, and they would not be deterred.

CHAPTER 47

The Moscow night breathed cold and heavy, a lingering frost dusting the edges of a apartment block that squatted among the shadows of the city's forgotten quarter. Nick Taylor, his frame still imposing despite the years etched into his weathered face, surveyed the silent building with an icy resolve. Flanked by Martin De Simone, whose dark eyes were sharp under the brim of his cap, they moved with purpose, their steps muffled against the snow-laden ground.

"Three minutes," Nick whispered, a smoky plume escaping into the chill.

Martin nodded, his breath visible in the air as he touched the earpiece nestled in his ear, coordinating their entry with Sergey and Michael positioned around the perimeter. The sound of his voice was a low murmur, barely discernible over the whispering wind.

Nick's gaze swept to Sergey Komutov, who fidgeted with a collection of wires in his hands—his thinning hair and focused expression illuminated by the soft glow of a nearby streetlamp. The ex-KGB mathematician's intellect was their wildcard, his love for complex problems now serving a more explosive purpose.

"Ready," Sergey confirmed, adjusting his glasses before moving towards the main entrance.

Approaching the door, Nick felt the familiar adrenaline surge, his senses heightened, alert. As Sergey set the charges, Nick admired the intricate dance of the man's fingers—each movement precise, deliberate. A testament to a life lived in pursuit of perfection, whether on the chess board or in the field of covert operations.

"Clear," Sergey said, stepping back.

The explosion of the grenades tore through the silence of the night like a beast unleashed. The door erupted inwards, fragments of wood and metal spiraling into the darkness beyond. Without hesitation, a smoke bomb followed—a ghostly wraith that slithered into the gaping maw of the violated threshold.

Nick led the charge, his body a blur of motion as he crossed the threshold, Martin closes on his heels, the pair moving with the synchronicity of long-practiced comrades-in-arms. Michael fanned out behind them, each step choreographed chaos, each movement a brush stroke in a violent masterpiece.

Within seconds, the apartment's interior materialized through the dissipating smoke—modern minimalism clashing with the stark realities of their intrusion. Clean lines and high-end furniture, the trappings of wealth acquired through blood money, lay in disarray from their explosive entry.

Alexey Zaprinski, the specter they had hunted, lay prostrate, his lean body sprawled across the marble floor. His once meticulous blonde hair now a tangled mess, his steely green eyes wide with shock and fear—two windows into a soul accustomed to being the predator, not the prey.

"Secure him," Nick barked, the command snapping through the tension like a whip.

As Michael and Martin pinned Zaprinski's arms behind his back, Nick decides, due to extreme volatile and dangerous situation after the attack in the Italian restaurant, to transform the space into an interrogation room. A designer table, its surface sleek and unblemished, was dragged into the center of the room, flanked by two chairs—one for the interrogator, one for the quarry.

Sergey stood back, observing, his calculating mind no doubt already anticipating the myriad ways the scene could unfold. As Nick took his place at the table, he felt Sergey's eyes upon him, the weight of their shared history lending gravity to the moment. Michael was covering them and observing any particular movements outside the windows.

"Let's begin," Nick said, his voice a low rumble, as much a part of him as the scars he bore—the marks of a life spent skirting the edge between light and shadow.

The atmosphere was electric, charged with the potential of what was to come. Zaprinski's disoriented state was palpable, his confusion rendering him vulnerable—an opening Nick was prepared to exploit. Every second mattered; every word spoken could be the difference between success and failure.

"Alexey Zaprinski," Nick began, his tone deliberately even, "you have information we need and a microchip we want."

Zaprinski's gaze darted between his captors, the once formidable assassin reduced to a cornered animal, seeking an escape that would not come. The game had changed, the hunter now the hunted, and in the quiet of that Moscow apartment, amidst the detritus of shattered security, only one truth remained: Information was power, and Nick Taylor intended to wield it without mercy.

Nick leaned in, his gaze laser focused on Zaprinski's disheveled figure. The man's once pristine shirt was now wrinkled and stained, a testament to the scuffle that had preceded this moment. It was an incongruous sight—this killer, known for his meticulous nature, appearing so unkempt and unguarded. But it was exactly this image that Nick intended to exploit.

"Alexey," he said, voice calm but edged with an unmistakable authority that bespoke years of experience, "you know why we're here. And I believe you also know that your cooperation is not just beneficial—it's essential."

Zaprinski's eyes, cold as the Moscow winter outside, met Nick's. There was a flicker there, a hint of calculation as he assessed his situation. Nick recognized that assassin look; it was the cogitation of a man who was always three moves ahead, even when the board was being reset.

"Your client don't take kindly to betrayal," Nick continued, shifting subtly in his chair, a maneuver designed to command attention. He spoke the truth confidently, laying the groundwork for doubt to creep into Zaprinski's mind. "But we can offer you protection. What we need from you are answers."

From behind Nick, Martin's presence was palpable. His broad-shouldered silhouette was a bulwark of solidarity, reinforcing the gravity of their purpose. In sync without a word, he produced photographs of the crime scene in New York and in LA—the latest evidence—and slapped them onto the table one after another. They showed the aftermath of Zaprinski's handiwork, stark and undeniable.

"See this?" Martin's voice was gruff, each word punctuated with controlled anger. "This is on you, Alexey. And unless you start talking, it's only going to get worse." "Check mate" added Nick.

Zaprinski's jaw tightened as he looked at the photos extracted from the CCTV Footage of the attempt of assignation of Diego Alvarez in LA, his facade beginning to crack. The images were intrusive, an invasion of his professional detachment, forcing him to confront the reality of his actions.

"Think about what you stand to lose," Nick added, his tone softer now, injecting a note of empathy—a psychological pry bar to widen the gap in Zaprinski's armor. "But also consider what you stand to gain by helping us. You're a smart man, Alexey. Make the right choice."

The apartment, with its sparse furnishings and utilitarian design, felt like an extension of the interrogation itself—a no-nonsense space stripped of all pretenses, its bare walls echoing the starkness of their conversation. Outside, the city hummed indifferently, unaware of the pivotal exchange taking place within.

Nick exchanged a quick glance with Martin, a silent acknowledgment of their small victory. They had cracked the shell, but the nut inside would require careful extraction. Nick was ready, though. It was the kind of challenge he lived for—the dance of wits, the battle of wills. And he was determined to emerge victorious.

CHAPTER 48

Nick leaned forward, his elbows resting on the cold metal table that separated him from Zaprinski. The room was stark, illuminated by a single overhead light that cast deep shadows across their faces, amplifying the tension in the air. The walls, a nondescript beige, bore the scuff marks and stains of countless previous interrogations. The smell of dust and lingering sweat hung heavily, adding to the claustrophobic feel of the space.

"Alexey," Nick began, his voice steady and controlled. "You know we can do this the easy way, or the hard way."

Zaprinski sat motionless, his hands cuffed in front of him. His posture was upright, almost defiant, though his eyes darted around the room, betraying an internal struggle. He was no stranger to interrogation tactics; after all, he had been on the other side of such exchanges before. But now, cornered and without an exit strategy, his usual coolness was showing cracks.

"Your silence won't protect you," Martin chimed in from behind Nick, his tone sharp. "We have evidence—"

"Your evidence means nothing to me," Zaprinski cut in abruptly, his Russian accent thickening with the rise of his emotions. His voice was a low growl, a bear cornered by hunters.

"Doesn't it?" Nick countered, unfazed. He observed Zaprinski closely, noting the slight twitch in his jaw, the clenching of his fists. "We're not just talking about your freedom here. We're talking about your life. You've crossed paths with some dangerous people, my friend."

Zaprinski scoffed, but Nick could see the uncertainty in his eyes. It was like watching a master chess player realizing he was in check—with limited moves left to escape the inevitable checkmate.

"Let's talk about the job from the dark web," Nick said, shifting gears and leaning in closer. "The hit on two Americans in LA and me in New York".

Zaprinski remained silent, but his breathing grew more rapid, his chest rising and falling visibly.

"Then there's the bomb in my home and the microchip stolen from my home." Nick's gaze hardened. "A microchip that holds more power than you can imagine."

"Even if I knew something..." Zaprinski started, his voice trailing off, his eyes searching the room as if the answer might be scrawled on the wall.

"Tell us about the client," Nick pressed, his patience wearing thin. "Give us a name."

"I... I don't have a name. It was all anonymous, encrypted. There was a map, pictures, details of daily routines—I received everything needed to carry out the job." Zaprinski's voice faded into a whisper, his resistance crumbling.

"Where is the microchip now?" Nick demanded, his tone sharpening like the blade of a knife.

Zaprinski hesitated, his lips parting but no words escaping. That's when Nick's open hand struck swiftly against Zaprinski's cheek, the sound echoing off the bare walls. Zaprinski's head snapped to the side, a red imprint forming on his pale skin.

"Where did you put it, Alexey?" Nick's voice was a harsh whisper, his eyes locked onto the man before him.

Zaprinski looked up, pain and defiance mingling in his steely gaze. "I don't remember," he lied, his voice barely audible.

Nick didn't buy it. He knew Zaprinski remembered perfectly well. It was only a matter of time and pressure before he cracked completely. And time was something Nick was willing to invest if it meant keeping that microchip out of the wrong hands.

CHAPTER 49

Nick's fingers drummed a steady rhythm on the cold metal surface of the interrogation table, the noise filling the cramped, dimly lit room. Zaprinski sat opposite him, bound to the chair that skidded slightly with each impact, his blonde hair disheveled and the bruise from Nick's hand blossoming like a dark cloud on his cheek.

"Let's go over it again," Nick said, his voice level but edged with impatience. "The microchip—where did you get the job to steal it?"

Zaprinski swallowed hard, the cords in his neck straining against the skin as if trying to break free from the fear that constricted them. "I told you... from the dark web," he murmured, his accent thickening with stress. "They paid well. One million dollars. Money transferred to an offshore account untraceable."

Martin stood a little way off, arms folded across his chest, his muscular build contained within a tailored suit that spoke of both functionality and finesse. His short, dark hair was styled meticulously, a stark contrast to the chaos around them. He watched the exchange with hawk-like intensity, ready to interject at any moment.

Nick leaned forward, his athletic frame casting a larger shadow over Zaprinski. "This microchip," he began, his tone softening to draw out the truth, "it details everything—the Medellin Cartel's operations, their transactions, shipments... It could dismantle them completely."

A flicker of understanding crossed Zaprinski's face, and for a moment, Nick sensed a shift in the air. The cautious optimism that had been bubbling beneath his disciplined exterior rose to the surface, visible only in the slight easing of his furrowed brow.

"Everything..." Zaprinski echoed, his voice a mix of awe and fear. "Every deal, every route from Colombia to the States. Names, contacts—it's all there."

"Exactly," Nick confirmed, his words clipped. "And it was hidden in my apartment, in a clock watch. My insurance—my life insurance against those cartel bastards."

Zaprinski looked up at Nick through steely green eyes, a hint of respect—or was it resignation? — flickering within. "That's why they want it so badly," he said, almost to himself.

"Who, Alexey?" Martin interjected sharply. "Who wants it so badly?"

"The client... I don't know who they are, but they're powerful. They have reach. If they find out I haven't delivered—" Zaprinski's words stumbled into silence as dread crept into his expression.

"Then help us stop them," Nick urged, his gaze unyielding. "You hand over the microchip, and we keep you safe from the fallout."

"Safe?" Zaprinski scoffed, bitterness seeping into his voice. "There's no safe when it comes to the Medellin Cartel. If I talk... if I don't deliver this chip..." His voice trailed away, leaving the threat unspoken yet palpable in the cramped room.

"Alexey," Martin said, stepping forward, his voice resonating with authority. "We can protect you. But you need to trust us."

Zaprinski's laugh was hollow, devoid of humor. "Trust," he repeated mockingly. "A luxury I can't afford."

Yet as Nick's determination met Zaprinski's fatalism, the latter's resolve seemed to waver. The tension in the room tightened like a wire about to snap, everyone holding their breath, waiting for the ex-KGB killer to make his choice.

CHAPTER 50

Nick leaned back against the cold, concrete wall of the nondescript apartment that had become their makeshift interrogation room. His eyes, sharp and assessing, never left Alexey Zaprinski's face. The steel-gray stare of the captured ex-KGB agent met Nick's gaze without flinching.

"Alexey," Nick began, breaking the silence that had settled over them, "where and when are you supposed to hand over this microchip?"

Zaprinski shifted uncomfortably in the metal chair, his hands cuffed behind him. The sparse light bulb hanging from a wire above cast deep shadows across his angular features, giving him an almost spectral quality. His blonde hair, cropped short in military fashion, seemed to blend into the pale walls around them.

"I... I don't have the details yet," Zaprinski admitted, a note of defeat threading through his voice. "The instructions were to come via the dark web. I check it daily."

Nick exchanged a glance with Martin, who stood off to the side, arms crossed and jaw set in determination. They could feel the atmosphere in the room begin to shift, the tension easing ever so slightly as Zaprinski's demeanor softened.

"Good," Nick nodded, his own body relaxing marginally. "You'll let us know as soon as you get the information?"

Zaprinski nodded, a reluctant ally. "Yes. As soon as it comes in, I'll tell you."

"See, Alexey," Nick said with a hint of warmth returning to his tone, "that wasn't so hard, was it? Cooperation is a two-way street."

Martin moved closer, his combat boots thudding softly against the concrete floor. He was a solid presence, ex-military bearing evident in his posture. His eyes remained fixed on Zaprinski, like a hawk watching its prey—not out of malice, but vigilant protection.

"Once we have the chip," Martin interjected, "we'll make sure you're out of reach from the Cartel's claws. That's our end of the bargain."

"Assuming you keep your word," Zaprinski replied, skepticism lacing his words even as he acknowledged their offer with a nod.

"Your life depends on it, just as much as ours," Nick pointed out, his voice steady. He turned away, signaling to the others that they could afford to ease up. Martin backed away, and their other allies—shadowy figures blending into the periphery—relaxed their watchful stances.

As the group prepared for their next move, Nick couldn't help but reflect on the strange twists and turns that had led them to this point. From New York to Moscow, and now on the trail of the Medellin Cartel, it seemed as though fate had chosen a particularly convoluted path for them to follow. But with each new revelation, the pieces of the puzzle were slowly falling into place, bringing them one step closer to dismantling the dangerous cartel and securing the safety of countless lives.

"Stay vigilant," Nick warned his friends, his voice steady and reassuring. "We may have made progress, but we can't afford to let our guard down."

With Zaprinski's cooperation secured and the promise of crucial information on the horizon, the group braced themselves for whatever challenges lay ahead, knowing that their combined knowledge, skills, and determination would see them through the darkest of times.

CHAPTER 51

Nick led the charge and go to pick up the microchip in the indicated location: his hand steady on the butt of his sidearm as they navigated the labyrinthine corridors of the apartment block near Belorusskaia Metro station. Brutalist architecture loomed oppressively, a concrete monolith that bore silent witness to countless clandestine operations in its time. His green eyes, sharp and calculating, missed no detail—from the peeling wallpaper reminiscent of a bygone era to the flickering lights that cast long shadows.

The number 303 glared back at them as they reached their destination. Martin, ever the reliable comrade, followed close behind, his dark eyes alert and muscles tensed for any sign of danger. He carried himself with an assuredness that only years in the field could grant—a predator poised for the strike.

With a nod from Nick, they breached the apartment door, a process more silent than one would expect from two men of such imposing stature. Inside, the scent of stale cigarette smoke mingled with a faint metallic tang—blood, fresh and pungent.

A figure lunged from the shadows, a blur of desperation and aggression, but Martin's reflexes were quicker. Two shots rang out from his SIG Sauer P320, precise and fatal, the assailant collapsing in a heap, his life extinguished before he could so much as graze them. The killer's body lay splayed, a last breath escaping his lips in a silent plea for mercy that would never come.

"Clear," Martin muttered, holstering his weapon as Nick moved towards the kitchen. It was a space frozen in time, the linoleum flooring worn thin and cabinets that had seen better days. The stark fluorescent lighting cast a sterile glow over the room, which now served as a cache for secrets worth killing for.

Nick's fingers traced along the underside of the kitchen counter, feeling for anomalies, his mind working through possibilities with the clarity of a chess grandmaster anticipating his opponent's moves. There it was—a panel slightly ajar. Inside, nestled between aging pipes, was the microchip, innocuous yet laden with information that could tilt the balance of power.

"Got it," Nick called out, his voice betraying none of the triumph that surged within him. This microchip was his life insurance against the

Medellin Cartel, a guarantee of leverage. Kaprinski was helpful but still dangerous.

They left the apartment as methodically as they had entered, descending to the waiting vehicle where Zaprinski sat, cuffed and guarded by Michael, his steely gaze fixated on some distant point. Sergey, the ex-KGB mathematician, had chosen the location near Sheremetyevo Airport for its strategic importance. His analytical mind always thinking three steps ahead, he was already coordinating their next move.

"Good job, everyone," Nick praised, tucking the microchip securely into his pocket. "Now let's get out of here." They knew that every second counted; any delay could give their enemies time to regroup and retaliate.

With Zaprinski in tow, they made their way to the safe new location Sergey had arranged. The night swallowed them up like a hungry beast, shielding them from prying eyes.

Zaprinski's phone buzzed, startling them all. He glanced at the screen before sharing the news: "The handover is scheduled for April 9th in Cartagena, Colombia."

"Colombia," Martin muttered, rubbing his chin thoughtfully. "That complicates things."

"Indeed," Nick agreed, his mind racing with strategic possibilities. "Sergey, we're going to need your help to arrange transportation to Cartagena via Cuba. Can you handle that?"

"Of course," Sergey replied confidently, despite the daunting task ahead. "I have some contacts that should be able to help."

"Excellent," Nick said, allowing himself a small smile. Despite the challenges they faced, he couldn't deny the thrill of being back in the game, working alongside his friends to bring down a dangerous enemy.

"Remember," he warned them all, his voice firm and resolute, "we're walking into the lion's den. We need to keep your eyes and watch each other's backs."

"Agreed," Martin nodded, his eyes meeting Nick's with unwavering determination. "We've come this far, and we're not backing down now."

CHAPTER 52

They arrive in the new safe house. The air inside the safe house was thick with tension, each member of the group acutely aware of the high stakes and the formidable opponent they were about to face. As Nick lay on a makeshift bed in the corner of the dimly lit room, he couldn't help but notice the subtle signs of anxiety etched on the faces of his allies. Martin paced back and forth, his strong jaw clenched in determination; Michael stood by the window, scanning the dark Moscow streets for any signs of danger; while Zaprinski, now a reluctant but still dangerous ally, sat slumped in a chair, visibly shaken by the threat of retribution from his mysterious client.

"Get some rest," Nick urged the others, his voice soft yet firm. "We'll need all our strength when we reach Colombia."

With a mixture of reluctance and exhaustion, the group began to settle down for the night, each finding a spot in the cramped room to claim as their own. Despite the discomfort, sleep came surprisingly easy for Nick, his training allowing him to switch off in even the most hostile environments. But tonight, his dreams were plagued by the specter of their enigmatic enemy and the deadly secrets hidden within the recovered microchip.

"Nick," Martin whispered urgently, shaking him awake. "It's time to move. Sergey's arranged our transportation."

"Good," Nick replied groggily, rubbing his eyes and swinging his legs over the edge of the bed. He glanced around to see the others already packing up their gear, their faces pale but resolute in the early morning light that filtered through the cracks in the blinds.

"Zaprinski," Nick said, addressing the former killer with a steely gaze, "you know the details of the handover. You're coming with us, so stick close and do exactly as you're told. No other dirty games or you will pay for it."

"Understood," Zaprinski muttered, his usual arrogance replaced by fear and resignation.

As they filed out of the safe house, Nick's mind raced with strategic plans and contingencies for their mission in Cartagena. He knew that the success of their operation hinged on their ability to outwit the mysterious client who had orchestrated this deadly conspiracy, but with each step closer to Colombia, the danger grew ever more palpable.

"Whatever happens," Martin said quietly, his eyes locked onto Nick's as they climbed into the waiting vehicle, "we're in this together."

"Agreed," Nick nodded, his resolve firming as they drove away from the safe house. "We'll bring this bastard down, no matter the cost."

Nick couldn't help but feel a surge of excitement at the prospect of facing off against such a formidable adversary. The adrenaline coursing through his veins was a reminder of what he loved most about his former life as a spy: the thrill of the chase, the high stakes, and the satisfaction of bringing justice to those who sought to evade it.

With the knowledge of the microchip's contents and the imminent handover in Colombia, the stage was set for a deadly game of cat and mouse. And as the plane's engines roared to life on the runway, Nick knew that the outcome of this battle would shape the course of their lives and the fate of countless innocent souls caught in the crossfire of this explosive l espionage thriller.

"Rest up," Nick advised Zaprinski, noting the fatigue etched onto the man's face. "We've got a long road ahead."

"Rest," Zaprinski echoed, the concept seeming foreign after the tumultuous events that had unfolded. But there was a glint in his eye now—a signal that perhaps, in this game of espionage and survival, there were still moves to be made.

As plans were set in motion for their journey to Colombia, Nick couldn't help but reflect on the unlikely alliance they had formed. Each person brought unique skills and strengths to the table, creating a formidable team united by a common goal: to expose the international conspiracy and protect innocent lives from its deadly grip. The road ahead would be treacherous, but together, they were more than ready to face whatever lay in wait.

Reaching his room, Nick flipped open his laptop. He began to draft an encrypted message, reaching out to a network that operated in the deepest shadows of global espionage. His previous Life. Suddenly, the laptop pinged—an incoming communication. Nick tensed his fingers poised above the keyboard. The message decrypted slowly, its contents materializing one character at a time. The words that appeared sent a jolt through his system, electrifying this last night in Moscow:

"Phoenix. The eagle watches you. Snakes will hurt you. Be careful"

Nick's breath hitched. Phoenix—his operative code name, known only to a select few. And the eagle?

That could only mean... This message was a warning. Nick doesn't understand the message and tries to decode the world " snakes", plural of "Snake". Which " snakes they are talking about? Anyway, Nick just turned off his laptop and tried to sleep a bit.

CHAPTER 53

Hours later, as the jet touched down at Havana Airport, Nick allowed himself a small sigh of relief. They'd done it – they'd managed to extract Zaprinki from the heart of Russia. But there was no time to celebrate; they still had work to do.

The sun dipped low behind the historic buildings of Havana as Nick, Martin and Sergey stepped off the Tupolev, with their hostage Zaprinski in tow. The tarmac's heat rose around them as they made their way to a discreet black van waiting nearby.

In the terminal, Edward Smith was waiting for them. "Good morning," Edward urged, leading the way to a waiting Van that would take them to the hotel in Center of Havana.

As the van navigated the narrow streets of the city, Nick couldn't help but notice the vibrant colors that adorned the walls of the colonial-style homes.

"Hi Edward, happy to see you, I hope everything is ready," Nick said, his eyes filled with both concern and determination. "We are ready, Nick" say Edward with enthusiasm.

"Alright, let's go over this 10 days time," said Martin, pulling out the fake microchip they had fashioned during the flight. It was carefully shaped from a lightweight plastic, a convincing replica designed to fool even the most discerning eye. "This is what we'll use for the handover."

With Zaprinski in tow, they made their way to the hotel. Zaprinski's phone buzzed, startling them all. He glanced at the screen before sharing the news: "The handover is scheduled for April 9th in Cartagena, Colombia Hotel Bella Mar at 6PM."

They arrived at a small, unassuming hotel tucked away in a quiet corner of Havana. Its crumbling façade hinted at a rich history, while the worn wooden door creaked open to reveal a modest lobby decorated with antique furniture. They checked in without paying attention and headed up to their shared room.

Once inside, the air was thick with anticipation as they debated the identity of Zaprinski's mysterious client. Nick, his graying hair slicked back from his forehead, studied the faces of his friends. He knew that trust was hard-earned in their line of work, and yet he was grateful for the loyalty and dedication each man brought to the mission.

"Martin and I are convinced it's the boss of the Medellin Cartel," Nick said, his sharp gaze unwavering. "All the signs point to him."

"Perhaps," countered Micheal his tall, lean frame leaning against the wall, arms crossed. "But Sergey and I have been considering another possibility. We can't ignore the potential existence of a new cartel – a merger between an Asian and South American syndicate."

Sergey nodded in agreement. "The world is changing," he said in his thick Russian accent. "Old alliances break, and new one's form. We must be prepared for anything."

"Whatever the truth may be," Martin interjected, his muscular build tensing with determination, "we'll find out soon enough."

CHAPTER 54

Morning came quickly, and Nick awoke early, as was his habit. Edward contacted their pilot, who confirmed the private plane would be ready for departure within the hour. The team gathered their gear and set off to meet the aircraft, each man focused on what lay ahead.

Their hearts raced as they boarded the plane and took their seats. The engines roared to life, and the aircraft began its ascent towards the sky, leaving Cuba behind them. Cartagena awaited – the next step in unraveling the dangerous web that surrounded Zaprinski's client.

"Time is of the essence," Nick thought, his mind racing with a mix of adrenaline and anxiety. "We have to be ready for whatever comes our way."

The muted hum of the private plane's engines filled the cabin as it sliced through the sky, casting long shadows over the landscape below. Nick leaned back in his seat, eyes focused on the passing clouds outside the window, his mind lost in thought. The mission had taken them from Cuba to Colombia, and the stakes were higher than ever. Time was running out.

"Alright, team," Nick began, breaking the silence that hung heavy in the air. "We need to plan our next move carefully. We've only got one shot at this, and we can't afford any mistakes." His sharp gaze scanned the faces of Martin, Michael, and Sergey, each man showing a mix of determination and apprehension.

"Martin, have you heard back from your contacts in the CIA?" Nick asked, concern creasing his brow.

"Yep, just got word," Martin replied, his fingers tapping away at a secured tablet device. "The boss of the Medellin Cartel is still hiding out in his heavily guarded compound. But there's still no sign of the other player in all this."

"Damn it," Nick muttered under his breath, his jaw clenched in frustration. "We're going to have to play this by ear. We know the handover location, but we still don't know who we're dealing with."

"Then we'll adapt" Edward interjected, his serious demeanor never wavering. "We'll make sure Zaprinski delivers the fake microchip to the client. And when the time comes, we'll take them both down. The Client of Zaprinski need to be obliterated."

"Agreed," Sergey chimed in, his intellect and experience shining through his otherwise quiet demeanor. "We must remain vigilant and be ready to act at a moment's notice."

"Let's go over the information Edward provided us about the handover location," Nick suggested, pulling up satellite images on his own tablet. The team huddled closer, their minds racing as they analyzed the layout of the area and planned their approach.

The plane finally touched down in Cartagena, its landing gear kissing the tarmac with a jolt. Nick, Martin, Michael, Edward, Sergey, and Zaprinski disembarked, met by the warm embrace of the Colombian sun. As they made their way across the airstrip, a woman approached them – Eva Standfield, their local contact, ex Mi5, hired for the purpose of the mission in Cartagena by Edward.

"Welcome to Cartagena," Eva greeted them, her voice confident and alluring. Her long, dark hair cascaded over her shoulders, framing her intelligent eyes. She handed Nick a small envelope containing crucial intel and digital 3D maps on the handover location. "This should help you get started."

"Thank you, Eva," Nick replied, his eyes scanning the contents of the envelope. The information inside would be invaluable for their mission – a testament to Eva's resourcefulness.

"Alright, team," Nick said, determination flooding his veins. "Let's get to work."

CHAPTER 55

The sun was beginning to set in Cartagena, casting an orange glow over the bustling streets and casting long shadows from the colonial buildings that lined them. Nick led his team through the vibrant cityscape, taking in the sights, sounds, and smells of the coastal city. The air was heavy with humidity and the scent of fresh seafood and spices wafted from street vendors as they passed.

"Remember, we want to blend in," Nick reminded his team, his eyes constantly scanning their surroundings for any potential threats. "We need to act like locals and not draw attention to ourselves."

"Got it, boss," Martin replied, adjusting the brim of his hat to better shield his face. As they walked, he couldn't help but feel a pang of nostalgia for their undercover days during their time at the CIA.

Eva led them through a labyrinth of narrow, cobblestone streets, expertly navigating the maze-like layout of the old city. They passed brightly painted homes adorned with intricate wrought-iron balconies overflowing with bougainvillea.

"Alright, here's where we'll set up," Eva said, pointing to a tumbledown building overlooking the square where the handover would take place in front of Bella Mar Hotel. Nick surveyed the area, nodding in approval.

"Martin, you'll be our sniper," Nick instructed, knowing his friend's steady hand and sharp eye made him the perfect candidate for the job. "Find yourself a good vantage point and get comfortable. We'll handle the rest."

"Understood," Martin replied, his voice firm and focused. He disappeared into the shadows, leaving Nick and the others to continue their preparations.

As they delved deeper into Cartagena's criminal underworld, Nick's thoughts raced. What had started as a mission to apprehend Zaprinski's client was quickly becoming something much larger – a sprawling web of corruption that threatened the global drug market.

"Eva, what do you know about the other power players in this city?" Nick asked, his voice low and intent.

"Cartagena has always been a hub for illicit dealings," Eva explained, her eyes darkening with sorrow. "But recently, there have been whispers of a new player on the scene – someone with connections that span continents. Also in the last two weeks we had few shooting like street fight and one big explosion at the building of the local bank. The situation start to bi chaotic".

"Could it be possible that we're dealing with an alliance between multiple cartels?" Sergey posited; his brow furrowed in thought.

"Anything's possible," Eva replied, her tone grim. "But one thing's for sure – whatever we've stumbled upon here goes far beyond just Zaprinski's client."

The stakes were higher than ever before, and they had to tread carefully if they wanted to expose the corruption without becoming its next victims.

"Stay focused, everyone," Nick warned, his voice steady despite the turmoil raging inside him. "We don't know who's involved or how deep this goes. But we'll bring them down, no matter what it takes."

CHAPTER 56

Nick Taylor adjusted the cuff of his crisp linen shirt, a habit from his days in the field when every detail had to be perfect. The Hotel Bella Mar's lobby thrummed with the quiet hum of conversations and the clink of fine China as wealthy guests sipped their afternoon tea amidst lush greenery that lent the space an air of tropical elegance. He surveyed the area with a practiced eye, noting the antique vases that dotted the room, remnants of a bygone era, yet meticulously maintained. His friends, all ex-operatives like himself, were scattered strategically throughout the lobby, their casual stances belying the tension beneath.

Eva's assistance had been invaluable; the local intel specialist had provided them extra 5 light armed people with cutting-edge surveillance gear. Their attire blended seamlessly with the patrons—linen suits and designer sunglasses for the men, airy summer dresses and wide-brimmed hats for the women—yet beneath the fabric, they concealed holsters and earpieces. They were a mix of intellectuals and athletes, each chosen for their unique skill set, forming a covert symphony of vigilance.

The air was heavy with the scent of salt from the nearby Caribbean Sea, mingling with the faint fragrance of jasmine from the hotel's manicured gardens. The grandeur of the building, its colonial Spanish architecture speaking to a history rich with intrigue and conquest, stood as a silent observer to the clandestine nature of their gathering.

The clock on the wall, with its ornate brass hands, crept towards 6PM. Nick's mind remained focused, recalling every scrap of intelligence on Zaprinski's client, his strategies honed over years of navigating political minefields.

Without warning, the serenity was shattered by the guttural roar of engines. Ten sleek black Mercedes G-Class cars, their tinted windows reflecting the dying sunlight, pulled up in front of the hotel's grand entrance. The vehicles, symbols of power and precision, lined up with military exactitude, momentarily eclipsing the sounds of leisure with their mechanical might.

In an instant, the atmosphere shifted. Hotel guests turned their heads, curiosity piqued by the sudden display of opulence and authority. Waiters paused mid-stride, their trays laden with crystal and silver wobbling precariously.

Nick felt the familiar surge of adrenaline, his heart steady but alert. He exchanged a brief glance with a colleague across the room—a slight nod barely perceptible to the untrained eye. Their plan, meticulously crafted and ready to spring into action, hung in the balance.

He thought of Zaprinski, likely upstairs preparing for the encounter, his stoic face masking the calculations within.

"Keep sharp," Nick murmured into his hidden mic, his voice low and even. "It's showtime."

Nick's pulse quickened as the first of the doors swung open, and a man emerged from the depths of the armored vehicle. The figure was unmistakably Mr. Zho, his silhouette casting a long shadow across the cobblestones of the hotel's courtyard. Tall and imposing, he moved with the controlled grace of a seasoned operative. His head was shaved to a sheen that matched the glint of his polished shoes, reflecting the harsh Colombian sun.

Mr. Zho's attire spoke volumes about the life he led—a tailored Armani suit that seemed to armor his muscular frame, its dark fabric absorbing light and attention alike. The air around him felt colder, charged with the undercurrents of his notorious reputation as North Korea's most elusive operator.

His eyes scanned the surroundings with mechanical precision, betraying nothing of his thoughts, which were no doubt as sharp and dangerous as the blade Nick knew he carried close at all times.

As if on cue, the other vehicles disgorged their contents, a throng of stern-faced men stepping out into the humid air. They fanned out in formation, each one dressed in nondescript black suits that did little to camouflage the bulges beneath their jackets—clear indicators of the firepower they carried. Their movements were synchronized, a silent ballet of security protocols enacted with deadly seriousness.

These men, many with faces carved from years of service under unforgiving regimes, bore the distinct marks of their trade: scars, both physical and unseen, etched into their expressions. Eyes swept through the crowd, hands subtly adjusting their coats to assure themselves of the readiness of their weapons. Their presence was a statement, a fortress of flesh and steel built around Mr. Zho.

Nick absorbed every detail from beneath the brim of his hat, his outward calm belying the tactical storm brewing in his mind. Each breath he took was measured; each blink calculated to miss nothing. He memorized their stances, the way they positioned themselves strategically around their charge, creating a living shield as impenetrable as the walls of the Hotel Bella Mar itself.

The hotel, with its colonial grandeur and air of faded opulence, became a stage for this unexpected ensemble. Its balconies adorned with intricate ironwork and walls bearing the patina of age stood in stark contrast to the modern menace before it. The lush greenery that embraced the building swayed gently in the breeze, an indifferent witness to the drama unfolding at its feet.

Nick edged closer to a towering palm, its broad leaves offering concealment and a vantage point. The scent of salt and blooming flowers mingled with something else fear, perhaps, or anticipation. In his earpiece, a voice chimed with updates, but Nick needed no reminders. His world had narrowed to the players before him, each one a piece in a game where the stakes could not be higher.

"Stay focused," he whispered to himself, the mantra grounding him. "This is just the beginning."

Nick's fingers brushed against the small device in his pocket, a subtle motion that would have gone unnoticed by anyone not attuned to his particular brand of silent communication. The slight pressure of his thumb triggered a vibration, sending an invisible alert to his team scattered throughout the vicinity of Hotel Bella Mar. Their response was immediate; postures subtly shifted, eyes narrowed, and hands moved closer to concealed weapons.

Martin, perched high on a neighboring building's rooftop, felt the buzz against his wrist. He knew it as the signal to be on high alert, ready to take the shot that could tilt the scales in their favor. From his vantage point, he had a clear view of the hotel entrance, his sniper rifle's scope tracing an invisible line from his eye to the heart of the target below. His breathing slowed; a controlled rhythm honed from years in the field. Every sense was sharpened, every muscle tensed for the moment that mattered.

Below, the hotel staff—dressed in crisp uniforms, their smiles practiced and professional—paused in their orchestrated dance of hospitality. A bellboy, cart laden with luggage, halted mid-step, his youthful face creasing in confusion. The concierge, a woman with an air of quiet efficiency, tilted her head ever so slightly, curiosity piquing as she took in the unusual cavalcade of black vehicles and the stern-faced men who emerged. Guests lounging in the lobby, some draped in colorful vacation attire, others in the casual chic that spoke of wealth and indifference, turned their heads toward the commotion, murmurs rippling through the crowd.

The hotel itself seemed to hold its breath—the grand chandeliers casting a warm glow over the polished marble floors, the lush potted palms standing sentinel, and the ornate tapestries depicting scenes of old-world charm mute witnesses to this intrusion of stark reality. Through the vast windows, the Caribbean sun streamed in, catching on the glint of polished gunmetal as the armed entourage filed into the lobby.

Nick moved like a shadow among the guests, his gray hair and distinguished features allowing him to blend with the affluent clientele while his keen eyes remained locked on Mr. Zho's procession. The whisper of silk from a woman's dress, the clink of ice in a glass of aged rum—such details were absorbed and cataloged, part of the tapestry of his surroundings. Each step he took was measured; each glance calculated to maintain the façade of an uninvolved observer.

"Be alert," he murmured into the discreet mic nestled against his throat, his voice barely above a breath as he addressed his unseen allies. "Eyes on the prize, people."

A waiter, balancing a tray of sparkling cocktails, weaved through the throng with effortless grace, his gaze lingering just a moment too long on the intruders before returning to his task. The tension hung palpable in the air, a delicate balance of fear and fascination that permeated the space.

In the midst of the opulence and tropical beauty, the game of espionage continued to unfold, a silent battle of wits and wills where every player held their cards close to their chest, waiting for the moment to reveal their hand.

CHAPTER 57

Nick's gaze was fixed on the cadre of men who emerged from the black Mercedes convoy with military precision. They fanned out in a protective cordon around Mr. Zho, their movements sharp and fluid, a choreographed dance of danger. Nick could almost feel the weight of the firearms concealed beneath their tailored suits, the subtle bulges against fine cloth betraying deadly intent. These were no ordinary thugs; they moved with the discipline of soldiers and the sleek lethality of panthers.

It was then that Nick felt a jolt of surprise ripple through him; his expectations had been upended in an instant. Zaprinski's client was not the feared Medellin Cartel boss as anticipated but rather an Asian gangster, whose reputation for ruthlessness was whispered about in dark corners and back alleys across continents. His blonde hair, normally a striking contrast to his dark suits, was now slicked back, adding to the air of menace that clung to him like a second skin. The presence of Mr. Zho is the evidence of something new in the air, a new player in South America, new player for the control of the rich narco market.

Mr. Zho's presence resonated with an unnerving calmness. He paused for a moment, surveying the plush lobby with its gleaming marble floors and opulent chandeliers that dripped crystals like frozen raindrops. His eyes, dark orbs set in an impassive face, scanned the crowd with the detachment of a predator assessing its domain. There was nothing superfluous about him; every inch, from his polished shoes to the crisp line of his jaw, spoke of a man who valued efficiency over excess.

Above the hum of whispered speculations and the muted clinking of cutlery at the hotel's café, the sudden thrum of helicopter blades sliced through the sky. Nick's instincts flared—the circling black chopper added an unexpected variable to the equation. Without hesitation, he tapped the tiny earpiece lodged deep within his ear canal.

"Martin, we've got birds in the sky. Stay out of sight," he instructed tersely, his voice a low whisper that belied the surge of adrenaline coursing through him.

From his concealed vantage point, Martin would have a clear view of the hotel's entrance and the surrounding area. The rooftop, littered with antennas and satellite dishes, provided ample cover, blending the sniper into the architectural chaos. The message was clear: hold fire, remain invisible.

As Mr. Zho led his contingent towards the elevator banks, their steps echoed against the pristine floor, a rhythmic drumbeat that seemed to sync with the pounding in Nick's chest. Room 808 loomed in his thoughts, a number now etched into the fabric of the day's events—a room where destinies would collide, and the unwritten chapters of their lives awaited penning.

Nick's gaze followed the rigid back of Mr. Zho as he paced forward, the heels of his polished Oxfords tapping out a staccato rhythm on the sun-warmed cobblestones. Each step seemed measured, deliberate—Zho's every movement was a study in disciplined control. His life story, whispered in intelligence circles, painted him as a survivor hardened by adversity, sculpted by a youth spent under the unforgiving tutelage of street skirmishes and the strict military doctrine of his uncle's household.

Nick discreetly adjusted the cuff of his linen shirt, a nondescript cream that blended seamlessly with the tropical chic of Cartagena's tourists. Underneath, the cool touch of metal—a concealed weapon—was a comforting weight against his forearm. His mind raced through scenarios, each one playing out like a game of chess where human lives were the stakes. He needed a gambit to neutralize Zho without triggering a bloodbath.

"Stay sharp," Nick murmured into the comms unit hidden within the weave of his collar, his eyes never leaving the backs of the armed entourage filtering into the hotel. "This is no Medellin street gang we're dealing with."

The Hotel Bella Mar's grandiose lobby stretched before them, an opulent display of old-world charm and new money. Gleaming marble floors reflected the golden afternoon light spilling in from the arched windows. Lush potted palms added a touch of verdant life amidst the antique furnishings that spoke of a bygone era of explorers and conquests. The atmosphere was a heady mix of coastal breezes and the faint aroma of rich mahogany.

As Mr. Zho's group moved with purposeful strides towards the bank of elevators, Nick and his team melded with the throng of guests. They drifted through the space with the nonchalance of seasoned travelers: Rachel casually flipping through a brochure on local attractions, Carlos's fiddling with the settings on a high-end camera, and Eva adjusting her wide-brimmed sun hat with an elegance that drew appreciative glances.

Their movements were a choreographed dance of subtlety, each step calculated to maintain a buffer of anonymity while keeping the North Korean contingent within their peripheral vision. Nick let his gaze wander, taking in the details of the scene—the way the light played off the polished bannisters, the soft murmur of conversations punctuated by laughter, the subtle clink of glassware from the café.

"Remember, we're just tourists soaking up the history," he reminded them through the comms, his voice low and steady. "Let Zho think he's the predator here, not the prey."

Through the corner of his eye, Nick watched as Zho paused momentarily, his head tilting ever so slightly as if tuned to a frequency beyond the ordinary bustle. It was the posture of a man who had navigated treacherous waters, whose instincts were honed by years of survival in the shadows.

"Easy... easy..." Nick thought, mentally urging his team to remain inconspicuous as they ascended the grand staircase, trailing the procession of danger that wrapped itself around Mr. Zho like an invisible cloak. Their positive thinking was their armor; they were the unseen sentinels in a theater of espionage, where every act could be their last.

Nick Taylor's eyes scanned the opulent lobby of Hotel Bella Mar as he trailed behind the enigmatic Mr. Zho. His every sense was alert, attuned to the sounds of leather soles against the intricate mosaic tiles and the rustle of expensive fabric brushing past polished mahogany furnishings. The air was scented with a fusion of fresh Colombian coffee and subtle floral notes from the grand centerpieces adorning the reception desks.

His friends, matching his pace, were undistinguishable from the other patrons in their linen shirts and chinos—standard tourist attire—but beneath that casual facade, they were coiled springs, ready to leap into action. Nick's gaze lingered momentarily on an antique clock by the concierge; its pendulum swung with a reassuring precision, much like the plan unfolding in his mind.

Zho's associate, a compact man bristling with quiet intensity, murmured something into his earpiece, prompting Mr. Zho to adjust the cufflinks on his tailored suit—a dark ensemble that spoke volumes of his lifestyle, one where power was currency and brutality a means to an end. The shaved head gleamed under the crystal chandeliers, a beacon of menace in the throng of unsuspecting hotel guests.

They reached the elevator, and Nick's team split up, as per their strategy. Some took the adjacent lift while others opted for the stairs, blending effortlessly into the ebb and flow of the hotel's heartbeat. Zaprinski, ensconced in room 808, would be expecting them; his keen intellect and years of KGB training had instilled in him a near-pathological need for control—an antidote to the nerves that now gnawed at his resolve.

"Stay sharp," Nick whispered into his hidden mic, his voice betraying none of the tension that knotted his stomach. "Eyes on the prize, and hearts light."

The elevator dinged softly, announcing their arrival at the eighth floor. Room 808 lay to the right, its door unassuming yet laden with unseen danger. Nick and his closest companion paused by an ornate vase hosting an explosion of tropical flowers. Their reflections stared back at them from the polished surface of the vase—two soldiers disguised in civilian garb, moments away from confronting the unknown.

"Positive outcomes only," Nick murmured, not for his team but for himself, as he adjusted the strap of his faux camera bag—a weightless prop compared to the gear he'd carried in darker times. A deep breath filled his lungs, taste of anticipation and the faint tang of sea air that drifted in from the open windows along the corridor.

Zaprinski's time in the KGB had ingrained a clinical detachment that served him well in moments like these, and though the silence from room 808 was deafening, Nick knew the ex-assassin was preparing for all possible scenarios with cold efficiency.

"Let's make history," Nick signaled with a nod, and together, they moved towards the door that stood between them and a confrontation that could shift the balance of international power. Their footsteps were silent, their minds razor-sharp—a testament to the years spent mastering the art of survival.

CHAPTER 58

The air in the room was thick with the heavy scent of old wood polish and tension. Kaprinski, a man whose once sharp features were now softened by age and worry, stood across from Mr. Zho, his hand extended as if offering peace. Between their outstretched palms lay the fate of nations: a tiny microchip, the weight of which seemed to press down on the room like an impending storm.

Mr. Zho, a human edifice carved from stone and steely resolve, eyed the chip with the calculated detachment of a chess grandmaster contemplating a pivotal move. His muscular build filled out the tailored suit perfectly, every thread seemingly aligned with his rigid posture. The dim light cast shadows over his shaved head, giving him an aura that was both enigmatic and foreboding.

Kaprinski's fingers trembled ever so slightly as he relinquished his grip on the silicon harbinger. Mr. Zho's own hand—a vice of flesh and bone—enclosed the microchip, and for a fleeting moment, their eyes locked. Kaprinski's held a flicker of defiance, a silent challenge to the unspoken threat that vibrated between them. Mr. Zho's gaze, however, was a void, devoid of emotion, unreadable and ice-cold.

The luxurious room, adorned with antique furnishings that spoke of a colonial past and power long held, seemed to contract, as though it too anticipated the coming storm. A stately grandfather clock ticked in rhythm with the pulse of the men who occupied the space, its pendulum swinging with a hypnotic precision that mirrored the heartbeat of the operation at play.

In the periphery of this exchange, cloaked in the shadow of discretion, stood Nick Taylor. His weathered face, etched with the experiences of a thousand covert operations, betrayed nothing. Yet beneath the surface, his mind raced, calculating every possible outcome. His athletic frame was poised, coiled with potential energy, ready to spring into action at a moment's notice.

As the silence stretched, becoming almost a tangible entity in itself, Mr. Zho's hand—a hand that had no doubt dealt death as easily as it dealt cards—moved with a suddenness that belied his bulk. In one fluid motion, the gun appeared, a metallic extension of his will, and barked fire and lead.

Zaprinski's expression shifted from challenge to shock, and then to nothing at all as his body crumpled to the floor, the richly patterned Persian rug beneath him drinking in the red that began to spread like a dark bloom. The sound of the gunshot reverberated through the high-ceilinged room, bouncing off gilded mirrors and priceless oil paintings, each echo a grim punctuation to Zaprinski's life.

Nick's heart lurched into his throat, his face a mask of horror etched with lines that spoke of both age and adrenaline. He felt the familiar surge, the call to action, but the shock rooted him momentarily. It was not just the abruptness of the execution that shook him; it was the cold efficiency, the brutal finality of Mr. Zho's betrayal.

In that suspended slice of time, where the world seemed to inhale sharply in unison, Nick knew that everything had changed. The mission they had so meticulously planned was unraveling before his eyes, and survival now hinged on his ability to adapt, to overcome the unexpected with the cunning and decisiveness that had kept him alive in this deadly game of espionage.

CHAPTER 59

Nick's world narrowed to a tunnel, the edges blurring as his focus sharpened on the unfolding chaos. Mr. Zho's gangsters, realizing their cover was blown, scrambled towards the stairs, their movements swift and practiced amidst the panic.

"Martin, take the shot!" Nick barked into his earpiece, urgency threading his voice. He could hear Martin's controlled breathing over the comm, a testament to years of training kicking in. There was a whisper of fabric from Martin's ghillie suit brushing against the concrete of the rooftop where he lay in wait, a human predator camouflaged among city detritus.

From his vantage point, Martin had Zho in his crosshairs. The rifle recoiled against his shoulder, a near-silent puff of smoke the only sign of the shot. Yet it wasn't meant to be; a sudden gust of wind, a fraction of a second's hesitation, a small movement from the target - the reasons didn't matter. The bullet missed its mark, embedding itself in the wall just as Zho ducked into the stairwell with his men, descending like rats fleeing a sinking ship.

"Damn it," Martin cursed under his breath, already sending the picture of Mr. Zho and his entourage to the CIA for identification. They needed to know who they were dealing with, and whether these gangsters were lone wolves or part of a larger pack.

"Plan B, Sergey, now!" Nick's command snapped through the comm, an order that Sergey and Maria's team executed with precision, attaching GPS trackers to the chassis of the G-Class Mercedes that roared to life below.

Nick's legs pumped as he bolted down the fire escape, the metallic clanging of his boots echoing in the stairwell. His mind raced, analyzing each motion before making it, the remnants of his shock transformed into fuel for his relentless drive.

"Martin, I'm heading to the garage. Where's my ride?" Nick gritted out between breaths.

"Meet you at the hotel garage. Eva left a gift – a black Dodge Challenger SRT8 Hellcat. You can't miss her," came Martin's reply, a note of dark amusement lacing his tone despite the gravity of their situation.

The grandeur of Cartagena's architecture blurred past him as Nick emerged into the balmy late afternoon air. The intricate colonial facades and flowering balconies might have charmed any other man, but for Nick, they were just part of the landscape he needed to navigate.

He arrived at the rendezvous point, the growl of the Hellcat reaching his ears before the beast came into view, gleaming black and formidable under the sterile lights of the garage. It was more than a car; it was mobile command center, a lifeline, and perhaps their only chance at staying in this deadly game.

"Let's hunt," Nick muttered, the taste of vengeance bitter on his tongue as he slid behind the wheel, ready to chase the specters that fled into the Colombian night.

CHAPTER 60

The garage was a cavernous space, the air thick with the scent of motor oil and the quiet hum of idling engines. Shadows clung to the corners where the fluorescent lights couldn't reach, creating pockets of darkness that seemed to watch and wait. Martin stood near an open bay, his frame outlined by the dim glow, his dark hair and muscular physique making him appear as a sentinel guarding the metallic cave.

"Got everything?" Nick asked, his voice steady despite the undercurrent of urgency that laced every syllable.

"Locked and loaded," Martin replied, patting the trunk where the geolocator and Berettas lay concealed within.

Nick's gaze swept over the black Dodge Challenger SRT8 Hellcat. It was a beast of American engineering, its curves and lines whispering promises of untamed power. The paintwork reflected the sparse light, mirroring the determination in his steely eyes. He slid into the driver's seat, the leather cool against his skin, and felt the car come alive beneath him.

He grasped the steering wheel, its leather grip familiar in his calloused hands. The interior was a blend of luxury and functionality—the dashboard a constellation of dials and screens, each glowing softly like stars in the pre-dawn gloom of Cartagena. The geolocator beeped, a green blip pulsating rhythmically on the screen—a digital heartbeat that led them to their quarry.

The twin Beretta M9s lay beside it, the moonlight glinting off their sleek barrels. These were not merely tools; they were extensions of his will, a promise of defense—or retribution.

As they exited the garage, the night enveloped the Hellcat. The streets of Cartagena were a labyrinth of history and modernity, colonial architecture fused with neon signs of progress. But for Nick, they were merely obstacles to be navigated, pathways to be mastered in this deadly race against time.

His fingers tightened on the wheel as he wove through traffic, the Hellcat responding to every touch, every shift with a predator's grace. Martin kept his eyes on the geolocator, calling out directions with clinical precision, his focus unwavering as Nick drove with the skill of a man who had long since melded machine with instinct.

The G-Class Mercedes Arcade they pursued was a specter in the distance, its location a constant reminder on the screen before them. Each turn brought them closer, each decision narrowing the gap between hunter and hunted.

Nick could feel the adrenaline coursing through him, the rhythmic thud of his heart a drumbeat spurring him onward. There was no room for hesitation, no moment for second-guessing. Every motion was fluid, every thought crystallized into action.

"Airport's twenty out," Martin said, checking his watch. "We need to close the gap but keep out of sight."

"Understood," Nick responded, his words clipped as he focused on the chase. The Hellcat roared down the boulevard, a symphony of horsepower and determination.

They were close now, so close he could almost taste the fumes from Zho's fleeing vehicle. Yet even as the airport loomed ahead, a sprawling complex of runways and terminals silhouetted against the starlit sky, Nick knew the true challenge lay beyond its gates, in the shadowy world where truth and lies danced a lethal tango.

And he would lead.

Nick's hands gripped the leather steering wheel, the Hellcat's engine growling like a caged beast eager for release. His eyes scanned the winding streets of Cartagena, the historic facades blurring into a tapestry of shadow and amber streetlights as he navigated the chase with the precision of a maestro conducting an orchestra.

"Zho's just ahead," Martin said, his voice calm yet edged with urgency. "Maintain this course."

The dashboard bathed Nick in a soft green glow, the geolocator blinking steadily. They weaved through the city, a ghost trailing another in the night. Nick's gaze was steely, each movement deliberate, betraying none of the turmoil that churned within him. The chase was a delicate dance on the razor's edge between pursuit and exposure.

"Freeman's got us covered from above," Martin murmured, his earpiece crackling with static as he communicated with their eye in the sky. "Satellite's tracking their every move."

"Good," Nick replied curtly. He could almost feel the orbiting technology zooming in on their quarry, an omnipresent guardian angel armed with high-tech surveillance.

Martin's phone vibrated, casting an eerie light on his rugged features. "It's Sergey," he said after a glance at the screen. Decrypting the message with swift fingers, his brow furrowed. "Zho's men are from Macao. They're Lee Chang's foot soldiers."

"Chang..." The name fell from Nick's lips, heavy with realization. The pieces of the puzzle were falling into place, each revelation etching a clearer picture of their adversary—a dragon lurking behind his lair, orchestrating chaos from afar.

"Lee Chang is escalating the game," Martin continued, relaying the information. "He's playing kingmaker—wants to control the drug trade across two continents."

"Then Zho's just a pawn," Nick concluded, his mind racing. A warlord masquerading as a businessman, Lee Chang was a force to be reckoned with, and they had just scratched the surface of his ambition.

"Exactly," Martin affirmed. "But if we can take down his pawns..."

"Checkmate," Nick finished the thought, a grim smile touching his lips. It was a high-stakes game, but Nick Taylor was no stranger to gambling with danger. His life had been a series of calculated risks, and this was one more bet he was willing to make.

The Hellcat surged forward, its tires hugging the cobblestone as they rounded another corner. Cartagena's colonial beauty was lost on them now; it was merely a battlefield, a chessboard upon which they plotted their next move.

"Stay sharp," Nick said, his voice a low growl to match the car's rumbling engine. "We can't afford any mistakes."

"Never do," Martin replied, his hand resting on the Beretta M9 at his side—a silent promise that he would do whatever it took to protect his friend and see justice served.

As the buildings gave way to the outskirts of the city, the dense foliage whispered secrets of the coming dawn, but for Nick and Martin, the night was far from over. Ahead, destiny awaited, cloaked in the guise of a G-Class Mercedes speeding towards uncertainty.

The Hellcat's engine growled a low, steady hum as Nick eased off the accelerator, guiding the beast of a car to a discreet halt just outside the perimeter of Rafael Núñez International Airport. The night air was thick with the salt of the Caribbean and the distant hum of jet engines preparing for their global ballet.

"Kill the lights," Martin murmured, and he promptly flicked the switch, plunging them into shadows. Nick's eyes, seasoned by countless nights of surveillance, adjusted swiftly to the darkness. He watched through the windshield, his gaze sharp and calculating, as the G-Class Mercedes glided toward a private hangar, its sleek form a whisper against the tarmac.

"Let's see what we've got," Martin said, his voice hushed but firm. He retrieved a pair of infrared binoculars from the glove compartment, the equipment cool and weighty in his hands. Raising them to his eyes, Martin scanned the hangar where a Gulfstream jet sat like a dormant predator, its silver wings catching the moonlight.

"Serial number Tango-Bravo-Six-Five-Niner," Martin recited quietly, relaying the information through a secure line to a contact at the CIA. His pulse quickened; steps had to be taken, and fast.

Within moments, the response crackled through their earpieces, "Confirmed. It's registered to a shell company in Hong Kong. Ties to Lee Chang's corporate network. Flight plan's logged for Macao."

"Damn it," Nick swore under his breath. His jaw tightened, muscles flexing with a mix of frustration and resolve. "Lee Chang's making a run for it."

"Then we're on the clock," Martin replied, lowering the binoculars. His face, etched with lines of experience, was set in grim determination. His dark hair, cropped close to his scalp, seemed to blend with the night around them.

Nick glanced over at him, noting the way his friend's body tensed, ready for action—a coiled spring in human form. Martin was a fortress of a man—muscular, solid, his very presence a statement of intent. In his steel-gray eyes, there flickered an unquenchable fire that spoke of battles fought and a lifetime committed to justice. This was more than a mission; it was personal.

"Options?" Nick asked, knowing full well that each choice they made now could mean life or death.

"Direct assault is off the table," Martin stated flatly. "Too risky without backup."

"Agreed. We need to track them, find out Lee Chang's endgame. " Nick's mind raced through scenarios, discarding them as quickly as they formed. "We'll need to get into that terminal, place a tracker on that jet before it takes off."

"Exactly. And I've got just the thing." Martin reached into the backseat, retrieving a compact device no larger than a credit card—the latest in covert tracking technology.

With a nod, they exited the Hellcat, slipping into the night like phantoms. Nick led the way, his feet silent on the grass, his movements fluid and assured. As they approached the airport fence, hidden from view by the cover of vegetation, the world seemed to hold its breath.

Their attire melded with the darkness—black tactical gear, lightweight yet resilient. Each man was a shadow, one with the environment. Nick, despite his age, moved with the grace and precision of a much younger operative, testament to years of rigorous training and an unyielding commitment to his craft.

Martin followed, his own expertise evident in the effortless way he navigated the terrain. Between them, a silent language flowed—an unspoken understanding honed through years of camaraderie and shared dangers.

They reached the terminal, the building itself a modern structure of glass and steel, its interior design a testament to luxury and exclusivity. But to Nick and Martin, it was merely another piece of the puzzle—a facade behind which darker deeds were plotted.

With deft fingers, Nick attached the tracker beneath the chassis of the jet, its presence betrayed only by a faint red blink before it went dark. "Tracker's set," he whispered.

"Good. Now let's vanish before—" Martin's words were cut short by a sudden interruption, but that was a trouble for another moment.

"Back to the car. We've done what we can here." Nick's voice was calm, but within him, a storm raged, thoughts already turning to their next move. They retreated into the night as silently as they had come, two ghosts dancing on the edge of war.

CHAPTER 61

"Wait," Martin interjected, his hand instinctively reaching for the Beretta M9 tucked in his shoulder holster beneath his black tactical jacket. The fabric stretched over his broad shoulders betrayed his readiness for combat. He pointed to the sky. "Chopper."

The whump-whump-whump of rotor blades sliced through the night, and an ominous silhouette descended upon them—an airborne predator with a sleek, matte finish that drank in the moonlight. The helicopter, a menacing harbinger of chaos, hovered above.

"Change of plans," Nick grunted, throwing the Dodge Challenger into gear. Tires screeched against asphalt as they lurched forward, the car's powerful engine roaring like a caged beast set free.

Gunfire erupted from the helicopter, the metallic clatter of AK-47 rounds punctuating the air. Bullets peppered the vehicle, biting into the muscular curves of the Hellcat, leaving behind pockmarks of destruction.

"Into the trees!" Nick affirmed, veering off the road. Branches whipped against the car as he navigated the dense Colombian forest, a terrain he knew only from satellite images but now felt beneath his wheels—a place where life thrived in wild abundance, untamed and indifferent to the follies of men.

He slammed the brakes, the car skidding to a stop amidst the foliage, leaves rustling in protest. "Get the Stinger," he ordered.

Martin flung open the trunk, revealing an arsenal fit for a small war. Among the weapons lay the FIM-92 Stinger, its surface a dull green that spoke of lethality without ostentation. Efficient, deadly—the tool of a professional. With practiced hands, Martin assembled the missile launcher, his movements precise, no motion wasted.

"Cover me," he said, slipping on the night vision goggles, their lenses cutting through the darkness, turning the night into day. He shouldered the weapon, the world narrowing to a single point of focus—the black specter in the sky.

"Clear backblast," Martin warned, and with a deafening roar, the Stinger missile leaped from its tube, a vengeful spirit streaking towards its target.

The helicopter, caught in the infrared crosshairs, had no time to evade. An explosion bloomed in the sky, a fiery chrysanthemum that briefly turned night into day. Burning debris rained down through the canopy, each piece extinguished by the damp earth as it landed.

"Got it," Martin breathed out, the night resuming its silent watch over the forest.

As the echo of destruction faded, a tremor of urgency seized Nick. "We've got to move," he said, his gaze shifting skyward. Through an opening in the lush canopy, he could see the private jet taxiing on the runway, the Hong Kong company's emblem glistening under the airport lights.

"Chang is getting away," Martin observed, the weight of the moment settling upon them both. "Let him—for now," Nick replied, his jaw set with grim determination. As the jet lifted into the night sky, its engines a distant thunder, he knew this wasn't the end. Cartagena was just the beginning. There was a war brewing, and he'd be damned if he let Lee Chang take the next battlefield unchallenged.

"Let's get back to the city. We have work to do," Nick stated, sliding back behind the wheel. The forest around them seemed to lean in, listening, the leaves whispering secrets of the chase to come.

"Yes Nick lets go back to the city, now Satellite has eyes on the jet," Martin's voice cut through the silence, as sharp and focused as the man himself.

"Good," Nick replied tersely, his blue eyes reflecting the determination that had become his signature. "We're not done yet."

They were an unlikely pair, the intellectual might of Martin's strategic mind perfectly complementing Nick's physical prowess. It was a partnership forged in the crucible of covert operations, one that had never shied away from the gritty, often unglamorous reality of espionage.

"Chang thinks he's won," Martin said, locking his tablet. "Let's prove him wrong," Nick responded, his voice infused with the cold steel of conviction. Standing up, he adjusted the holster at his hip, ensuring the Beretta M9 was within easy reach. The weapon was an extension of himself—sleek, reliable, and deadly when necessary.

"Next stop, Macao," Martin affirmed, his eyes meeting Nick's. There was no need for further words; their shared history spoke volumes.

"Checkmate in three moves," Nick said, the ghost of a smile playing on his lips. It was a sentiment echoed in the set of Martin's jaw—the game was indeed interesting, and they were ready to make their final play.

As they drive back into the urban labyrinth, the city's ancient colonial architecture loomed above them. Balconies adorned with intricate ironwork and buildings washed in faded pastels told stories of a time long past, but Nick and Martin were focused on the narrative yet unwritten—one that would unfold thousands of miles away, in the neon-lit streets of Macao.

In the distance, the private jet soared higher, a silver speck vanishing into the vastness of the heavens. But Nick and Martin didn't watch it go. They were already plotting its downfall, their minds whirring with strategy and anticipation. Because for men like them, the chase was never over until justice was served.

CHAPTER 62

Nick Taylor's grip on the steering wheel was firm, the leather contouring his callused palms as he navigated the sleek, black sedan through the humid night air of Cartagena. Martin De Simone sat beside him, his posture rigid, eyes scanning the darkened streets with trained vigilance. Theirs was a silence born of years in the field, where words were often superfluous, and understanding ran as deep as shared scars.

The Hotel Hyatt Regency stood like an illuminated monolith against Bocagrande Avenue's nightlife. Its grand facade, bathed in soft golden light, projected an aura of tranquility that belied the chaos unfolding in the city. They pulled into the underground parking, the car's headlights briefly illuminating the stark concrete before they settled into their designated spot.

Exhaustion weighed on Nick's broad shoulders as he followed Martin through the plush carpeted corridors, silent save for the muted echoes of their footsteps. The décor spoke of old-world elegance, with antique furnishings accentuating the opulence of the establishment. They exchanged terse nods with the night staff, their own attire – dark, functional clothing with concealed holsters –

contrasting sharply with the employees' crisp uniforms.

Once inside Nick's suite, the transition from the ornate hallway to the modern luxury of his room was seamless. Every piece of furniture was carefully selected for comfort and style, from the sleek leather couches to the minimalist art that adorned the walls. Sliding doors opened to a balcony that overlooked the ocean, the sound of waves providing a soothing backdrop to the tension that clung to both men.

"Rest up," Nick said, his voice low and gravelly, "We hit it hard at first light."

Martin only nodded, disappearing into his own room without another word. Nick took a moment to himself, standing out on the balcony and letting the sea breeze clear his thoughts. Then, without ceremony, he stripped down to his undershirt and boxers and sank into the king-sized bed, sleep claiming him almost instantly.

CHAPTER 63

The sunrise brought with it a resurgence of purpose. The Sunlight pierced through the sheer curtains of Nick Taylor's suite at the Hotel Hyatt Regency, casting a golden hue over the opulent surroundings. The room was an expanse of old-world luxury, its walls adorned with rich tapestries that whispered of history and grandeur. Antique furnishings dotted the space, each piece meticulously crafted and polished to a warm sheen.

Sergey Komutov, Michael Freeman and Edward Smith arrived there early and entered joined his suite, bringing with them the scent of fresh coffee and pastries. Together, they sat at the round dining table, a contrast of personalities united by a common cause. Sergey's thinning hair was combed neatly to one side, his eyes sharp behind wire-framed glasses as he studied the documents before him. Michael, ever the FBI agent, ate with methodical precision, his short black hair and stern features softened slightly in the morning light.

As they fueled their bodies, the television droned in the background, a constant reminder of the urgency of their mission. The newscaster's voice, somber and steady, spoke of terror attacks that had shaken the foundations of Cartagena and Medellin, the images on the screen depicting plumes of smoke and the aftermath of violence.

"Time to make the call," Nick announced, his breakfast untouched. His satellite encrypted phone felt cold and heavy in his hand as he dialed Tim Stratton, the ex-CIA South America specialist. Martin watched silently, his analytical mind already piecing together fragments of intelligence, while Marcos took diligent notes.

"Tim, it's Nick. We need everything you've got on the Cartagena and Medellin incidents," Nick's tone was all business as he paced the length of the suite, his athletic frame poised and ready for action.

Meanwhile, Sergey's conversation in hushed Russian provided a counterpoint to Nick's English, his FSB contacts offering another perspective on the intricate web they were untangling. With every piece of information, they constructed a clearer mosaic of motivations and machinations.

As Nick ended the call, he spread out the satellite tracking data across the glass-top coffee table, a constellation of digital breadcrumbs that he sifted through with expert precision. He cross-referenced timestamps with CCTV footage, his brain running through possible scenarios with a tactician's finesse.

"Look at this," he pointed at a cluster of dots on the map, "Same van, three locations, each within minutes of the blasts." His finger traced the route, eyes alight with the thrill of the chase.

"Good catch," Martin affirmed, leaning over the table, his own gaze following the pattern Nick had discovered. His mind, always searching for justice in the midst of chaos, found solace in the clarity of evidence.

Together, the four men delved deeper into the labyrinth of intelligence before them, their collective resolve unwavering. It was a battle fought not with guns or fists, but with minds sharp as blades, cutting through the fog of war that threatened to engulf the cities they sought to protect.

Nick, tall and imposing even in repose, stood by the expansive window, his athletic frame silhouetted against the morning light. His graying hair, once as dark as the Colombian coffee he sipped, was neatly combed back, revealing sharp eyes that surveyed Bocagrande Avenue below. Despite the tranquility of the vista, his mind was a tumult of strategy and analysis.

"Rival gangs could be making a play," Martin, ever the pragmatist, mused as he lounged on a leather armchair that seemed to swallow his more modest build. His casual attire, a stark contrast to the suite's grandiosity, did nothing to diminish his authoritative air.

"Or political factions seeking leverage," Sergey added, leaning against an ornate mahogany desk, his features etched with the rigor of Russian intelligence training.

"Lee Chang doesn't strike me as a man who would share power." Nick's voice was firm, reflecting a certainty honed by years in the field. "His ego demands control. The chaos in Colombia... it's a smokescreen, a ploy for revenge and domination."

"Chaos as a ladder," Sergey chimed in, stroking his chin thoughtfully. "Classic strategy."

Nick nodded, his gaze flitting to the flatscreen television where images of turmoil flickered. The air was thick with the scent of fresh croissants and fruit, remnants of their breakfast now forgotten in the urgency of their mission.

"Tim will have something on Lee Chang's past dealings with the Medellin Cartel. He understands the narco chessboard better than anyone," Martin declared, confidence threading his words as he straightened in his seat.

Over a thousand miles away in Washington, Tim Stratton sat ensconced in his study, surrounded by stacks of dossiers and the hum of encrypted servers. His fingers danced over a keyboard, coaxing secrets from the digital shadows. Tim's face, lined with the wisdom of countless covert operations, was illuminated by the glow of multiple monitors as he delved into the enigma of Lee Chang.

The distant click of keys punctuated the silence of the suite as the men waited for the report that would unravel the threads of conspiracy. In this high-stakes game, knowledge was the currency of survival, and they were investing heavily.

"Keep digging," Nick urged, his determination palpable. "Every connection, every whisper of Lee Chang's name in the dark corners of power... it's vital we understand his moves before we make our own."

"Agreed," Martin said, his own resolve mirroring Nick's. "We need to anticipate his next step, not just react to it."

"Then it's settled," Nick concluded, his mind already racing ahead to the confrontation that awaited them. "We find the puppet master behind this chaos, and we cut the strings."

The quartet's collective intellect was a force to be reckoned with, their synergy born of shared battles and hard-won trust. As they plotted their course, the Hyatt suite became less a sanctuary of rest and more a command center, the eye of a storm that was sweeping across Colombia with a fury that only the calculated mind of Lee Chang could orchestrate.

CHAPTER 64

Nick Taylor's hands, steady despite the years and scars etched into his rugged skin, carefully manipulated the fragments of the device that had torn through the heart of Cartagena. The suite's luxurious decor—a tapestry of colonial elegance intertwined with modern sleekness—contrasted sharply with the brutality of their task. Martin De Simone stood over Nick's shoulder, his dark eyes as focused as a hawk's on the remnants of twisted metal and circuitry laid out like an autopsy of terror on the mahogany table.

"RDX-based," Nick murmured, lifting a shard with tweezers, examining it under the magnifying glass. "Military grade, but not standard issue. This is custom work."

Martin leaned in, his muscular frame tense with concentration. "See these etchings? That's precision engineering, beyond your average bomb-maker's skill set."

"Signature work?" Nick suggested, his mind already sifting through the implications.

"Has to be," Martin replied, turning the fragment in the light. "There's pride in this craftsmanship.

Whoever did this wants it recognized—just not easily."

"An ego hidden within anonymity," Sergey Komutov chimed in, his voice tinged with the accent of his Russian past. He approached the table, pushing up the rimless glasses perched on his nose. The calculated movements of Sergey's chess-honed mind were evident as he scrutinized the evidence, his thinning hair a mere afterthought to the intensity of his gaze.

"Could be a calling card," Edward interjected from the room's edge, his voice a calm counterpoint to the tension hovering in the air. His sharp features softened slightly with thought. "But why would Chang leave such a trace?"

"Perhaps it's not Chang's doing directly," Nick posited, shifting his focus to the electronic components. "He may have outsourced this part, kept his hands clean while ensuring his message was clear."

"Let's piece it together," Martin said, moving to the room's expansive windows overlooking the bustling streets below. "The 'how' is starting to shape up, now we need the 'why' behind these attacks."

"Power vacuum," Sergey offered, crossing his arms. "Chang could be using the chaos to stage his own ascent, dismantling the Medellin Cartel's influence."

"Or it's misdirection," Michael countered, leaning back against the plush armchair. "Maybe there's another player we haven't considered."

"Both are plausible," Nick conceded, eyes narrowing. "It's a two-front war—public fear and underworld upheaval. We're dealing with someone who knows how to manipulate both arenas."

"Control the streets, control the narrative," Martin added, his tactical mind dissecting the strategy. "Create enough panic, and people clamor for a new order—any order."

"Which brings us back to Chang," Nick concluded. The data points were converging, threads weaving into a tapestry of intrigue and ambition. Each man brought his unique perspective to the table, their collective experience painting a broader picture of the labyrinth they navigated.

"Alright, let's assume Chang is our maestro," Martin said, rolling his shoulders to relieve the tension. "The question remains: what does he gain by igniting this firestorm?"

"Let's not get ahead of ourselves," Nick cautioned. "First, we confirm the players, then we unravel their motives. Piece by piece, the truth will emerge."

"Like a grandmaster positioning his pawns before the decisive strike," Sergey mused, his metaphor drawing a brief, knowing smile from Nick.

"Exactly," Nick affirmed. "We'll lay out the board and anticipate the moves. In this game of shadows, foresight is our greatest weapon."

In the sanctuary of the Hyatt suite, amidst the opulence of velvet drapes and oil paintings whispering of a storied past, four minds melded into a singular force. Their dialogue was more than mere words; it was the alchemy of intellect and instinct, refining raw data into strategic insight. With each revelation, they edged closer to piercing the veil that shrouded their enigmatic adversary.

"Let's keep at it," Nick urged, his resolve steely as the Colombian sun dipped below the horizon, casting long shadows across the room that mirrored the darkness encroaching upon the city they sought to protect.

CHAPTER 65

Nick's eyes were locked onto the screen, fingers dancing over the keyboard as he pored over the encrypted files that had taken them days to crack. The suite's air was tense, heavy with the weight of their collective focus. Sunlight filtered through sheer curtains, casting a golden hue on the antique furnishings that adorned the room—a stark contrast to the modern technology sprawled across the table.

"Got something," Nick announced, his voice slicing through the silence. Martin leaned in, his muscular frame tensed like a coiled spring. Sergey's brow creased in concentration as he adjusted his glasses, peering at the data that could redefine their mission.

"Lee Chong," Nick began, pointing to a series of transactions onscreen, "has been funneling money to an offshore account linked to none other than Senator James Hargrave."

"Christ," Martin muttered, running a hand through his dark hair. "The same Hargrave who golfs with the President?"

"Exactly," Nick confirmed. "This isn't just about drugs; it's a political power play." The implications were chilling, and for a moment, the weight of the conspiracy seemed to press down upon the ornate oak-panelled walls of the room.

"Chong's making a move to shake the geopolitical chessboard," Sergey added, his voice steady but grave. "Which means we need more intel," Nick declared, standing up. His gaze was resolute, his mind already racing with strategies. "We need to talk to the Boss of Medellin face-to-face."

"Could be risky," Martin cautioned, but his eyes held a spark of adrenaline-fueled excitement. "Risk comes with the territory," Nick replied, a wry smile touching his lips. He'd lived on the edge of danger for most of his life; this was no different.

"Eva and the others will set up our Macao angle," Nick continued, his mind shifting gears to logistics. "Sergey, we need that jet ready."

"Consider it done," Sergey said, tapping away on his phone to secure transportation.

Nick took a deep breath, feeling the familiar thrum of anticipation. This was what he lived for—the thrill of the chase, the puzzle unraveling piece by piece, and the relentless pursuit of justice. It was almost poetic, the way the room spoke of history and battles fought long ago—now they were embarking on a new kind of warfare, one of shadows and secrets.

"Let's pack up. We leave for Medellin within the hour," Nick instructed, his tone leaving no room for argument.

Martin nodded, his movements efficient as he stowed away sensitive equipment. They dressed in nondescript attire, blending utility with anonymity—jeans, sturdy boots, and lightweight jackets to conceal their gear. Every item they chose was deliberate, from the sunglasses perched atop Nick's head to the tactical watch strapped to Martin's wrist.

As they exited the suite, the scent of the sea mingled with the lush greenery that encased the hotel's grand facade. The Hyatt Regency stood like a silent sentinel amidst the chaos, its neoclassical architecture imposing yet elegant, a fortress of luxury in the heart of Cartagena.

"Medellin won't know what hit it," Martin said, a smirk playing on his lips as they descended the marble staircase.

"Let's hope not," Nick replied. "But if they do, we'll be ready for them."

They stepped into the bright Colombian day, the sun high in the sky, casting its watchful eye over them. It was a beautiful day for truth-seeking, they thought; a perfect day to confront shadows with the light of revelation.

CHAPTER 66

Nick gripped the steering wheel of the Dodge Charger, feeling the powerful engine's vibration resonate through his bones as he navigated the Colombian roads to the serpentine roads leading to the hills of Medellin. His gray eyes, normally sharp and clear, were narrowed in concentration, a testament to the gravity of their mission. Beside him, Martin checked the encrypted GPS on his phone one last time before slipping it into his pocket, assuring they were on the right path.

After a four hours' drive, "Three kilometers out," Martin announced, his voice steady despite the adrenaline that Nick knew pulsed just as strongly in his old friend's veins. The lush greenery of the Colombian landscape blurred past them, a stark contrast to the dark purpose of their journey. As they neared the compound, the Dodge's headlights illuminated towering walls crowned with barbed wire—an imposing fortress meant to deter unwanted guests. But tonight, Nick Taylor and Martin De Simone were not to be dissuaded.

"Check the EMP device," Nick instructed without taking his eyes off the winding road ahead. Martin reached into the backseat and retrieved a matte-black case, flipping it open to reveal a sleek piece of technology that looked out of place against the rustic backdrop of the Colombian countryside.

"Charged and ready," Martin confirmed, his muscular build tensed in anticipation. He had foregone his usual tailored suits for gear more fitting for their night op, yet he carried himself with the same assuredness he always did.

"Good," Nick said, the corner of his mouth twitching upwards. Positive thinking wasn't just useful; it was essential when you were about to plunge into darkness.

As the clock struck midnight, the hills of Medellin loomed before them, silhouettes against the starry sky. They navigated the final stretch, the headlights cutting a swathe through the night until they arrived at a secluded compound nestled within the embrace of the looming mountains.

"Here we go," Nick whispered, killing the headlights and pulling the car to a stop beneath the cover of dense foliage. The villa sprawled before them, its opulent architecture a stark contrast to the natural beauty surrounding it. Balconies adorned with intricate ironwork jutted out from walls of stucco, and windows glowed with the warmth of life inside — soon to be snuffed out by their hands.

Martin activated the EMP device, its soft whirring sound barely audible as an invisible wave of energy pulsed from it. Within moments, lights flickered and died, plunging the villa into sudden darkness, a tangible blanket of silence falling over the area as even the hum of electricity ceased.

"Good. Let's move," Nick replied, parking the car in the shadows of the dense foliage that surrounded the estate.

They exited the vehicle, their movements fluid and silent, blending into the night like phantoms. Dressed in dark clothing that hugged their athletic frames, they looked every inch the seasoned operatives they were—two men shaped by years of covert operations and clandestine service.

Approaching the perimeter, Nick surveyed the high wall, noting the absence of the usual buzz of electrified barriers. He pulled a grappling hook from his backpack and launched it expertly over the wall, securing their entry point. With a nod to each other, they scaled the obstacle with the agility of men half their age, dropping silently onto the manicured lawn on the other side.

The sprawling villa loomed before them, a mixture of modern luxury and traditional opulence. Its facade was a combination of sleek glass and rustic stone, designed to impress and intimidate. Now, however, it stood silent in the darkness, its usual vibrancy subdued by the absence of light.

Nick and Martin moved with purpose, their boots barely making a sound against the soft grass as they navigated around sculpted hedges and past ornate fountains now stilled. They communicated with hand signals, a language forged in the fires of countless missions—a silent ballet of tactical precision.

Reaching the main building, they found the heavy wooden door unlocked, an invitation—or perhaps a challenge—from Rodrigo Carlos himself. Inside, their senses were assaulted by opulence. Thick Persian carpets muffled their steps, while the faint scent of tobacco lingered in the air. Antique furniture dotted the grand hallway, gilded frames showcasing artwork that would make a museum curator weep with envy.

At the end of the corridor, a large mahogany door stood ajar, golden light spilling from its edges. Nick and Martin exchanged a glance, reading the unspoken agreement in each other's gaze. They advanced, weapons drawn but held low, ready for whatever lay beyond.

Pushing the door open, they stepped into a study that reeked of power and wealth. The room was lined with bookshelves filled with leather-bound volumes, a massive desk dominated the space, and in the far corner, a globe bar stood open, bottles of aged spirits glinting dully in the dim light.

And there, seated behind the desk, was Rodrigo Carlos—the Boss. He was a man whose very presence commanded attention, his robust frame clad in an impeccably tailored suit that spoke of his taste for the finer things in life. His face was stern, with deep lines etched by the weight of his empire, and his dark eyes regarded them with a cool, calculating gaze.

"Señores Taylor y De Simone," he greeted in a voice that was both cultured and menacing. "I've been expecting you."

Nick stepped forward; his posture relaxed but alert. "We need to talk, Rodrigo," he said, his tone leaving no doubt that this was not a request.

The boss nodded slowly, gesturing to the chairs across from him. "Then let's talk."

CHAPTER 67

In the dim-lit expanse of Don Rodrigo Carlos' palatial office, mahogany bookshelves lined with leather-bound tomes cast long shadows over the Italian marble floor. The air was heavy with the scent of Cuban cigars and aged tequila that lingered on the breath of the man who ruled this fortress. Rodrigo reclined behind a grandiose desk of dark wood inlayed with gold leaf patterns.

Nick Taylor's sharp gaze surveyed the room, taking in the opulence that surrounded him—the gilded frames embracing masterful paintings, the ancient swords displayed like trophies from bygone eras. The physical embodiment of his own history as a retired CIA spy, Nick was all sinew and experience, his gray-flecked hair a testament to his years in service. Opposite him, Martin De Simone's athletic form tensed, every muscle coiled and ready, visibly uncomfortable amidst such extravagance.

"Rodrigo," Nick began, his voice measured but firm, "we need to clear the air about Colombia. What's your stake in it, and what's the deal with the Cobra—Lee Chang?"

Rodrigo steepled his fingers, a smile playing on his lips that didn't reach his calculating eyes. He leaned forward slightly, the light catching the signet ring—a family crest—on his finger. "Mr. Taylor, imagine if you will, a chessboard. The pawns are scattered, chaos reigning across the board. This is Colombia now—not my doing, I assure you. The Cobra slithers through the tall grass, unseen yet orchestrating the pandemonium. Lee Chang is no pawn; he is the player moving the pieces to his advantage."

"Qui prodest the Chaos in Colombia and South America in the business of the drugs?" he posed the question almost philosophically, letting it hang heavily in the air.

Nick and Rodrigo locked eyes, an unspoken understanding passing between them. They needed each other; this was a hunt that required a merging of resources, skills, and perhaps most importantly, a shared ruthlessness.

"Help me find Chang, eliminate the threat he poses to us both, and our... partnership will prove mutually beneficial," Nick offered, extending his hand across the desk.

Rodrigo's laughter filled the room, deep and resonant, as he accepted the handshake. "Agreed. We cut off the head of the Cobra together."

As the meeting drew to a close, Martin, unable to contain his impatience, interjected with a question that sliced through the congenial facade. "Rodrigo, we know Lee Chang has been funneling money to an offshore account linked to Senator James Hargrave. Do you know him, and why is this happening?"

Rodrigo's chuckle morphed into a full-throated laugh, echoing against the vaulted ceilings, offering no answer but leaving a chilling sense of foreboding lingering like the smoke from his cigar.

Later, beneath the arches of the villa's castle-like corridors, the boss led them to a fortified chamber tucked away like a hidden sanctum. Here, the walls were adorned with antique weaponry, maps spread across tables, and screens displaying encrypted communications. It was a war room designed for a modern crusade.

They were joined the following day by Sergey Komutov, Michael, Edward and Eva. Sergey, the ex-KGB chess player, appeared deceptively unassuming with his thinning hair and spectacles, yet his mind was a labyrinthine enigma capable of outwitting any adversary.

"Each of you brings a vital piece to this puzzle," Rodrigo addressed them, his voice echoing off the stone walls. "Together, we will dismantle Lee Chang's empire, brick by brick."

Assignments were handed out with surgical precision: Martin to oversee tactical operations, Sergey to unravel the digital web of Chang's finances, Michael to infiltrate the ranks, and Eva to manipulate the technological battlefield. Each role carefully crafted to exploit their strengths, a symphony of espionage orchestrated by necessity and vengeance.

With every detail meticulously planned, they turned their collective gaze toward Macao, where the Cobra lay coiled within his lair, oblivious to the strike force amassing against him.

CHAPTER 68

In the shaded confines of Don Rodrigo's war room, a hive of activity thrummed with urgency. Nick, with his lean, military-bred physique clothed in nondescript tactical attire, leaned over the table strewn with maps and digital tablets. His eyes, sharp as hawk's, scanned satellite images that painted a real-time picture of Lee Chong's Macao fortress—its high walls casting long shadows like silent sentinels.

"Here," Martin pointed, his fingers tracing the outline of an auxiliary entrance obscured by the lush canopy of a manicured garden. His voice was low, a deep baritone that resonated with the confidence of a man who had navigated through countless covert operations. He straightened, the light catching on his weathered face, highlighting the scars that were testimonies to battles past.

Sergey, hunched over a laptop, his fingers dancing across the keyboard, projected a complicated financial network onto the screen. The ex-KGB agent's attire was inconspicuous—a simple sweater vest over a pale shirt, the very picture of an academic rather than a spy. Yet his mind was alighting with the thrill of the chase, equations and algorithms his weapons of choice as he delved into the abyss of Lee Chong's encrypted assets.

"Tim Stratton just sent these over," Eva announced, her voice a velvet purr that contrasted sharply with the intense focus in her eyes. She relayed the blueprints of the villa's interior, each room detailed with meticulous care. Her slender fingers swiped through the images on her tablet, her posture poised, every inch the lethal enigma draped in a fitted black ensemble that whispered of danger beneath its elegance.

"Good. We've got eyes everywhere now," Nick murmured approvingly, absorbing every pixel of information that could give them an edge. "We'll know if a fly lands on Chong's window."

Michael, silent but observant, checked the radio satellite communication equipment laid out like a surgeon's tools ready for operation. Compact and rugged, his build spoke of agility, and his hands moved with practiced ease over the devices. His attire was casual, yet every piece was chosen for utility—a knife hidden here, a lock pick there. He was the street-savvy warrior, ready for urban jungle warfare.

"Comms check. Encryption protocols are up," Eva confirmed, his head nodding toward the array of sleek earpieces and transmitters.

"Let's go over the gear," Martin directed, his attention shifting to the arsenal that lay before them. Customized firearms, suppressors affixed, lay alongside non-lethal options and specialized ammunition. Each item was chosen for silence and efficiency—the tools of their deadly craft.

"Remember, we're not going in loud. Precision is key," Nick stated firmly, eyeing the weapons with the discerning gaze of a connoisseur. Every piece was a testament to their grim purpose, and he handled them with the reverence of one who knew their cost.

"Everything has been triple-checked," Eva assured him, her role extending beyond the cyber realm. She understood the importance of flawless execution, her own experience in the field melding seamlessly with her technical prowess.

"Then it's time we put this plan into motion," Nick declared, the finality in his voice mirroring the resolve etched on each of their faces. As they packed their gear, the weight of their mission settled upon them—a mantle they bore with the gravity it deserved.

The war room, once abuzz with planning and strategizing, quieted to a solemn stillness as the team departed, leaving behind the ancient weapons and maps for the modern arsenal they carried into the night. They stepped out under the stars, the cool air of anticipation mingling with the warm breeze that carried the scent of the surrounding orchards—an olfactory reminder of the paradise that housed their battleground.

Together, they moved like phantoms toward their destiny, their minds laser-focused on the task at hand. Macao awaited them, and with it, the serpent they aimed to strike at its heart.

CHAPTER 69

The day after was the last day of planning and exercise. Nick Taylor's fingers danced across the blueprint of Lee Chong's villa, spread out like a tactical canvas on the mahogany table. The room was dimly lit, casting long shadows over the intricate design, each line and curve a potential death trap or a path to victory. Martin De Simone leaned in, his intense gaze fixed on the maze of corridors and chambers, memorizing every detail with the precision of a chess grandmaster visualizing moves ahead.

"Entrance through the east wing here," Nick pointed, tapping a secluded part of the layout, his voice low and steady. "Tim says it's less guarded at night."

"Right," Martin agreed, his muscular frame tense as if ready to sprint into action. "We cut the power here, create a blind spot. Then slip in undetected."

Their attire was utilitarian—dark cargo pants and fitted black shirts, chosen for mobility and blending into the night. Each man wore a watch with multiple time zones, synchronized down to the second—a silent nod to the global nature of their quest. On Nick's wrist, the second hand ticked away with relentless urgency.

"Once inside, we need to control these chokepoints," Nick continued, tracing a route through the villa. His finger paused at various intersections. "Sergey's team will handle the west corridor. Eva will jam communications starting from 0300 hours."

"Precision is key," Martin interjected, his analytical mind dissecting every angle. "No room for error. We have to be ghosts."

"Exactly," affirmed Nick, their shared history at the CIA bonding them in unspoken understanding.

Outside, the grounds of Don Rodrigo Carlos' estate lay shrouded in evening's embrace, the manicured lawns and exotic flora exuding an almost ethereal beauty. Yet beneath this serene veneer, fifty fighters honed their skills under the watchful eyes of Nick and Martin.

"Again! Move like you mean it!" barked Michael, one of the trusted cartel members, as he led a squad through a drill. Their movements were sharp and deliberate, boots thudding softly against the earth. Sweat glistened on sun-kissed skin, testimony to their exertion and commitment.

"Stealth teams, check your gear," called Eva, her blonde hair pulled back in a no-nonsense ponytail, her blue eyes scanning her subordinates with the precision of a hawk. She moved among them, double-checking each weapon, each piece of technology. Her background in cyber espionage was evident in the meticulous care she took with the equipment.

"Remember, speed and silence," Nick reminded them, his voice carrying the weight of experience. "Chong's guards are elite—they'll hear a pin drop a mile away."

"Understood, sir," came the collective response, a chorus of determination.

As twilight deepened, the villa's simulated model glowed under the touch of portable work lights. The team gathered around, studying the 3D representation of their battleground, committing every nuance to memory.

"Here," Nick said, pointing to a miniature courtyard, "is where we expect the highest resistance. Use flashbangs, but keep it tight. No stray shots—we can't afford any alarms."

"Got it." Martin nodded, his jaw set in resolute lines. It was a dance of death they were choreographing, and every step had to be executed with flawless grace.

"Check your comms," instructed Eva, her tone leaving no room for debate. She handed out earpieces calibrated to evade detection, her expertise ensuring seamless coordination when silence would be golden.

"Tomorrow, we strike," Nick concluded, his eyes sweeping over the team. There was no fear in those depths, only the calm before the storm, the quiet confidence that came from years of navigating the treacherous waters of espionage.

"Let's make sure Chong's last taste of wine is bitter," Martin added, a grim humor touching his lips.

The team dispersed, a symphony of subdued movements and hushed tones, their thoughts focused on the mission ahead. In the sanctuary of the orchards, the scent of ripening fruit belied the tension that hung in the air, a stark contrast to the deadly purpose that drove them forward.

Inside, the villa's opulent interior stood in stark contrast to the rustic charm of the orchards. Rich tapestries adorned the walls, each thread woven with the history and pride of the Carlos family. Antique furniture gleamed under the soft glow of chandeliers, the dark wood polished to a mirror finish. But the luxury served only as a backdrop to the scheme unfolding within, the elegance of the surroundings at odds with the lethal planning taking place.

"Get some rest," Nick finally said, his voice low but authoritative. "We move at zero dark thirty. Sharp. Get ready for Macao".

With that, the men retired to their quarters, the villa's grandeur giving way to simple, spartan rooms where they could steel themselves for the trial to come. Tomorrow, they would face not just Lee Chong's defenses, but the culmination of their own fears and hopes—an operation where success and survival hung by the slenderest of threads.

CHAPTER 70

The muted hum of the Tupolev's engines provided a steady backdrop to the fervent activity within its cavernous belly. It was a leviathan of steel and purpose, cutting through the night sky toward Macao. In the sparse light of the cargo hold, shadows danced across the faces of the operatives as they reviewed their plans. Nick's gaze swept over the assembled team, a motley crew bound by a singular intent.

Sergey adjusted his glasses and pored over a satellite map splayed out before him. His fingers traced routes and positions with the precision of a grandmaster moving chess pieces across a board. His intellectual rigor never wavered, a beacon in the sea of uncertainty that this mission had become.

"Remember," Sergey's voice resounded with clarity, "timing is as vital as silence. Each second, each breath must be accounted for."

Nick nodded, feeling the weight of every decision upon his shoulders. The stakes were clear; any misstep could unravel everything. He turned away from Sergey and peered out of the small window at the dark clouds below, contemplating Macao's Sky that would soon test their mettle.

As the plane touched down in the stillness of predawn, the hangar loomed ahead, a monolithic structure where Sergey had assured them they would find sanctuary and finality of purpose. They disembarked swiftly, their movements a choreography of discipline and resolve.

Inside the hangar, the air was cool and smelled faintly of oil and metal—a stark contrast to the tropical humidity outside. Harsh fluorescent lights flickered on, bathing the concrete floor and the high rafters in an unforgiving glare. This was their last haven, their final moments of quietude before the storm they were about to unleash.

"Check your gear," Martin commanded, his athletic frame poised with an energy that hinted at his military background. "Once we step out of this hangar, we're ghosts in the city."

Weapons were checked, communication devices secured, and disguises donned. Eva, the blonde seductress whose beauty belied her lethality, slid a silenced pistol into the holster hidden beneath her tailored jacket. Her eyes held a steely determination that matched the men's. There was no room for error, no space for hesitation. They were all predators cloaked in the guise of night.

By the time darkness enveloped the city, they had melted into the urban tapestry of Macao, unseen but ever-present. The neon glow of casinos and bars cast a surreal light on their path, but they navigated the alleys and byways with the confidence of those who have already walked these paths in countless mental rehearsals.

Nick led the group with silent footsteps, the subtle communication of hand signals enough to guide his comrades. Every corner turned, every shadow utilized, they were phantoms flitting through the city's veins, propelled by the adrenaline that coursed through them.

They passed beneath the ornate balconies of colonial buildings, their facades a blend of European and Chinese influences—whispers of history that went unnoticed by the team focused solely on the present moment. The scent of street food and the murmur of nightlife reached them, but they remained undistracted, their senses attuned only to the mission.

As they approached the outskirts of Lee Chong's stronghold, the air grew tense, electric with anticipation. Here, in the domain of their enemy, each breath felt heavier, each step a deliberate dance with danger.

"Positions," Nick whispered into his mic, the word barely a breath, yet it carried the weight of command. Like shadows dispersing at the break of dawn, the team spread out, each to their assigned role in the intricate ballet of espionage and infiltration.

Above them, the stars twinkled indifferently, while below, the game was set, the players ready. Tomorrow's sun would rise on a world changed by their actions tonight—for better or worse, only time would tell.

CHAPTER 71

The moon hung low and indifferent in the night sky, casting an illusory tranquility over the opulent villa that sprawled before Nick Taylor and his team. Pockets of light from within the compound pierced the darkness like watchful eyes, and the scent of frangipani wafted over the high walls that promised both luxury and secrecy. Encased in shadows, the team converged upon the estate, their movements precise and purposeful.

"Echo team, you're up," Nick's voice was a tightly controlled whisper, its timbre resonating with years of command and field operations. He watched as two figures detached from the group like ghosts peeling away from the darkness itself. They were clad in tactical gear that melded into the night, faces obscured by night-vision goggles that gave them an otherworldly appearance. Their task: to disable the state-of-the-art security systems that Lee Chong prided himself on.

Martin De Simone stood beside Nick, his muscular frame tense, ready to pivot into action at any sign of trouble. His hand rested casually near the concealed holster under his dark jacket—a testament to his readiness for whatever lay ahead. With short, dark hair mussed from the infiltration, he scanned the area with keen eyes that missed nothing—not the slight rustle of leaves in the gentle breeze nor the distant bark of a guard dog.

Nick and Martin, flanked by three trusted colleagues whose loyalty had been forged in the crucible of covert operations, advanced toward the heart of the villa. The architecture of the palatial residence bore the hallmarks of old-world aristocracy mingled with modern opulence—Doric columns stood sentinel at the entrance, while sleek glass surfaces reflected the moonlight, creating a mosaic of light and shadow.

The rest of their 25-man commando followed suit—silent figures, each a specter with a purpose, their faces set in determination beneath night-vision goggles. The narco boss of Medellin had played his part well, providing them with a high-stakes entry into this treacherous ballet of espionage.

"Check your gear," Nick murmured, his voice barely above a whisper, yet carrying the authority of a man who had stared down death more times than he cared to count. His men complied without question, adjusting straps on bulletproof vests, ensuring that silencers were firmly attached to their sleek submachine guns.

Sergey Komutov, with his thinning hair and intellectual aura, led the second commando alongside Michael. Sergey's eyes, usually alight with the thrill of a chess match, now scanned the environment with mathematical precision. In another life, he might have been found in a dimly lit room, hunched over a board of sixty-four squares. Tonight, however, he was a field operative, his mind attuned to the deadly stakes at hand.

As Sergey's group fanned out, creating smaller units to maximize their infiltration potential, Nick's team approached the fortress from a different angle. The structure loomed ahead, an imposing edifice of cold stone and fortified walls that seemed to mock their mortal efforts. Yet, there was no hesitation in their steps; their resolve was unbreakable.

They moved with the stealth of seasoned predators, their movements choreographed by countless hours of training and hardened by experience. Each man carried not just ammunition and weapons but also the tools of silent war—wire cutters, grappling hooks, and encrypted radios, all testament to their readiness for the attack that lay ahead.

Nick paused, signaling his team to hold position. His sharp gaze swept over the fortress, taking in the high walls and the watchtowers that pierced the sky like accusing fingers. His mind raced with tactics and contingencies, his senses alert to the faintest sound or shift in the wind. This was the world he understood, a world where every detail could mean the difference between life and death.

"Remember what we're here for," he said, his voice steady, instilling confidence in his men. "We do this by the book—quick, clean, no mistakes."

Martin nodded, his own expression mirroring Nick's intensity. They shared a bond forged in the fires of conflict, a brotherhood that went beyond words. Together, they would face whatever awaited them within those walls, united by a cause greater than themselves.

With a final check of their surroundings, Nick gave the signal, and his commandos resumed their advance. The fortress of Lee Chong beckoned, its secrets hidden behind layers of security and deceit. But Nick Taylor was no stranger to such challenges. He was a master of the shadowed path, a warrior-poet of the modern age, ready to etch another chapter into the annals of covert warfare.

"Green across the board," Martin confirmed, his fingers deftly running over the sleek, compact equipment strapped to his body. A slight nod from Nick, and they both activated their earpieces, establishing a silent line of communication with their team.

The plan had been meticulously crafted, every possible outcome accounted for with the precision of a chess grandmaster. Now, as they waited for the synchronized watches on their wrists to tick closer to the hour, Nick allowed himself a brief moment to reflect on the magnitude of their task. Killing Lee Chong was not just about dismantling a criminal empire; it was about restoring balance to a world teetering on the brink of chaos.

"Time to move," he said, the words clipped and decisive. Together, they rose from their hiding spot, their movements synchronized and fluid, the result of years of training and countless missions that had honed their skills to near perfection.

As they approached the perimeter of the villa bunker, the natural sounds of the night seemed to fall away, replaced by the thumping of their own heartbeats. Nick's hand moved instinctively to the hilt of his combat knife, the grip familiar and reassuring in his palm. He scanned the expanse before them, noting the subtle shift in the breeze that carried the scent of the sea mingled with the exotic fragrance of the flowering vines that climbed the fortress walls.

At precisely midnight, as prearranged, they were in position, ready to breach the sanctuary of one of the world's most dangerous men, " Thew Cobra". There was no turning back now. The game was set, the players poised, and Nick Taylor, with Martin De Simone at his side, was ready to make his move.

CHAPTER 72

Nick Taylor's senses operated at maximum capacity, the cool night air carrying with it a cocktail of anticipation and danger. He and Martin De Simone moved like shadows across the uneven terrain toward the secret tunnel that promised access to Lee Chong's fortress-like villa. The moon, partially cloaked by scudding clouds, cast an intermittent silver glow on their path, lending an ethereal quality to their clandestine approach.

Martin's dark eyes, usually warm and reflective of his compassionate nature, were now hard as flint, mirroring the seriousness of their mission. His body, accustomed to the adrenaline that comes with the prospect of confrontation, was taut and ready, every muscle coiled for action. His attire, a blend of tactical utility and night camouflage, whispered of his military precision and the silent promise of violence only if necessary.

Nick's gaze, meanwhile, swept over the palatial estate with its blend of oriental magnificence and modern defensiveness. The villa was a fortress, boasting antique elegance with its terracotta roof tiles that gleamed under the celestial light, juxtaposed against the high-tech surveillance that peppered its ancient walls. It was a statement of power, a testament to Lee Chong's influence that bridged centuries and continents.

The scent of the encircling pine trees mingled with the salt from the distant sea, crafting an aroma that spoke of both tranquility and decay. It was as though nature itself was in on the conspiracy, providing cover and comfort to those who dared challenge the status quo.

Suddenly, the tranquil night erupted into chaos as Sergey Komutov initiated the diversion. Distant booms and the crackling of automatic gunfire punctuated the stillness, transforming the serene landscape into a battlefield of sound and fury. It was a calculated cacophony designed to draw the attention of Lee Chong's guards away from Nick and Martin's ingress point.

Sergey, the ex-KGB mastermind, had lived a life steeped in cerebral challenges, his thin frame and receding hairline deceptive indicators of the ruthless strategist within. He played this moment as he would a grandmaster chess move; each explosion and burst of gunfire was a pawn advancing, a knight leaping, creating openings in the enemy's defense.

"Go," Nick breathed, his voice barely audible above the din. The command was unnecessary; Martin was already in motion, moving with the lethal grace of a panther. Years of trust and shared experiences meant words were often superfluous between them; they functioned as extensions of one another, each knowing the other's thoughts and intentions.

They reached the perimeter undetected. In the distance, the silhouette of a solitary guard patrolled the grounds, a rifle slung over his shoulder—an unwitting sentinel unaware that the hunters had become the hunted. With a hand gesture from Nick, another operative peeled away from the group, melting into the foliage with predatory grace, to neutralize the threat.

Nick exchanged a look with Martin, a wordless conversation passing between them. It was a look that conveyed trust, camaraderie, and the unspoken knowledge that their shared history had led them to this moment.

"Let's find our snake," Nick murmured, the determination in his voice enough to steel his comrades for the confrontation ahead. Together, they moved forward, each step bringing them closer to the heart of darkness that housed Lee Chong—their quarry in this deadly of cat and mouse.

Their advance through the tunnel was swift, their progress measured and silent despite their hearts thundering in their chests.

Nick Taylor swept forward, his gaze darting between the shadows that clung to the opulent interior of Lee Chong's villa. The grandeur of the place was a stark contrast to the violence about to unfold. Intricate carvings adorned the mahogany panels lining the walls, and delicate silk tapestries fluttered slightly with the disturbance their team brought inside.

"Contact left!" Martin De Simone barked, his dark eyes sparking with alertness as two guards emerged from a concealed doorway, their assault rifles raised. The lethal elegance of their tailored black suits did nothing to mask the threat they posed.

The narrow hallway erupted in a cacophony of gunfire, echoing off the polished marble floors like a thunderclap. Nick felt the familiar adrenaline rush, his instincts honed by years in the field taking over. He pivoted, returning fire with practiced precision, his movements fluid despite his age. His silver hair, usually a mark of his years, now seemed like a deceptive camouflage against the youthful assailants.

Martin, built more like a bulldozer than a man accustomed to the clandestine world of espionage, moved with surprising agility. His muscular frame absorbed the recoil of his weapon as he systematically dismantled the opposition's resolve with disciplined bursts.

Beyond lay a network of tunnels, each one more lavish than the last. Hand-painted murals adorned the walls, depicting serene landscapes that clashed violently with the reality of their mission. Crystal chandeliers hung from the ceilings, casting prismatic light across their path, their beauty lost on the men whose lives depended on navigating this maze.

"Left flank, clear," Nick called out, his voice a low growl as they cleared each corner with ruthless efficiency. He couldn't help but admire the strategic mind that had designed such a fortress—every turn, every opulent room, was a potential deathtrap.

"Got him," Nick replied, steadying his aim and squeezing the trigger. The guard's body jerked once before slumping over the banister, a lifeless marionette severed from its strings.

They pressed on, the echoes of their own gunfire a grim metronome marking their advance. Every so often, the glint of antique vases and the shimmer of rare paintings caught Nick's eye, reminders of the wealth and power that fueled Lee Chong's empire.

"Almost there," Martin panted, the strain of combat etching lines deeper into his weathered face. "Stay sharp."

Nick's determination was a palpable force, driving him forward, a relentless tide eroding the defenses of a man who believed himself untouchable. Each step was a promise, each breath a commitment to ending the tyranny of the half-Chinese, half-North Korean mogul whose ambition had cost too much, for too many.

"Ready?" Nick asked, pausing at the threshold of what they believed to be Lee Chong's sanctuary.

"Always," Martin affirmed, his expression steely and resolute.

As they neared the end of the tunnel, they could hear the faint sounds of classical music filtering through the walls, a surreal soundtrack to the impending confrontation. Nick's hand rested lightly on the pistol at his hip, a reassuring weight against his thigh. The time had come to face the enigma that was Lee Chong, and they emerged from the shadows, not as predators, but as deliverers of justice in a world held hostage by fear and corruption.

CHAPTER 73

After the secret tunnel, inside the Villa bunker, start the battle to sanitize the location and kill all Cobra's affiliate. "The Palace needs to be secured" Nick was murmuring to himself.

The villa erupted into a cacophony of chaos; the night sky lit by intermittent flashes of gunfire that cast stark shadows across Nick's grim visage. He and Martin crouched behind an ornately carved marble balustrade, the cool stone a fleeting respite against their heated skin. Bullets chipped at the edges, sending fragments skittering across the polished floor like deadly hail.

"Left flank, two tangos!" Martin's voice was calm, despite the adrenaline that surged through them both, his words clipped and professional. Nick nodded, acknowledging the callout with a brief glance as he assessed the situation.

With precision born of countless missions, Nick returned fire, his Beretta 92FS an extension of his will. The gun recoiled in his hand, a familiar dance of metal and might as he picked off the assailants with disciplined ease. Martin, equally adept, dispatched another with a silenced shot from his compact Glock 19, the weapon's muted report barely audible above the symphony of violence.

Together, they moved like a fluid shadow through the opulent halls of the villa. The stench of cordite mingled with the faint aroma of exotic woods and the lingering scent of imported cigars, creating an olfactory map of wealth and indulgence turned battleground.

"Staircase, clear?" Nick murmured, eyes never ceasing their vigilant sweep of the grand foyer adorned with menacing gargoyles leering from high corners.

"Clear," confirmed Martin, his own gaze sharp as obsidian.

Ascending the staircase, the intricate wrought iron railing cold under their touch, they encountered the plush, crimson carpet that muffled their steps. Above them, a colossal crystal chandelier hung like a frozen waterfall, casting prismatic light across the battle-worn faces of antique statues and oil paintings of stoic ancestors.

Nick's mind was a fortress of focus, every sense heightened to its peak. He could almost feel the intentions of their enemies, predicting movements before they happened, his body responding with trained alacrity. Their progress was a tactical ballet, each step choreographed by years of experience and honed instincts.

During the fray, a momentary lull allowed Nick a glimpse through a floor-to-ceiling window, the sprawling gardens bathed in the soft glow of moonlight, a stark contrast to the brutal conflict within. But there was no time for reverie; this mission was everything.

"Watch your six!" Martin's warning came just in time, as Nick pivoted on the balls of his feet, narrowly avoiding the swing of a combat knife. His response was immediate, disarming the assailant with a swift motion before incapacitating him with a well-placed strike to the solar plexus.

"Thanks," Nick grunted, the closest approximation to gratitude in the heat of battle. They shared a brief nod, an unspoken acknowledgment of their interdependence. This was not just a mission; it was a testament to their bond, a promise to watch each other's backs against all odds.

Together, they pressed forward, through the labyrinthine corridors lined with ancient tapestries depicting heroic battles of yore—an ironic backdrop to their current endeavor. Every corner held potential peril, but Nick and Martin navigated the dangers with an almost telepathic synergy, their movements synchronized, their goals singular.

Lee Chong, the elusive kingpin who had orchestrated terror from the shadows, was close now. Nick could feel it in his bones. And when they finally confronted their quarry, it would be more than a clash of arms—it would be a meeting of destiny, the culmination of a journey paved with sacrifice and resolve.

Nick's body was a coiled spring, every muscle primed for the next encounter. His faded olive combat boots, laces double-knotted with precision, dug into the lavish Persian carpet that lined the hallway of Lee Chong's villa—a stark contrast to the brutal reality unfolding around them. The walls, adorned with antique sconces casting a muted glow, seemed to watch in silent judgment as Nick and Martin advanced with lethal purpose.

"Clear," Martin whispered, his breath barely audible over the distant cacophony of conflict. They had trained for this—years of experience distilled into a symphony of controlled violence. Nick's eyes, the color of storm-tossed seas, scanned the foyer where white marble met gold leaf in an ostentatious display of wealth. It was quiet here, too quiet, but they proceeded, communicating with hand signals that could be understood in the pitch-black of a moonless night.

They turned a corner and were met by two of Lee Chong's personal guards, dressed in suits that did little to hide the bulging outlines of concealed firearms. In a fluid motion, Nick drew his combat knife; a relic from his military past, its blade honed to a whispering edge. He feinted left, then ducked under a clumsy jab, using the guard's momentum against him. A twist, a pivot, and the guard crumpled, his consciousness slipping away with Nick's precise strike to the carotid artery.

They exchanged a nod, partners not just in battle but in a shared vision of justice. With that silent agreement, they prepared to face the heart of the viper's nest, where Lee Chong awaited, unaware of the storm that was about to break upon him.

Nick Taylor's boots barely made a sound on the marble floor, a testament to his years of training. They were in the belly of the beast, a place where Lee Chong, the viper himself, lay coiled.

As they entered the capacious study, the scent of old leather and mahogany filled their nostrils. Books lined the walls, a library fit for a king or, in this case, a tyrant. Amidst it all, Lee Chong sat behind a monumental desk like Napoleon after Austerlitz Battle, the very image of composure. His suit was perfectly tailored, accentuating broad shoulders and a lean frame—a wolf in designer clothing. His fingers caressed the stem of a crystal wine glass, red liquid swirling like blood. He was not looking as defeated men!

CHAPTER 74

"Mr. Taylor, Mr. De Simone," Lee Chong greeted them, his voice smooth as silk but with the underlying menace of a hidden blade. "I must commend your tenacity. To have come this far is... impressive."

"Game's over, Chong," Nick replied, his voice steady despite the adrenaline coursing through his veins. Every muscle in his body was tensed, ready to spring into action. Martin stood beside him, equally prepared, his gaze never wavering from their target.

"Is it?" Lee Chong mused, taking a leisurely sip of his wine. "You see, gentlemen, you might think you have me cornered, but I assure you, I am not without resources."

"Your guards won't be coming to your aid," Martin stated flatly, his dark eyes missing nothing.

"Guards? My dear Martin, you underestimate me," Lee Chong said with a thin smile.

Nick's hand hovered near his weapon, calculating angles and movements, his mind painting a picture only decades of shadow operation and espionage could illustrate. He knew the moment of truth was upon them, and the weight of justice bore down on his trigger finger.

"Any last words, Chong?" Nick asked, though he knew men like Lee Chong were never short on rhetoric.

"Only that chaos is a ladder, and I am its master," Lee Chong replied, setting his wine glass down with a resonant clink.

Nick Taylor's silhouette cut through the dimly lit villa, his Beretta 9mm extended before him with lethal precision. At the center of the Livingroom stood Lee Chong, an enigma wrapped in the trappings of luxury. The half-Chinese, half-North Korean billionaire, named " The Cobra", was dressed in a tailored Armani suit that whispered of silk and expense, his sharp features were set in an expression of amused contempt. This was a man unaccustomed to facing the consequences of his actions—until now.

"Lee Chong," Nick said, his voice reverberating off the concrete walls, "why the slaughter in the USA? Why provoke the Medellín cartel? And the microchip—what's your endgame?"

Lee Chong's smile never wavered, his dark eyes glinting with the reflection of Nick's weapon. "Mr. Taylor," he began, his English tinged with an accent that spoke of international boarding schools and diplomatic soirees, "do you truly believe you have the upper hand here?"

Nick's finger tightened on the trigger, his resolve steeling. He could almost taste the acrid smell of gunpowder that would soon permeate the air. But his mind, honed by decades of espionage, questioned every possible outcome. Killing this man could unravel layers of international conspiracy, yet the specter of unseen chess pieces gave him pause.

As if on cue, the shrill ring of a phone pierced the static tension. Nick flinched, his focus fracturing for a moment as the nostalgic sound of a rotary phone echoed in the hollow space. The incongruence of the interruption was like a crack in the meticulously crafted tableau of their standoff.

"Are you going to answer that?" Lee Chong asked, the mirth in his voice now laced with something darker.

Nick hesitated; his gaze locked onto the figure before him. Every instinct screamed it was a distraction, a ploy from a man whose resources matched his ambition. Yet, the possibility that the call held answers clawed at him. With a scowl etched across his weathered face, he reached into his pocket, withdrawing a secure satellite phone—

a lifeline to his past life in the CIA. His thumb pressed the answer button, and the warehouse fell silent except for the distant sound of his own heartbeat pounding in his ears.

CHAPTER 75

Nick's thumb hovered over the green icon on the screen, a gateway to another unforeseen twist in this already labyrinthine operation. He pressed down, and the phone call connected with a click that seemed to reverberate off the warehouse's corrugated metal walls.

"Taylor," he said, his voice a low growl of caution. The line crackled, a storm of static before it cleared into the unmistakable timbre of authority.

"Nick, this is the President."

The words sent a jolt through Nick's hand, almost making him drop the phone. He had anticipated threats, perhaps a desperate plea from an ally, but not this. The weight of the office behind the voice transformed the dusty air around him, infusing it with a gravity that bore down on his shoulders like the leaden sky outside.

"Mr. President." Nick's response was automatic, the training of countless briefings and emergency calls kicking in despite the maelstrom of confusion brewing within him.

"Abort, Nick. Stand down immediately." The President's tone was not just urgent; it was granite-hard and brooked no argument. It was the sound of world-shifting decisions made before dawn, of codes entered and buttons readied.

"Sir?" Even as he spoke, Nick's mind raced. Abort? Now? When Lee Chong was finally within reach, a specter that had haunted the intelligence community for years?

"Your orders are to abort the mission. Extract yourself. That is a direct order from your Commander-in-Chief, Nick."

Nick could practically see the President in the Oval Office, surrounded by the trappings of power—the flags standing sentinel, the historic Resolute desk, the stoic portraits of past leaders gazing down. This was a man who knew the crushing responsibility of life-and-death decisions, whose every word could trigger ripples across the geopolitical landscape.

"Understood, Mr. President." Nick's reply was terse, but he was anything but resolved. His finger lingered on the 'end call' button as if it were a detonator. The President's directive clashed with the culmination of Nick's relentless pursuit, the narrowing path to justice he'd carved out through sheer will.

The satellite phone felt like a lead brick in his hand, its weight disproportionate to its size—a physical manifestation of the monumental choice laid before him. With a reluctant press, he severed the connection to the most powerful man in the free world.

Lee Chong, still bound and blindfolded across from him, shifted uncomfortably on the cold cement floor, oblivious to the seismic shift that had just occurred. Nick's eyes narrowed, a renewed sense of purpose stealing his resolve. Despite the President's command, the ghost of his old CIA contact's warning whispered in his ear: "The eagle watching you."

In the clandestine world where shadows danced and allegiances shifted like sand, Nick Taylor would have to navigate the treacherous path ahead with nothing but his wits and an unshakable dedication to what he believed was right. For now, that meant adapting to survive—capturing, not killing, Lee Chong. But as he moved forward, the ominous implications of the President's involvement loomed over him like a dark cloud threatening to burst.

CHAPTER 76

Nick's square jaw clenched as the silence left by the President's command echoed through his mind. His gaze was locked onto Lee Chong, whose chest rose and fell with shallow breaths. The beretta in Nick's firm grip was no longer pointed at the man who had orchestrated chaos across continents; it now hung by his side, a symbol of the orders he could not bring himself to obey.

"Dammit," Nick muttered under his breath, the internal struggle painting lines of conflict across his weathered face. The mission had been clear: eliminate the threat. But now, the directive from the highest office muddied the waters, challenging his allegiance to the core.

"Martin, I need a second opinion urgently. We are in trouble" Nick whispered into his encrypted earpiece, his voice strained but controlled. His eyes never left Lee Chong, watching for any sign of movement.

"Nick, we've got our hands full out here," Martin's response crackled with urgency over the line. Even without seeing him, Nick could picture Martin's dark hair matted to his forehead with sweat, his muscular frame tense as he navigated the battlefield. "Sergey's boys took hits. We're bleeding out here."

"Orders from the top are to abort. To let this... mastermind walk." Nick's hand unconsciously tightened around the beretta. "I can't—I won't let that happen."

"Listen, brother, you know as well as I do, we can't just ignore a direct order from the President," Martin reasoned, his voice a blend of frustration and desperation. "But maybe there's a middle ground. Capture and secure Chong. It buys us time to figure this out."

"Kidnap him?" Nick's sharp gaze flickered as he assessed the risks. The collapsing trust in the chain of command wrestled with his unyielding sense of duty. To disobey would mean crossing lines that couldn't be uncrossed. Yet, to comply felt like abandoning justice.

"Nick, we need to decide—now!" Martin's tone was insistent, piercing through Nick's hesitation. Taking a deep breath, Nick looked around the dilapidated villa they were holed up in. The walls were streaked with grime, the air thick with dust and the stench of decay. It was a far cry from the polished corridors of power where decisions were made and fates decided. Here, in the raw reality of their situation, Nick knew that every choice carried weight.

"Fine," Nick finally conceded, his voice barely above a whisper. "We'll take him alive."

As he moved toward Lee Chong, Nick's movements were precise and efficient. He handcuffed the billionaire's wrists with a click that resonated throughout space. A blindfold followed, rendering Chong even more vulnerable.

"Nick Taylor," Lee Chong spat, his voice laced with venom even as it trembled with indignation. "You think you've won?"

"Shut it, Chong," Nick commanded, his tone leaving no room for argument. There was no victory here, only the path forward—a path shrouded in uncertainty and shadowed by the ominous presence of the eagle's gaze.

Nick Taylor's eyes locked with those of Lee Chong, the tension between them as taut as a tripwire. The air in the opulent villa was thick with unspoken threats; luxury and danger intermingled like the exotic scents wafting from the incense burners perched atop intricately carved mahogany furniture. Nick's athletic frame, honed from years of disciplined training, was coiled and ready for whatever might come next. His gray hair, usually a mark of distinguished experience, now lay plastered to his forehead with sweat, betraying the intensity of the moment.

Lee Chong stood opposite him, an enigmatic statue in a tailored suit that screamed of wealth and meticulous attention to detail. The cut was European, but the fabric held the sheen of Asian silk, a testament to his mixed heritage and international connections. His imposing demeanor was as much a weapon as the rumored arsenal hidden within the villa's vaults.

The walls themselves whispered of conspiracies; adorned with ancient tapestries and modern abstract art, they bore witness to the countless secret meetings that had taken place within their confines. Gilded frames housed oil paintings of landscapes, capturing nature's wild beauty—a stark contrast to the man-made storm brewing in their midst.

"Nick, it's not too late to walk away from this," Lee Chong said, his voice smooth as the aged scotch that rested untouched on the bar cart nearby.

Nick's sharp gaze never wavered. "I'm afraid we're past the point of no return, Chong."

CHAPTER 77

Suddenly, without warning, the world erupted into chaos.

A deafening roar shattered the standoff, sending vibrations through the floorboards and shaking the very foundations of the villa.

A Tomahawk missile, dispatched by a silent predator lurking beneath the waves of the South Pacific Ocean, found its mark. In an instant, the opulence around them transformed into a hellish landscape of fire and brimstone.

Nick felt the force of the explosion hurl him backward, his instincts barely giving him time to shield his face from the flying debris. He crashed to the ground amidst the ruins of what had once been a symbol of power and control. Dust choked the air, turning it into a murky fog through which screams and the groan of twisting metal could be heard.

He tried to push himself up, his hands slipping on the slick marble tiles now strewn with shards of broken antiques and splintered wood. The villa, once a masterpiece of interior design blending the traditional with the contemporary, was now a grotesque collage of destruction.

In the villa Bunker, his friends—men and women who shared his sense of duty—grappled with the disorientation, their training kicking in as they fought to stand amidst the rubble. Panic was a luxury they couldn't afford, even as the reality of their situation became grimly apparent.

Nick knew one thing for certain—their mission had just taken an unexpected turn, and time was running out. He was collateral damage, or he was the target.

Nick Taylor's world blurred into a cacophony of ringing ears and fading consciousness. His body, once the epitome of physical resilience, betrayed him as a jagged piece of shrapnel found its mark, tearing through his left shoulder with a searing heat that pulled a grunt from his lips. He staggered, his vision tunneling, the peripheral sight crowded out by encroaching shadows.

"Nick!" The voice seemed distant; a lifeline thrown from afar. But he could not reach it, his knees buckling beneath him, the cold embrace of the floor coming fast to claim him.

His mind, a vault of experiences drawn from years in the field, now scrambled to make sense of the chaos—a futile endeavor as darkness clawed at the edges of his thoughts. Nick succumbed to the void, his graying hair matted with sweat and blood, his athletic frame sprawled in defeat among the ruins of opulence turned to wreckage.

In the midst of anarchy, figures clad in tactical gear materialized like phantoms from the smoke. They moved with intent, the sleek lines of their body armor and the understated menace of their carbines painting a stark contrast against the baroque extravagance of Lee Chong's villa. Muted greens and tans of their uniforms melded with the shades of destruction, a testament to their clandestine nature.

"Target acquired," one of them murmured into a comms device nestled discreetly behind his ear, his gaze fixed on the disoriented figure of Lee Chong. The billionaire stood rooted, his sharp features twisted in disbelief, his usual air of control dissolved in the aftermath of the explosion.

"Package is secure," another operative confirmed. They swept in, precision guiding their movements as they secured Lee Chong with practiced ease, the man's cunning smile wiped clean, replaced with the shock of vulnerability.

"Exfil route bravo. Move out," commanded a voice, barely above a whisper, yet carrying the weight of authority. The unit, swift and silent, disappeared into the remnants of once-lavish corridors with their high-value cargo in tow, leaving no trace but the displaced air of their passage.

The opulence that had defined Lee Chong's sanctuary was now a memory, the decor of wealth and power reduced to dust and echoes. Intricate tapestries lay shredded, portraits gazed out from cracked frames, and every surface told a story of upheaval. The natural light that once danced through the grand windows was now choked by debris, casting the scene in a pall of gloom.

As the special forces vanished, Nick's unconscious form remained, a symbol of sacrifice amidst the rubble, his journey far from over, his mission now written in the uncertainty of survival.

CHAPTER 78

Martin's fingers trembled as he punched the numbers into his satellite phone, a lifeline amidst the chaos. The device, surprisingly intact, connected with a crackle and hum to the other side of the world.

"Sergey, it's Martin. It's all gone to hell," he barked into the receiver, urgently lacing his words. He could barely hear his own voice over the ringing in his ears, the aftermath of the explosion still reverberating through his skull.

"Martin? What has happened?" Sergey's voice was calm, a stark contrast to the pandemonium that surrounded Martin.

"Lee Chong... he's been taken. Special forces, I think. They came out of nowhere, precision like clockwork," Martin explained, his chest tightening as the reality sank in. "And Nick... he's bad, Sergey. We need to get him out, now."

"Understood," Sergey replied with the efficiency of a man who had spent his life calculating variables and outcomes. "I'm on my way. Hold tight."

Martin clicked off the call, slipping the phone back into his pocket. His gaze swept across what remained of the villa, his mind racing. Once a bastion of luxury and power, the stately structure now lay in ruins, its walls cracked open like the fractured shell of an egg. Plumes of dust rose from the rubble, swirling in the air and painting everything with a grim patina.

The grand entrance, where dignitaries and criminals alike had once been welcomed, was now nothing more than a gaping wound in the building's façade. Marble tiles, imported from the quarries of Tuscany, were strewn about like leaves after a storm. A chandelier, dripping with crystals that had once twinkled under the soft glow of evening soirees, now lay shattered, its remnants sparkling amidst the debris.

Martin's heart ached as he surveyed the scene. This was not just the destruction of a building; it was the dismantling of an empire. Lee Chong's empire.

Twenty minutes later, as promised, Sergey arrived together with Michael in a stolen sedan that had seen better days, its paint job marred by the city's hustle and scrapes from narrow escapes. Yet, its engine roared with the promise of salvation.

"Quickly!" Sergey called out, stepping out of the vehicle with the poise of a man who had navigated far worse than a mere extraction. He rushed over to Nick's prone form, assessing his condition with a mathematician's eye for detail.

Nick, whose body bore the testament of his loyal service, was a patchwork of past encounters and fresh wounds. His gray hair, once meticulously combed, now clung to his forehead, matted with sweat and blood. The once sharp lines of his jaw were slack, his skin pallid beneath the grime and soot. But it was the steady rise and fall of his chest that gave Martin hope.

"Help me with him," Martin instructed Sergey, his voice firm despite the quiver of fear that threatened to break through.

Together, Sergey and Michael lifted Nick with care that belied the urgency of their actions, maneuvering his large frame into the back seat of the car. As they settled him, Martin couldn't help but notice the paradox of Nick's peaceful expression amidst the turmoil that had claimed his consciousness.

"Sergey, Now Drive," Martin said, slamming the door shut after him. "Fast and low profile, we can't afford any attention."

Sergey nodded, his thinning hair barely moving as he revved the engine and pulled away from the wreckage. His hands were steady on the wheel, betraying none of the concern that shadowed his analytical gaze.

As Sergey and Michael sped toward the airport, the sounds of approaching sirens merged with the cacophony of their escape. Martin's thoughts were already turning to their next move, the chessboard of international intrigue demanding their next play. But first, they had to save Nick, the man who had always stood unwavering at the frontlines of their battles for justice, both visible and veiled.

CHAPTER 79

Martin decides to go back inside the villa and search for answers. Eva join him. With each step, his boots crunched over shattered glass and twisted metal, the remnants of Lee Chong's empire. Eva, lean and hawk-eyed, flanked him, his sharp instincts attuned to the task at hand.

All around the dust settled like a grim shroud over the remains of the once opulent villa, its marbled surfaces cracked and smeared with the soot of destruction. Martin De Simone, his sturdy frame casting a determined silhouette against the chaos, moved with purpose through the debris.

"Over here," Martin called out, his voice cutting through the thick silence. Together with the haggard survivors of the cartel, they navigated corridors that bore the scars of betrayal and conflict. The air was heavy with the smell of burnt electronics and gunpowder, but beneath it all lingered the faintest trace of the jasmine incense Lee Chong favored, an incongruous note in the symphony of destruction.

They arrived at what used to be the communication room, a space where sleek technology had once hummed with power and potential. Now, it lay in ruin, screens blinked erratically, their displays distorted. Cables, like wounded serpents, snaked across the floor, severed from their sources.

"Start collecting the hard drives," Martin instructed, his voice steady despite the adrenaline coursing through his veins. He knew this operation had taken a turn into uncharted waters, and every piece of evidence could be the key to unraveling the web of corruption they were entangled in.

Eva and the rest of the commando set to work, prying open panels and extracting data storage units with meticulous care. Meanwhile, Martin surveyed the remnants of Lee Chong's digital arsenal—a testament of a man's obsession with surveillance and control. The multiple monitors, though now fractured, still echoed images of maps, financial transactions, and clandestine communications.

"Martin, you need to see this," one of the cartel members beckoned, holding up a partially damaged laptop with reverence.

"Good find," Eva replied, his eyes scanning the device for signs of life. He flipped it open, the screen flickering to life under his touch. There, amidst the chaos of code and encryptions, lay a trove of emails and documents that could expose the arteries of Lee Chong's operations.

"Get everything uploaded to my server in Switzerland. It's secure, out of reach from prying eyes," Martin ordered, his mind racing with the implications of their discovery. This data could very well be the compass leading them through the murky waters of international conspiracy.

With practiced skill, Eva connected a small, unassuming device to the laptop, initiating the transfer of data. The indicator light blinked steadily, a beacon of hope amid the wreckage. Eva watched the progress bar inch forward each kilobyte transmitted a step closer to understanding the full extent of Lee Chong's treachery.

"Let's keep moving," Martin urged, his gaze shifting towards the labyrinthine heart of the villa. Every second mattered; they were racing not just against the clock, but against unseen forces that would stop at nothing to retain their grip on power.

The group pressed on, their movements shadowed by the knowledge that, although they had lost the battle to capture Lee Chong, they might yet win the war with the secrets they were uncovering.

CHAPTER 80

In the ashen aftermath, with dust swirling like specters in the dimming light, Martin De Simone cast a final glance over the ravaged opulence of Lee Chong's villa. The grandeur that once whispered secrets of power now screamed a silent requiem, the intricate hardwood floors splintered, and priceless antiques lay shattered amidst the debris.

"Time to move out!" Martin's voice was firm, tinged with the gravel of urgency. He appeared unflappable, his muscular frame weather-beaten but unbowed by the day's trials. His eyes, sharp and calculating, scanned the chaos for signs of life among his crew, their loyalty forged in adversity.

Eva emerged from the shadows, his face smeared with soot, his cartel attire ripped and stained, the embodiment of the havoc wrought upon them. "All set," she confirmed, patting the encryption device now safely secured in his tactical vest.

The survivors—each one a chiseled testament to the rigors of clandestine warfare—nodded in solidarity, their expressions a tapestry of relief and grim resolve. As they tread lightly through the remnants of wealth and conspiracy, the once lavish corridors echoed empty promises and forsaken dreams.

Outside, the twilight caressed the villa's broken silhouette, nature's indifferent beauty juxtaposed against human ruin. The creeping vines that had once artfully embraced the stone walls now seemed to strangle the life out of the crumbling edifice.

"Keep your heads down," Martin instructed, blending the role of conductor and comrade as he led his team into the encroaching night. Their movements were purposeful, their steps measured to avoid detection.

The sirens crescendo, a cacophony of impending confrontation, heralding the approach of authorities eager to dissect the evening's explosive events. Martin could almost taste the bitter tang of gunmetal and bureaucracy that would soon envelop the place.

"Here," Eva said, handing Martin a sleek satellite phone. Its black casing was nondescript, yet within its circuits flowed the channels of insurgence and rebellion. Martin punched in a sequence of numbers his fingers steady despite the adrenaline that coursed through him.

"Base camp, this is Black Swan. Extraction needed at secondary rendezvous. Tango is mobile but compromised. Over." His words, crisp and succinct, carried the weight of command and the promise of retribution.

"Copy, Black Swan. We're on the move. Keep your signal hot. Over and out."

As the ensemble slipped through the villa's wrought-iron gates, a sense of fleeting victory washed over them. They had not captured the elusive Lee Chong, but they carried with them the seeds of his undoing—a digital trove that held the potential to unravel the web of deceit.

Martin felt it then, the duality of their existence—the relentless chase and the elusive quarry, the clarity of purpose amid the fog of war. It was a world where every shadow could harbor an enemy, and every piece of evidence was a step closer to the truth.

"Let's double-time it," Martin urged, his voice barely above a whisper. The sirens' wail was a siren song itself, beckoning them to evade, to survive, to fight another day.

With each stride towards sanctuary, Martin's mind was already plotting, strategizing for the battles to come. For in the world of espionage, the end of one ordeal was merely the prelude to the next.

Martin's boots crunched over gravel as he led the remnants of his team through the labyrinthine of the forest of Macao's Hills, the humid air clinging to their skin like a sodden shroud. He was the archetype of rigor under pressure—a man whose intellect was matched only by the sinewy strength that coiled beneath the fabric of his tactical attire.

"Martin," Sergey's voice broke through the encrypted earpiece, the Russian accent thick but composed, "I have secured an exit strategy. My contacts in the FSB have arranged for a cargo ambulance plane. It will touch down at Macao airport within two hours, escorted by fighter jets."

A flicker of hope sparked in Martin's chest. Sergey, the ex-KGB operator turned ally, might have looked unassuming with his chess player's calm and scholarly demeanor, but his connections were as vast as his intellect. Michael's connection with the Pentagon was silent. The operation black swan, this was the name Michael was using was unsuccessful and actually create a collateral damage: serious injury of his honorable friend Nick. Martin was just happy somebody would take care of this exhausted armada.

"Copy, Sergey. I'll regroup everyone at the airstrip. Keep the channel open," Martin replied, the subtext clear: they were not out of the woods yet. His mind was already racing through the variables, calculating risks, and devising contingencies.

The group maintained a brisk pace, their boots muffled against the ever-moist pavement, the air punctuated by distant sirens growing fainter behind them. They were ghosts flitting through an urban wilderness, every movement deliberate, every breath measured.

As they arrived at the desolate outskirts of the airport, the structure loomed like a behemoth of steel and glass. Its modern facade was a stark contrast to the lush greenery that bordered it—an oasis of technology on the edge of nature's untamed domain.

"Stay sharp," Martin instructed tersely, his gaze sweeping the perimeter. "We're almost home free."

The wait was a tapestry of tension and silent prayers until the silhouette of the cargo ambulance plane emerged, a leviathan against the tangerine streaks of the dusk sky. The sleek design of the aircraft spoke of efficiency, its interior a sterile sanctuary fitted with the latest medical equipment, ready to tend to Nick's wounds.

All the survivors and Nick boarded swiftly; the cabin's interior bathed in a soft blue light—a cocoon of security amidst the chaos they had left behind. Martin settled into a seat, feeling the weight of his responsibility tether him to reality. This was more than an extraction; it was a lifeline. All the survivors of the little armada take also place in the plane and the wounded one received the necessary medical treatments.

With a roar that swallowed all other sounds, the plane hurtled down the runway. Martin watched Macao shrink away, the cityscape blurring into a tapestry of lights as they ascended into the heavens. When the landing gear retracted with a definitive clunk, he allowed himself that rare luxury—a deep, steadying breath.

"Next stop, Moscow," Sergey announced, his voice imbued with a quiet confidence that seemed to spread throughout the cabin.

As the cargo ambulance plane pierced the velvet night, disappearing into the starlit abyss toward Russia, Martin closed his eyes momentarily. In the darkness of his own mind, he plotted, planned, and prepared. The game of espionage had many moves left, and he was ready to play.

CHAPTER 81

The relentless rain pattered against the cold, unforgiving tarmac of Moscow Sheremetyevo Airport as the ambulance cargo plane's wheels screeched to a halt. Martin, Diego, and Sergey emerged from the aircraft's belly, their faces etched with fatigue and concern under the stark white floodlights that cut through the dreary evening mist. They watched anxiously as paramedics hastened to unload stretchers, among them Nick Taylor—motionless, his pallor a stark contrast against the crimson that had stained his bandages.

A convoy of ambulances, their red and blue lights painting the wet concrete in urgent flashes, awaited the wounded. Police cars with heavy-set men inside, eyes vigilant behind their rain-spattered windshields, flanked the emergency vehicles. Above, a solitary helicopter churned the icy air, its rotors slicing through the drizzle as it prepared to escort the procession through Moscow's labyrinthine streets.

As the sirens wailed their mournful song, the caravan rolled out towards Botkin Hospital, the most advanced medical fortress in the heart of Russia's stoic capital. The city itself seemed to shiver, its grandiose buildings and ancient spires standing sentinel in the downpour, their facades weeping with the skyline's tears.

Inside the hospital, a flurry of activity ensued. The reanimation unit was a hive of life-saving precision, where every second mattered, and every breath was a battle. Igor Vasilyev, the chief surgical maestro, stood at the epicenter, directing his team with the meticulousness of a conductor leading an orchestra through a symphony of scalpels and sutures.

"Scalpel," he commanded, his voice steady even as his hands performed a delicate ballet over Nick's wounded left shoulder. The surgery was textbook perfection, each incision made with the deft assurance of countless hours in the operating theater. Around him, monitors beeped their mechanical hymn, affirming life amidst the sterile scent of antiseptics.

Days later, Nick lay in his hospital bed, his body a patchwork of healing flesh and bruised spirit. The "raketa" coursed through his veins, a potent cocktail of vitamins and steroids that reignited the fire in his once-dulled eyes. He could feel the strength returning, the familiar hum of a soldier's resilience.

But with consciousness came the questions. Why? Why had the President turned on him? Why the desperate scramble to abort the operation? His mind, once clouded by painkillers and trauma, now sharpened into focus, analyzing the absurdity of his predicament.

"Could it be a rogue element within our own government? What is the role of Senator James Hargrave?". Nick pondered, his gaze fixed on the room's antique clock, its ticking a metronome to his thoughts. "Or is this the work of a deeper, more insidious conspiracy? Qui prodest? Who will take advantage of this situation?" This is the question.

His friends had risked everything to bring him here, away from the jaws of death. Yet as the luxurious fabrics of his room whispered the comforts afforded to few, Nick couldn't shake the dread that clung to him like a second skin. He felt like a pawn in a game played by shadowy figures who moved pieces across a global chessboard.

"Who truly stands to gain from this chaos?" he mused aloud, though no one was there to answer. Each hypothesis gave birth to another, a never-ending maze of deceit and political machinations. But one thing was clear: he would not rest until justice, whatever its true form, was restored.

Nick's fingers brushed against the fresh bandages, a tactile reminder of his narrow escape. He knew that the road ahead was fraught with peril, but he was not alone. Martin, Michael, Eva and Sergey were more than just allies; they were brothers-in-arms, united against an unseen enemy. As the storm outside rattled the windowpanes, Nick steeled himself for the fight to come.

CHAPTER 82

The sterile scent of antiseptic and the low hum of medical equipment provided an unlikely setting for a reunion. But as Martin, Michael, Eva and Sergey entered Nick's private room at Botkin Hospital, the atmosphere shifted palpably. Their faces, etched with lines of concern and fatigue, brightened upon seeing Nick propped up in his hospital bed, the pallor of his skin beginning to yield to the faint blush of recovery.

"Nick," Martin said, his voice a mix of relief and joy as he approached. His eyes, usually sharp and calculating, softened considerably. Martin's clothes were well-tailored yet practical, a reflection of his lifestyle which balanced intellect with action. He extended a hand, gripping Nick's firmly.

"Hey, brother," responded Nick, his voice stronger than expected. The gratitude in his steel-blue eyes was unmistakable. Despite his athletic build being temporarily confined to a bed, his presence remained commanding.

Michael, always the more casually dressed of the trio, with his penchant for functional clothing suited for sudden departures, gave a nod and a wry smile. "You've looked better, amigo, but it's damn good to see you alive."

Sergey, carrying the air of a chess grandmaster contemplating his next move, adjusted his glasses and gave a curt, respectful bow. "It is fortunate that your resilience matches your reputation, Nick."

"Martin, what's the situation?" Nick asked, his mind swiftly transitioning from patient to operative.

Martin took a deep breath, glancing at Eva, who began fiddling with an advanced tablet device. "The assault on Lee Chang's villa... it was worse than we feared. Many didn't make it out." His words were heavy, laden with the weight of lives lost.

"Damn it," Nick swore under his breath, his jaw setting firm. "And the files?"

"Right here," Eva interjected, holding up the tablet. "I'm still going through them, but there's a trove of information about Cobra's operations—both sides of the law. Communications with someone at the Pentagon, codenamed 'Eagle.'"

"Good work," Nick praised, then grimaced. "We need justice for those who died, for all of this madness."

"Justice..." Martin echoed, frustration lacing his tone. "It seems so elusive when the very institutions we trusted are involved."

"Then we'll find our own way to it," Nick asserted, his gaze flinty with resolve. "Help me recap everything. Start from the beginning."

"Okay," Martin agreed, pacing slightly. "First, the bomb in your apartment—"

"Intended to silence me," Nick interjected. "But they have bad luck."

"Right. Then, the Russian operative who tried to take you out and the retrieval of the microchip that started all this," Martin continued.

"Which led me to Colombia, to Zho," Nick added, piecing together the chain of events. "Lee Chang's right-hand man, The Cobra himself."

"Exactly," Martin nodded. "You received encrypted warnings from 'Eagle'—'stay away from the snakes.' Cryptic, but pointed."

"Then that call... from the President," Nick recalled, his brow furrowed. "Telling me to abort the mission."

"And moments later, a missile strike hit the villa. In the chaos, Lee Chang was extracted by an unknown team—a stealth operation within an operation,"

Martin finished, the implications hanging heavily in the air.

"Someone wanted him alive, and us dead," Nick concluded, the pieces forming a disturbing picture in his mind. "We have to expose the truth, no matter how high up this goes."

"Agreed," Eva said firmly, tapping away at the tablet. "And we will. Together."

They shared a look among them, one that needed no words. It spoke of trust, commitment, and an unyielding desire to right the wrongs that had been done. They were united, not just by friendship, but by a cause that transcended borders and bureaucracies.

"Alright, let's get to work," Nick declared, the strategist within him taking over. "We have a conspiracy to unravel and a justice to restore."

Nick's eyes were sharp and alert as he lay propped up in the hospital bed, the sterile white of the room serving as a stark contrast to the dark, complex web of international intrigue they were discussing. Martin paced back and forth, his hands animated as he spoke, while Diego sat hunched over his laptop, his fingers flying across the keyboard.

"Control, distribution, power—it all comes down to those," Martin murmured, his voice a low growl.

"The President's involvement isn't just incidental. It's strategic. The Asian mafia's grip on the Medellin Cartel is no hapless coalescence of crime; it's orchestrated."

"Orchestrated with chilling precision," Nick added, his athletic build tensing beneath the thin hospital blanket. "Lee Chang's ambition married to the power of the Oval Office—it's a formidable beast."

"Qui prodest?" Diego interjected, his dark eyes lifting from the screen. "Who benefits? That's what we need to keep asking ourselves."

"Exactly." Martin halted mid-stride, turning to face Nick. "It's not just about the flow of narcotics. This plot has tendrils reaching into the very sinew of international politics."

"Which means," Nick said, grim determination etching his features, "we have to be smarter, faster. Time is against us."

"Here's what we've got," Eva announced, swivelling the laptop around for them to see. Documents, financial transactions, and encrypted communications filled the screen, painting a damning picture. "The Mexican standoff with the DEA gave Lee Chang and our own CIA the opening they needed. But it's more than that—the President himself with the help of the Senator James Hargrave appears compromised."

"Compromised or complicit?" Martin pondered, his short, dark hair seeming to bristle with the intensity of the question.

"Either way," Nick replied, the gray at his temples standing out like war paint against his seasoned complexion, "it's betrayal at the highest level."

They absorbed the gravity of the evidence, the silence heavy with the weight of their next steps. Finally, Nick spoke, his voice steady with resolve. "Justice might be an elusive concept in this case, but I'll be damned if I let corruption fester at the core of our system. We expose them, no matter how powerful they are."

"Agreed," Eva said, closing the laptop with a decisive snap.

"Then we're in agreement," Martin stated. "We go after the truth. Full throttle."

"Full throttle," echoed Nick, a fire kindling in his gaze. He was a man reborn from the ashes of his old life, each revelation fueling his drive to fight back against the shadows that had almost consumed him.

"Let's start pulling on threads," Nick suggested, his mind already racing with strategies and contingencies. "We need to unravel this before more lives are lost to these power-hungry vipers."

"Starting with one thread in particular," Diego added, reopening the laptop to reveal a matrix of information. "Cobra's transactions. They could lead us straight to the top."

"Then it's settled," Martin concluded, his muscular frame conveying a readiness to leap into action. "We pull at Cobra's strings and watch the mighty fall."

"Pull hard enough," Nick mused, "and the whole rotten structure comes crashing down."

They shared a somber nod, understanding the road ahead would be fraught with danger. Yet, within that perilous path, there lay a chance to right grievous wrongs—a chance they were willing to take, together.

CHAPTER 83

The room was silent as Sergey leaned forward, his fingers tented in contemplation. A sliver of Moscow's grim daylight filtered through the blinds, casting long shadows across the sterile white walls of the hospital room. Nick, propped up on an array of pillows, watched Sergey with hawkish intensity. The graying at his temples seemed to have deepened since his ordeal, yet his eyes retained their sharpness—a testament to his unwavering resolve.

"Comrades," Sergey began, his voice low but clear, "the Kremlin has been... attentive." His thinning hair did little to distract from the intelligence that gleamed in his eyes. He dressed plainly, a simple sweater and slacks, yet there was nothing simple about the way his mind worked.

"Attentive how?" Nick's question cut through the air, betraying none of the pain he felt beneath the bandages and stitches that crisscrossed his shoulder.

"Operation 'Black Swan. The tentative of capture the Cobra"—it was under surveillance by Russian services. We intercepted communications, including what you believed to be a call from your President."

Martin, solid and stoic, shifted in his chair, his dark eyes reflecting a storm of thoughts. Michael, whose casual attire belied his acute mind, frowned deeply, sensing the weight of Sergey's revelation.

"The call..." Nick prompted, leaning in despite the pull at his wound.

"Ah, yes. It originated not from the desk phone in the Oval Office, but elsewhere." Sergey paused, allowing the implication to sink in. "And the missile that tore through Lee Chang's villa—it was launched from a US Navy vessel stationed in the South Pacific."

"Are you saying our own President didn't make that call?" Martin interjected, his brow furrowing.

"He was making the call from another location. We don't understand why. Also, We are working to uncover who truly gave the order for the strike. Something is amiss, and it stinks of deception."

Nick's jaw tightened. The pieces were falling into place, forming a picture more complex and sinister than he'd imagined. "Sergey, your insights are invaluable," he said with genuine gratitude. "We knew the stakes were high, but this..."

"Russia," Sergey continued, "is not blind to the shifts in the drug trade's power structure. We seek understanding, perhaps even involvement. After all, such machinations affect us all."

The somber realization of the tangled web they were facing settled over them like the chill that gripped Moscow's streets outside. Confronting the President, unraveling the conspiracy's full scope—it was daunting. Yet, here they were, each man driven by a desire for truth, justice, or both.

"Thank you, Sergey," Michael said earnestly. "We're piecing together a puzzle that spans continents and climbs to the highest echelons of power."

"Indeed," Sergey acknowledged with a nod. "Remember, the political elite of the G20 have vested interests in the narcotics chessboard. Their influence extends further than most dare to imagine. We think there is more than just political interest."

They sat there for a moment, silence wrapping around them like a shroud. Each man lost in his thoughts; they contemplated the magnitude of what lay ahead. Nick's gaze settled on the rain-streaked window, watching droplets race down the glass in unpredictable paths, much like the mission they had before them.

"First, we must investigate further. Understand the involvement of The President with the G20 elite powers" Nick stated resolutely. "Then we pull back the veil on why the world's power players covet control over the drug trade's dark tendrils."

"Rest now, Nick," Martin advised, concern etching his features. "You'll need every ounce of strength for the battles to come."

"Agreed," Nick said, standing to leave. "Time is of the essence, and I will continue to provide whatever aid I can from my end."

As Sergey exited, the quiet hum of medical equipment filled the space he left behind. Nick, Martin, and Michael remained, a trinity bound by purpose, ready to challenge the shadowy puppeteers orchestrating global vice.

Nick's eyes narrowed as he processed Sergey's offer. The sterile white walls of the Botkin Hospital room seemed to close in around them, a stark contrast to the dark, complex web they were about to traverse.

"Thank you, Sergey," Nick said, his voice gravelly but firm. "We need all the intel we can get. Your Kremlin contact could give us the edge we've been looking for."

Sergey, with his thinning hair combed meticulously to the side, offered a slight smile that didn't quite reach his analytical eyes. "I will set up a meeting with our best counterparty" he assured, his Russian accent flavoring each word. "And I believe this will significantly accelerate our investigation and solution of the situation."

"Good." Martin rubbed his jaw, the stubble there rasping under his palm. His muscular frame was coiled with tension, like a spring wound too tight. He looked every bit the seasoned operative, ready to leap into action. "We'll use our own channels. Time to see who's still loyal."

Michael, always the more casually dressed of the trio with his penchant for Philipp Plein leather jackets and jeans, nodded in agreement. His athletic build, honed from years of fieldwork, shifted restlessly. "CIA, DEA, FBI, NSA... Someone has to know something that can help us connect the dots."

"Exactly," Martin concurred. "We dig deep, stay under the radar. Can't afford any leaks or slip-ups."

"Agreed," Nick replied, pushing himself up slightly in the hospital bed, ignoring the twinge from his freshly stitched shoulder. The determination in his sharp gaze was mirrored by his friends. "Let's regroup here in two days, share what we've found."

"Be careful," Sergey warned, his expression serious as he buttoned up his coat, preparing to face Moscow's biting cold outside. "These are treacherous waters, and not all sharks swim in the open."

"Always are," Nick responded with a ghost of a smile. "See you in two days, Sergey."

With a final nod, Sergey departed, leaving his friends enveloped in the silence of the room. Outside, the relentless Moscow rain continued its symphony against the windows, a reminder of the grim atmosphere that hung over the city.

"Two days," Michael reiterated, his tone resolute. "Let's bring some truth to light."

"Truth," Nick echoed, his mind already working through the list of contacts he would need to discreetly probe. "Justice might be a longer road, but it starts with uncovering the lies."

"Rest up, Nick," Martin advised again, his protective nature evident in his steady gaze. "We're going to need you at your best."

"Rest when this is over," Nick quipped, though the warmth in his eyes conveyed his appreciation for Martin's concern.

As Michael moved to check the security measures one last time, Martin settled into a chair, pulling out his encrypted phone. They were a team once more, albeit one facing an adversary more formidable than any they had known before. Each man knew the stakes were high, and the path perilous, but they shared an unspoken vow to see this through to the end, whatever it took.

CHAPTER 84

Nick Taylor's eyes, sharp as ever beneath the furrows of a weathered brow, skimmed over the array of documents spread across the white plastic desk. The hospital was quiet today. Nick was now in a separate area of the hospital in a "hospitalized apartment'. That was his new headquarters.

Seated in a leather chair that squeaked under his athletic build, Nick's fingers traced the labyrinthine web of financial transactions displayed on his laptop screen. Diego, perched on an antique sofa with upholstery that whispered of bygone opulence, monitored incoming data on his own device. The juxtaposition of cutting-edge technology and antique surroundings was not lost on them; this was a modern hunt grounded in historical conspiracy.

"Look at this," Nick said, his voice a low rumble of authority that matched the steady cadence of rain beginning to tap at the windowpanes. "The money flows from the President's ex-associate right into the coffers of front companies we know are linked to Lee Chong."

Michael leaned forward, his keen gaze meeting Nick's. "And these transactions coincide with the dates of the attacks," he added, his finger following the timeline they had pieced together. He was younger than Nick by a decade, but his eyes held the same kind of relentless determination.

"Exactly," Nick replied. His mind was a steel trap, every detail a spring-loaded mechanism waiting to snap shut on the truth. "It's more than coincidence. It's a pattern."

The apartment's high ceilings echoed with the clink of ice as Martin, their link to European agencies, poured chilled water into a glass etched with delicate vines. Physically less imposing than either Nick or Michael, Martin's intellectual prowess was his weapon of choice. He returned to the table, his movements precise, deliberate.

"Chong is using a network of shell companies to collect and pay of funds," Martin chimed in, pushing up the sleeves of his crisp white shirt, which contrasted starkly with the room's aged grandeur. "Tracing them back is like following a trail of breadcrumbs straight to our hidden wolf."

Nick nodded, absorbing the information while his green eyes remained locked onto the laptop screen. "Lee Chang," he mused aloud, the name tasting like venom on his tongue. "The mediator between the President's and other counterparties.

We need to find him, catch him and interrogate him and after kill him".

"I'm just going in this direction," Michael interjected, pulling up a satellite image on his tablet. "There's a compound here, nestled in the mountains north of Chengdu. No official records, but it fits the profile for a place Mr. Lee would consider secure."

"Remote, defensible, and outside of any legal jurisdiction we could exploit," Nick assessed, leaning in to study the topography. "But I think is too easy to be true. I'm not sure it's where we'll find Lee Chang."

"Yes, is true," Martin confirmed, as the trio shared a look of mutual understanding." I think the Russians are one step ahead" added Nick." Let's wait the meeting with Sergey's contact in Kremlin and after we will make the final decision where to move " Nick ordered with the calm assurance of a man who had faced down danger more times than he cared to count. "We're going hunting."

As the sun set beyond the secure apartment's windows, casting long shadows through the wrought-iron grilles, the operation was set into motion. With every step they took, Nick, Michael, and Martin were acutely aware that they were walking a tightrope stretched taut over a landscape of political intrigue and international conspiracy. But Nick's resolve only strengthened; for him, there was no turning back from the path of justice.

Nick's fingers danced across the keyboard, his eyes flickering between lines of code and encrypted files. In the dimly lit room of their safe medicalized apartment nested in a separate area of the Hospital, only the glow of multiple monitors illuminated his weathered features. The apartment was unusual, it was a collector's paradise, with relics from bygone eras adorning every corner: Italian rugs, oil paintings of pastoral landscapes, and shelves lined with first-edition books that spoke to an intellectual sanctuary. Yet, for Nick, it was just another battleground.

"Got something," he murmured, his voice as steady as his hands. He'd uncovered a digital trail—a series of clandestine meetings logged in obscure corners of the dark web.

"Let's hear it," Martin said, leaning on the mahogany desk, muscles tensing beneath the fabric of his tailored shirt. His athletic build, usually poised for action, was momentarily still focused on the intelligence Nick unearthed.

"Meeting transcripts... look at the dates. They align with the G20 summits," Nick pointed out, highlighting sections of the text where pseudonyms masked real identities. "And these cryptic references—'The Architect'... 'Operation Grand Castle.' It's like they're playing chess with global economies."

"Cross-reference those nicknames with our intel from the French DGSE," Michael suggested from across the room, his angular face serious, eyes squinting as he pieced together the puzzle from the shadows. He was the thinker, always three moves ahead, his lean physique belying his mental strength.

"Already on it," Nick replied, his keystrokes echoing through the silence. A connection emerged from the fog of data, a pattern that painted a picture far more complex than any of them had imagined.

"Look at this," Nick said, zooming in on a spreadsheet. "These transactions aren't just pay offs; they're investments. Shell companies tied to government officials—Italy, Spain, Germany, France, Holland, the UK—all leading back to one entity: Lee Chong."

Martin's fist clenched involuntarily. "So, the President's war on the Medellin Cartel..."

"Isn't about drugs," Nick cut in. "It's a power play. He's using Chong to destabilize rivals and centralize control. Cocaine is just the currency of influence. The President probably made a secret deal with other European Government representatives to form the Club that govern and manage the business of drugs. No more laws, No more fight. Just share the profit. "This is the deal" added Nick with resolutive voice.

"Consolidating power in the criminal underworld to manipulate geopolitical and financial spheres" Michael concluded, his tone laced with disgust.

"Exactly. Around the world nobody fights anymore the drug trafficking and now we know why" Nick leaned back, the chair creaking under his tall frame. "They are constructing a drug Empire in the shadows managed by the G20. Money for everybody to finance political campaigns, parties and the political elite of the top 20 richest Nations of the World".

"Then we bring it into the light," Martin declared, standing upright. "Expose the conspiracy, dismantle the operation."

"Before more lives are lost," Michael added, his resolve hardening.

"Agreed," Nick said, closing the laptop with a definitive snap. "We move at dawn. Prepare yourselves—it's going to be a hell of a fight."

"Wouldn't have it any other way," Martin said, the corner of his mouth lifting in a rare smile.

"Justice doesn't sleep," Michael added, his eyes meeting Nick's with shared determination.

In the heart of darkness, surrounded by the silent witnesses of history, the trio stood united. Their cause was righteous, their spirits unbreakable, and their mission clear. They would strike at the core of corruption, no matter how entangled its roots. For Nick Taylor, this was more than espionage; it was redemption—a chance to right the wrongs of a world teetering on the brink. And when dawn broke, they'd be ready to chase it towards the light.

CHAPTER 85

The day after, Nick's gaze was the steely calm of a winter sea as he watched Sergey approach, his gait measured and deliberate. The Russian ex-KGB man wore an austere suit that seemed to blend into the bleakness of the hospital walls, his thinning hair meticulously combed back. His eyes, sharp with intellectual vigor, betrayed nothing of what churned beneath his stoic exterior.

"Ready?" Sergey's voice was flat but not without warmth.

"Let's do it," Nick replied, rising from the stiff hospital chair, his body protesting slightly after two days of recuperation. He straightened his fitted navy blazer over a crisp white shirt, the fabric stretching across his broad shoulders. Despite his age, the athletic build of his younger years had not abandoned him entirely.

Together, they stepped outside where a black Aurus Senat, the presidential limousine, awaited, its polished surface reflecting a dreary Moscow sky. As they slid into the opulent leather interior, the car moved with purpose, escorted by unmarked vehicles with tinted windows. The silent choreography of security spoke volumes of the gravity of their destination—the Kremlin itself.

The heart of Russian power loomed before them, its red walls and golden domes an imposing testament to history's weight. They passed under archways more accustomed to the tread of boots than the soft steps of diplomats, entering a fortress that had witnessed centuries of intrigue.

Their escort led them through ornate corridors, the air heavy with the scent of old wood and wax polish. Paintings of stern-faced leaders observed them from gilded frames, their eyes following the duo into a room devoid of grandeur or warmth.

Vladimir Romanov, a man whose name was synonymous with Russian intelligence, stood alone in the center of the sparse, windowless space. His presence filled the room like a chilling draft, his suit impeccable, his face an unreadable mask carved from years of clandestine operations.

"Mr. Taylor, Mr. Komutov," Romanov greeted, his Russian accent precise, his tone commanding immediate attention. "Three minutes."

"Understood," Nick answered, his own voice betraying no hint of the adrenaline coursing through him.

Romanov spoke succinctly, each word dropping like a stone into still water. "Lee Chang is in Rome, protected by elite mercenaries on loan from the Chinese Triads in connection with Italian Mafia. You will receive logistical support—satellite imagery, blueprints, local intelligence. Your operation must be swift, silent."

He paused only to let the gravity of his words take hold before continuing. "Lee Chang becomes our asset. Russia demands this." There was no room for negotiation in Romanov's cold gaze.

"Agreed," Sergey affirmed, his mind already racing through equations of risk and strategy.

"White Swan Down" was all Romanov said before turning on his heel, effectively ending the meeting. Nick and Sergey were silently ushered away, spirits undeterred despite the weight of the ultimatum.

Back in the limousine, Nick reflected on the dangerous path ahead. Romanov's information was a gift wrapped in barbed wire—valuable yet fraught with peril. He trusted Sergey's brilliant mind to unravel the complexities of their stealth mission. As the vehicle glided through Moscow's arteries, he felt a kinship with the city—both battle-scarred, both enduring.

"Two days to prepare, then we bring down the swan," Nick said, determination etched in his voice.

"By the book, Nick. We'll make it count," Sergey assured, his analytical brain already at work.

As the car disappeared into the labyrinth of the city, Nick found solace in the thought that justice, though often obscured, was within reach. And they, its unwavering champions, would chase it into the light.

CHAPTER 86

Meanwhile, Michael worked tirelessly in a dimly lit room, surrounded by screens displaying intercepted communications and surveillance footage. His keen eyes scanned through hours of recorded material, pausing, rewinding, documenting every nuance. An audio wave spiked, and he leaned forward, isolating the conversation—a damning exchange between the President and an unknown operative.

The replay button clicked as the voices echoed in the confined space. "Ensure our interests are protected," the President's voice intoned sharply. Michael's fingers flew across the keyboard, notes compiling into a dossier of truth.

"Got you," he murmured, satisfaction lacing his whispered words. The evidence was irrefutable; it painted a picture of betrayal so vivid; the canvas of national security would be forever stained.

CHAPTER 87

The Day after, Nick Taylor stood in the apartment; its concrete walls stripped of any adornment—a stark testament to the gravity of their undertaking. The chill in the air mirrored the cold resolve in his heart. This was not just an apartment; it was a strategic hub, clandestinely nestled within the bowels of Moscow, where the fate of nations could be steered.

He surveyed his team: Michael, with his keen analytical mind, sat at a makeshift desk littered with papers and electronic devices. His eyes, sharp as a hawk's, were glued to the screens, every so often flicking to the dossier that held the President's dark secrets. Sergey, ever the stoic intellectual with chess grandmaster precision, leaned against an aged filing cabinet, his arms crossed as he pondered their next move like a game of geopolitical intrigue.

"Timing is crucial," Nick began, his voice steady but commanding. "We have one shot to expose the President without triggering a backlash we can't contain."

Michael nodded, pushing back a lock of hair that had fallen over his brow in concentration. "The evidence is solid. It could dismantle his entire administration."

"Then it's settled. We'll confront him after 'White Swan down'. The public needs to see the full extent of his treachery," Sergey added, his Russian accent adding a layer of depth to each word.

Nick walked over to a large, military-grade map sprawled across the table. Fingers tracing the route to Rome, he envisioned every step of their operation—'White Swan down'. The plan was to abduct Lee Chang with precision, avoiding unnecessary casualties while penetrating the protective shell of criminal elements surrounding him.

"Preparations begin now. We have 48 hours to ensure our tactics are watertight," Nick declared, his gaze lingering on the location marked on the map. "Sergey, I need you to coordinate with Romanov's operative. We'll need every resource at our disposal."

"Consider it done," Sergey affirmed, his posture unwavering, the epitome of Russian military discipline.

"Michael Freeman, continue compiling the evidence. Once we have Chang, it'll be time to move quickly," Nick instructed, glancing towards the younger man who had become indispensable to their mission.

"Everything will be ready," Michael assured, his fingers already dancing across the keyboard in a symphony of impending justice.

The meeting adjourned with silent nods, each man lost in his own thoughts about the days ahead. They understood the risks; they could almost taste the danger. But the mission was greater than any one of them. It was about truth. It was about justice.

As Nick turned to leave, the sparse light caught the stern lines of his face, casting deep shadows that seemed to reflect the weight of their burden. He paused for a moment, allowing himself the briefest instance of vulnerability before the mask of leadership settled back into place.

"Let's bring the swan down finally!" he said, his voice low but filled with an unshakeable conviction. And with those words, the room sprang into action, alive with the hum of a plan set into motion—a plan that would either restore balance to a world teetering on the edge or send it spiraling into chaos.

CHAPTER 88

"48 hours," Nick muttered, running a hand through his graying hair. His eyes, which had witnessed more than most could dream, scanned the documents with a predator's precision. "That's all we have."

"By then, we'll be ready," Martin replied, his voice as steady as his hands. He was dressed in dark jeans and a simple black turtleneck that clung to his muscular frame—a stark contrast to the opulent surroundings of Romanov's provisioned hideaway. The room was an echo of old Russia, with heavy curtains and walls lined with books that whispered tales of tsars and revolutions.

"Every angle's been considered, every contingency planned for," Martin continued, adjusting the gun holstered discreetly at his side.

Nick nodded, absorbing the weight of his friend's words. The room seemed to close in around him, like claustrophobic. The ornate ceiling pressing down like the very sky they were about to storm. He approached a window, gazing out at the dense forest that shielded them from prying eyes. Leaves rustled in the wind, speaking of change, of upheaval.

"Are you sure about the non-lethal approach?" Martin asked, breaking the introspection. "Lee Chang won't afford us the same courtesy."

"Romanov was explicit, and I gave him my word," Nick affirmed, his jaw set. "We need Chang alive for answers—and leverage. Dead men tell no tales."

"Then we take him alive," Martin stated, matching Nick's resolve. "But what about the cell protecting him? They're not going to welcome us with open arms."

"Diversion and infiltration," Nick answered, tapping a point on the map. "We hit them fast, hit them hard. Non-lethal rounds, flashbangs, disorientation tactics. We extract Chang before they even realize what's happening. This time nobody will help him".

"Sounds like a plan," Martin smiled wryly, the corner of his eye crinkling. "A private jet to Rome, eh? Almost sounds like the good old days. But we need also a helicopter for the extraction."

"Except this time, we're not sanctioned by any agency. It's just us, our wits, and what's right," Nick added, locking eyes with his friend.

"Let's make it count," Martin said, standing up and extending his hand. Nick clasped it firmly, a silent pact between warriors. Michael stepped forward, joining the bond.

"This is the first important step to destroy the grand Castle.," Nick chimed in, his youthful confidence a beacon of hope amidst the encroaching storm.

As they finalized their plans, the room hummed with the electricity of impending action. Outside, the natural world went about its business, indifferent to the human drama unfolding within. Nick took one last look at the serene landscape before turning back to his comrades.

"Prepare yourselves, gentlemen," he instructed, his voice imbued with a gravity that belied his positive outlook. "In 48 hours, we bring 'White Swan' down."

CHAPTER 89

The morning sun glinted off the sleek, private jet's metallic surface as Nick Taylor strode confidently towards its yawning hatch, the brisk Moscow air biting at his exposed skin. His graying hair, a testament to years in clandestine service, sat neatly combed back, and his eyes, sharp and scrutinizing, scanned the tarmac with the practiced vigilance of a hawk. He was dressed for action in a tailored black jacket that concealed his athletic frame, honed from years of disciplined training.

Beside him, Martin De Simone's stocky silhouette moved with an assuredness that spoke of countless covert operations. His dark hair had been cropped to a practical length, matching his no-nonsense demeanor. The lines etched on his face were not just from age but from the burdens of moral responsibility he carried like armor.

Sergey Komutov followed, a stark contrast with his thinning hair and less imposing stature. His gait was measured, the mind behind the bespectacled eyes always whirring, calculating. Though lacking the physicality of his companions, Sergey's attire—a crisp, button-up shirt tucked into smart slacks—hinted at a man who approached life as he did chess: with precision and forethought.

Michael, their silent shadow, was last to board, his presence almost ghostly saves for the purposeful steps he took. In black tactical gear that seemed to blend into the surroundings, he was the embodiment of the unseen hand, the decisive strike.

As they boarded, the cabin's interior revealed itself to be a fusion of functionality and luxury. Plush leather seats promised comfort during their flight, while the polished mahogany tables bore no fingerprints, showcasing the meticulous care of the vessel's upkeep. Every detail within the jet was designed to cater to those accustomed to power—and the discretion necessary to wield it effectively.

"Roma won't know what hit it," Nick murmured, a faint smile playing on his lips as he settled into his seat, fastening the belt with a soft click. He exuded a calm that came from years of facing down danger, a leader who inspired confidence through his mere presence.

Martin nodded, cracking a wry grin. "Lee Chang is about to have a very bad day," he said, his voice low but threaded with anticipation. The light-hearted comment belied the gravity of the mission ahead.

"Assuming all variables remain constant," Sergey chimed in, adjusting his glasses with a thoughtful frown. "Our preparations must account for every potential contingency."

"Preparations are my middle name," Michael finally spoke, his voice a deep timbre that resonated within the confines of the plane. He checked his watch, a high-tech piece of equipment that mirrored his own specialty in gadgets and weaponry.

Their camaraderie was palpable—a bond forged in the fires of mutual trust and shared ideals. As the engines roared to life, the aircraft began its ascent, leaving the Russian landscape behind. Before them lay Roma, a city steeped in history, about to become the backdrop for their daring capture of Lee Chang, The Cobra. With every mile that passed beneath them, the quartet drew closer to the culmination of their meticulous planning.

In the belly of the beast, they were four men united by a singular goal, their resolve as unyielding as the steel wings that carried them forward.

CHAPTER 90

The private jet sliced through the atmosphere; a silver bullet aimed at the heart of Roma. Nick Taylor, ever vigilant, observed the clouds that painted a quilt over the land below. His eyes, those of a hawk, didn't miss the slight shudder of the aircraft's wing as they hit an air pocket. The tremor was brief, a reminder of the uncontrollable variables in play, just like the ones he anticipated on the ground.

"Bit of turbulence," Martin remarked casually to Nick, his voice steady despite the jolt. The two men exchanged a look, their history giving them an unspoken language that needed no words.

"Nothing our bird can't handle," Nick replied with a tight-lipped smile, feeling the weight of the mission pressing against his chest.

The bumpiness receded, and peace resumed its reign within the cabin. Outside, the sun dipped lower, casting golden hues upon the clouds, turning them into a fiery canvas only nature could conjure. The team used the remaining hours to review plans silently, each lost in their mental rehearsals.

As the plane began its descent into Roma, the city unveiled itself beneath them, a tapestry of ancient glory and modern bustle. They touched down with the grace of a feather, the wheels kissing the tarmac in a whisper of rubber. The door opened, releasing them into the Italian warmth, a stark contrast to the Russian chill they'd left behind.

Stepping off the Falcon 6X, a sleek black Mercedes S awaited, its black sheen standing out against the vibrant city life. As they slid into the leather seats, Nick couldn't help but appreciate the Russians' logistical prowess.

The chaotic symphony of Roma greeted them. Car horns sang impatiently, scooters weaved through traffic like dancers in a frenetic ballet, and voices clamored in a blend of excitement and everyday haste. The sun cast a brilliant glow over the cobblestone streets and terracotta roofs, shadows stretching long as the day began to wane.

"Russians sure know how to make an entrance," Martin quipped, his enthusiasm thawing the edge of tension that had settled over the team. Nick merely nodded, his mind already tracing the steps ahead.

After one hour they arrive at The Hotel Splendide Royal, nestled in the pulsing heart of Rome, rose before them—a monument to luxury and a fortress of opulence. The hotel loomed grandly, its façade a testament to Roman architectural splendor. Its interior, a sanctum of elegance, whispered of power and secrets. Murmurs of history echoed off marble floors, and the intricate frescoes adorning the walls bore silent witness to the countless tales spun under its roof.

Nick inhaled deeply, the scent of polished wood and faint perfume lacing the air. Despite the outward calm, his senses remained attuned to every nuance around him—the discreet glances of hotel staff, the soft clicks of heels across the lobby, the measured breaths of his comrades.

"Quite the setting for an operation," Nick mused, a sense of readiness settling over him like a second skin. "Let's get to work."

Martin nodded, his dark eyes reflecting the same resolve that had always defined their brotherhood. With each step they took through the hotel's opulent corridors, their purpose became more tangible, the stakes higher.

"Every detail counts," Nick reminded himself silently. "Every second, every move."

And with that thought anchoring him, Nick Taylor moved forward, ready to dance with danger in the eternal city.

CHAPTER 91

In the palatial suite of Hotel Splendide Royal, the air was thick with anticipation. Marco Markoff, his frame solid and imposing even within the grandeur of the room, set down two suitcases with a precision that spoke of countless drills and clandestine operations. Each clasp of the cases clicked open with a promise of what was to come—a symphony of impending action.

"White Swan Down," Marcoff announced, his voice a low rumble as he flipped the lids to reveal the neatly arranged armaments. Guns, magazines, explosives—each piece lay in perfect order, a testament to the gravity of their mission.

Nick Taylor's gaze swept over the arsenal before meeting Marcoff's steely eyes. Despite the opulence around them—the gold leaf gilding the ceiling, the priceless antiques that adorned the space—it was the tools of their trade that now commanded their attention.

"Everything you'll need," Marcoff added, his Russian accent coloring the words with a harsh edge.

"Good work," Nick responded, his mind cataloging every item. His fingers itched to check the balance of a Beretta, to feel the familiar weight of duty in his hands.

Martin, ever the tactician, leaned in closer, his brow furrowed as he surveyed the equipment. "And the escape routes?" he queried; his focus razor-sharp.

"Planned and accounted for," Marcoff assured, unfolding a map of Rome across an antique mahogany desk. The streets sprawled out like veins, each one a potential lifeline or dead end.

"Via delle quattro Fontane," Marcoff pointed to the map, near Piazza Barberini. "Chang will be there tonight."

Michael peered over the map, committing the twists and turns to memory. "Back alleys, checkpoints, everything is mapped out?"

"Like chess pieces on a board," Marcoff confirmed, his finger tracing paths only they could see.

"Let's talk contingencies," Nick said, the leader in him surfacing. They huddled close, their heads bowed in serious discussion. "What's our Plan B?"

"Plan B is here," Marcoff tapped another street, a shade darker than the rest. "Coded messages, safe houses, secondary extraction points. We leave nothing to chance."

The energy in the room crackled; they were operatives, shadows moving through a world that thrived beneath the surface of everyday life. The luxury that surrounded them was but a façade, a mere backdrop to the theater of espionage in which they were the lead actors.

"Remember, we strike at midnight," Nick reminded them, his voice firm. "Timing is critical."

"Understood," Martin replied, the soldier in him responding to the call.

"Let's gear up," Michael added, his hand already reaching for a matte-black helmet.

The sun outside cast long shadows across the ancient cobblestones of Rome, unaware of the plot unfolding within the walls of the Splendide Royal. As evening approached, the city hummed with life, oblivious to the fact that, within its heart, a dangerous game was about to begin.

The clock's hands converged on midnight, and the four men stood in silence, a black veil over their intentions. Nick's eyes, sharp as ever beneath his helmet's visor, scanned the faces of his comrades. "This is it," he whispered, his voice a low thrum of conviction that cut through the night. "One last dance with danger, then we can all walk away from this life."

Martin nodded, the muscles in his jaw tightening. His dark hair was slicked back, a few strands defying order, much like the man himself. Michael's face was set in determination, mirroring the steadfastness that had earned him a place among these veterans.

"Remember why we're here," Nick continued, his words not just a reminder for the others but a mantra for himself. "We fight for truth and justice—our creed, our burden, and our honor."

"Always," Martin affirmed, clasping his friend's shoulder with a gloved hand.

"Let's move out," Nick commanded.

CHAPTER 92

Two Ducati Panigale V4R motorcycles, sleek and predatory, lay dormant under the shadow of an ancient Roman building close to the apartment of Lee Chang. Marcoff sat in the driver's seat of the black Alfa Romeo Stelvio, his presence silent yet commanding. The 4 operatives dispersed, slipping into the darkness like wraiths hungry for retribution.

Their footsteps were whispers against the cobblestone as they closed in on Via delle Quattro Fontane 10. The first floor, apartment number 4—their target. Each movement was deliberate, a testament to years spent honing the art of stealth. Nick led the small commando, his Beretta M92A1, an extension of his will.

They converged at the door, three shadows becoming one. A small but efficient explosive charge—a compact device designed for discretion—was placed with surgical precision by Michael. Amidst the deafening heartbeat of Rome at night, the detonation would be a mere gasp.

"Ready?" Michael's voice crackled through the earpiece.

"Do it," Nick ordered.

The door erupted inwards, a controlled chaos that gave way to the smoke bombs flying from Nick's steady hand. A fog of war filled the space as he and Martin burst through the threshold.

Two guards—an unexpected but calculated risk—rose to meet them. They were dispatched within seconds; two muffled shots, two bodies crumpling to the ground, their blood seeping into the rich tapestry that adorned the marble floors.

Thick smoke curled around ornate furnishings and priceless artifacts, the spoils of Lee Chang's empire. The opulence was suffocating, but Nick's focus was unyielding, cutting through the haze like a blade.

"Clear!" Martin's confirmation echoed faintly.

"Secure the asset," Nick replied, gunfire still ringing in his ears.

Thirty seconds had passed since the door's obliteration, but in the world of espionage, thirty seconds could be an eternity—or salvation.

Nick's boots tread softly on the shattered remnants of the doorway, his senses heightened as he surveyed the chaos they had wrought. The interior of Lee Chang's apartment was a stark contrast to the violence that had just erupted outside its walls—an obscene display of wealth and power. Majestic oil paintings of Caravaggio e Michelangelo adorned the walls, each brushstroke a testament to the artists' mastery and Chang's vanity. Gilded edges caught the light from modern recessed fixtures, glinting off polished surfaces, while original precious vases from distant dynasties stood untouched by time or strife.

"Check him," Nick whispered.

Martin moved swiftly to the prostrate figure of Lee Chang, still dazed from the explosion, sprawled face down amidst the opulence. They were efficient, methodical. Handcuffs clicked into place, securing the wrists of 'The Cobra' behind his back. A black hood shrouded the man's vision, sealing him in darkness. Without hesitation, Martin administered the serum, a concoction guaranteed to render their captive pliable.

"Move out!" Nick commanded, the adrenaline coursing through him, a mix of victory and the tense anticipation of what was yet to come. The extraction was the crux; they all knew it.

They hoisted Chang between them, a featherweight burden compared to the gravity of their task. Exiting the apartment, they found Marcoff waiting with the car, its engine purring like a predator in the quiet of the night.

"Go, go, go!" Michael urged, as he and Sergey piled into the Alfa Romeo Stelvio, the black vehicle now containing the fruits of their daring operation.

Nick and Martin mounted their Ducati, the powerful machine a dark steed against the cobblestone streets. As they drove, the wind was a tempestuous symphony around them, carrying the thrill of success and the perilous uncertainty of escape.

With engines roaring, The Alfa Stelvio escorted by the two Ducati's sliced through Rome's sleeping arteries toward Villa Borghese, the city's grand park. It sprawled over 80 hectares, a verdant heart in the midst of urban splendor. Ancient trees whispered secrets of centuries passed as sculptures and fountains emerged from the shadows, ghostly sentinels to their flight.

But the respite was fleeting. Headlights splashed across the rearview mirrors—a cavalcade of vehicles, the minions of Mr. Zho, hungry for retribution. Bullets sang through the night, a metallic chorus chasing them down the winding paths.

"Contact rear!" Sergey's voice crackled in Nick's earpiece.

"Keep moving! Draw them away from the package!" Nick barked back, veering his motorcycle to intercept the pursuers.

The street battle unfolded with ferocious intensity. Lead zipped through the air, nicking stone and metal. Nick leaned into the turns, his bike an extension of his will, weaving a deadly dance between adversary fire.

"Extraction point up ahead!" called Martin.

The helicopter's rotors beat a thunderous rhythm, the Augusta Westland AW139 slicing through the Roman sky. As it touched down in the middle of Villa Borghese Park, eight Russian operatives spilled out, weapons at the ready to secure the landing zone.

"Clear!" one shouted, as Marcoff and Sergey hustled Chang aboard the aircraft.

Nick revved his engine, drawing the last of Zho's men away. Shots rang out, precise and fatal. One by one, they fell until silence reclaimed the night.

"Package is secure," Marcoff confirmed, his voice a growl of triumph.

"Take off!" Nick ordered, watching as the helicopter ascended, its cargo destined for Moscow. As it vanished into the night, Nick and

Martin put Florence in their sights, the roar of their Ducatis a fading echo in the eternal city.

CHAPTER 93

Conrad Washington Hotel stately modern facade juxtaposed against Washington's historic backdrop, projected an air of discreet luxury. As Nick Taylor strode through the revolving doors, his keen gaze swept over the opulent lobby adorned with rich colored panels and ornate Oriental carpets that whispered underfoot. Despite the three-day lull since their Roman escapade, he remained a coiled spring, senses alert to every detail.

Nick's athletic frame moved with practiced ease, his posture upright yet relaxed, a testament to years of disciplined training. His graying hair, cropped short in a no-nonsense style, lent him a distinguished air, while the faint lines etched around his eyes hinted at a life spent squinting into scopes and scanning horizons for threats unseen.

He was dressed in a tailored navy suit, the cut impeccable and befitting the five-star establishment. The subtle sheen of his silk tie caught the soft lighting as he approached the private conference room reserved for their meeting.

Inside, Martin De Simone was already present, standing by the window overlooking the cityscape. His muscular build was barely contained by the casual elegance of his designer sweater and slacks. The room's antique furnishings—a grand mahogany table centerpiece and leather-bound chairs—echoed his blend of strength and sophistication.

"Nick," Martin greeted with a nod, his dark eyes alight with the anticipation of their next move. Despite the fatigue that shadowed his features, there was an unmistakable spark of excitement; the thrill of the chase was an elixir none of them could renounce.

"Martin," Nick replied, clasping his friend's outstretched hand firmly. "How are we looking?"

"Ready for phase two," Martin assured, a strategic gleam in his eye. "We've got the layout, the intel, and the assets. All we need is to set the play."

Their conversation was interrupted as Sergey Komutov entered, his thinning hair slightly disheveled, as if he'd just left a complex equation half-solved on a chalkboard somewhere. He carried himself with the quiet confidence of a man who found comfort in numbers and patterns rather than words.

"Nick, Martin," Sergey nodded, adjusting the glasses perched on his nose. His attire was less refined, a simple tweed jacket and corduroy trousers, but it suited his academic demeanor.

"Good to have you, Sergey. How's the traffic in the neural pathways?" Nick asked, knowing full well that Sergey's expertise would be critical in the hours to come.

"Smooth as the algorithms I run," Sergey responded, a corner of his mouth tilting upward in a rare semblance of humor.

They settled around the table as Michael and Marcoff made their entrance. Michael, sleek and nimble like a panther in his form-fitting black attire, exuded an air of lethal grace. Marcoff, on the other hand, had the broad-shouldered bulk of a bear prepared for battle, his suit straining at the seams yet failing to mask the deadly intent behind his steely gaze.

"Alright, gentlemen," Nick began, his voice firm and authoritative, carrying the weight of their shared purpose. "Let's talk about 'The Castle'. We've extracted The Cobra, but this is far from over. We need precision, we need stealth, and above all, we need commitment. The Castle, the Lobby formed by numerous Countries they decide to own the

Medellin Cartel, The Cobra is like there manager or administrator"

"Phase two won't be without its risks," Nick continued, locking eyes with each man in turn. "But remember why we're doing this. For justice, for peace... for the damn good of everyone who can't fight this fight themselves."

"Here's to taking down The Castle for good," Martin raised an imaginary toast, the sentiment echoed by the group's determined nods.

"Then let's get to work," Nick declared, the group leaning in over the plan, their collective resolve as solid as the antique walls surrounding them. The second phase was about to begin, and they were ready to face whatever lay ahead together.

CHAPTER 94

Nick Taylor and his partners stood in the dim light of a Grand suite room of Conrad Hotel nestled within the quiet enclaves of the Center of Washington DC, his tall frame casting a long shadow across the room. The space was sparsely furnished, with utilitarian pieces that spoke of functionality over comfort. A few high-backed chairs circled a sturdy oak table, its surface laden with papers, photographs, and digital screens flickering with encrypted data streams.

The soft glow of a single desk lamp bathed the room in an amber hue, casting long shadows against the walls lined with bookshelves that groaned under the weight of leather-bound volumes and antique trinkets from across the globe. In the heart of Washington's historic district, within a brownstone townhouse that had seen two centuries pass through its doors, Nick Taylor paced over the Persian rug, his steps muffled by the thick weave.

"Look at this," Nick said, unfolding a spread of photographs across the dining table. The graying at his temples lent him a distinguished air, but the intensity in his sharp gaze spoke of a life spent in the shadows of espionage.

Martin De Simone, his features stern and eyes keen, stood behind him, arms folded over his chest—a fortress of muscle and resolve. His short, dark hair was neatly combed back, giving him a polished look that belied the coiled readiness of a man trained to react at a moment's notice.

Michael, the wiry tech wizard whose fingers danced across the keys of a rugged laptop, paused to consider the evidence displayed before them. "It's all connected," he murmured, pushing up the sleeves of his rolled flannel shirt, revealing tattoos that snaked up his forearms like silent stories of his past deeds.

The hotel room was a reflection of Nick's life—functional yet cultured. A chess set with pieces carved from ivory and ebony engaged in eternal battle on a side table. A decanter of Scotch, aged and peaty, sat next to crystal glasses that had listened to many a clandestine conversation.

"Italy, France, Germany and UK In Europe, Brazil, Argentina and Mexico in South America and Australia, Canada US five, plus China, India, Indonesia, Japan, Korea, Russia, Saudi Arabia, South Africa and Turkey , this are the countries shareholders of the Grand Castle..." Michael began, tapping into a database that flickered across his screen with the speed of light. "Their trails overlap with the attacks, the money flow from affiliates and representatives of this governments and parties to Lee Chang for financing the deal and to secure the control".

"Lee Chang, the Maestro is now and forever in the hand of the Russians," Nick replied, his voice laced with disdain as he recalled the Russian's steely green eyes, devoid of warmth or mercy. "Now we need to play a deeper game. We need to take down the castle and intercept this corrupt member of this Club of Powers."

"The members of the Club have illimited resources," Martin added thoughtfully, his analytical mind piecing together the complex puzzle before them. "The members of the club are shadows in the obscure World of Corruption. Wherever the Architect goes, destruction follows. It's a big conspiracy with the Elite of the Elite of the Powers sitting in the most lucrative business of the World: The Drug."

Nick nodded; his jaw set in determination. "They orchestrated the chaos, used Zaprinski as their scalpel. But the Architect, The US President, "The eagle"... he's the linchpin. Without him, nothing was possible."

"So, Let's focus on the endgame," 'The Architect'... 'Operation Grand Castle. The head of this is the

President and Senator James Hargrave " Martin interjected, his positive thinking cutting through the tension. "We expose the truth; they lose their power. The Grand Castle will be on fire for destruction."

"Alright, let's piece this together," Nick said, his voice steady as he traced the web of information laid out before them with a graying finger. Martin De Simone, a formidable figure with close-cropped dark hair, leaned forward attentively, his biceps taut beneath the sleeves of his fitted henley shirt, the very image of contained strength.

Michael Freeman, a man with a wiry build, nodded along, his agile mind absorbing every detail. Sergey Komutov sat back, his thinning hair and scholarly demeanor giving him the air of an intellectual warrior, fingers steepled as if contemplating a grandmaster's next move on the chess board.

"The President at the heart of it – 'The Architect,'" Nick continued, "Orchestrating everything from the shadows." He pointed to a grainy image of Senator James Hargrave, whose silver hair and tailored suit belied the corruption they now knew lurked beneath. "And Hargrave, his right hand."

"Medellin Cartel's microchip, my apartment bombing, Chang's power play in Colombia, Shain's assassination attempt in LA," Martin recounted methodically, his eyes sharp with indignation. "It's all connected. And yet, we need more than just these scattered pieces."

"Direct confrontation," Nick asserted, locking eyes with his comrades. "We blow the lid off this thing publicly. But first, we secure undeniable proof directly implicating 'The Architect'."

"Senator Hargrave's penthouse," Martin suggested resolutely, "High security, sure to be brimming with evidence. If we can break in..."

"Suicide mission," Michael interjected, but without fear. Instead, there was a hint of excitement in his tone, the thrill of the chase igniting his spirit.

"Then we do it for justice and for democracy," Nick affirmed, his own resolve unshakable. "We owe it to the ones who've suffered under their greed."

The men exchanged knowing looks, each aware of the perils that lay ahead. They were about to infiltrate a fortress protected by forces loyal to a man who had turned the highest office into a high lucrative business to finance the political elite.

"Gear up," Nick instructed, the leader within him surfacing. "We leave at dusk."

"Time to dance with the devil," Martin muttered, a wry smile playing on his lips, the anticipation of action awakening his innate desire to set right what had been wronged.

They each retreated to their respective corners of the grand suite, lost in their preparations. Nick checked the chamber of his pistol, the weight of it both a comfort and a reminder of the path he'd chosen. Martin meticulously packed a compact toolkit filled with lock picks and electronic disruptors, while Sergey consulted algorithms on his laptop, seeking patterns that might aid their endeavor. Michael, ever the pragmatist, loaded extra ammunition and secured their getaway vehicles.

As twilight approached, the group reconvened, dressed in black tactical gear that clung to their hardened physiques like second skins. They moved with the silent precision of seasoned operatives, their shared purpose galvanizing them into a formidable unit ready to infiltrate the lion's den.

"Remember, we get in, we get the proof, we get out," Nick commanded, his gaze piercing through the gathering darkness. "No heroics."

"Understood," came the chorus of replies, each man's determination mirroring that of their leader.

"Let's move out fast," Nick ordered, and as one, they stepped out into the encroaching night, their silhouettes disappearing into the urban jungle. Ahead of them awaited the gilded sanctuary of Senator Hargrave, the repository of secrets that could dismantle a presidency and shatter a conspiracy that spanned continents. Tonight, they would strike at the heart of 'The Castle.'

CHAPTER 95

The night air was still, a deceptive calm that belied the tension gripping Nick and his team as they approached the high-rise that housed Senator James Hargrave's penthouse. The building was a monolith of concrete and steel, floodlights casting harsh silhouettes across its facade. Nick observed from the shadows, his eyes tracing the patterns of the patrolling guards with the precision of a chess grandmaster planning several moves ahead. He adjusted the micro earpiece snug within his ear canal, Martin's subtle static a reassuring presence.

Nick, a seasoned operative with the weathered grace of a man who had navigated countless perils, led Martin and Michael through the shadows. They moved with purposeful strides, their boots barely making a sound on the damp concrete. Each man was an embodiment of determination; from Martin's focused gaze that missed no detail to Michael's stoic demeanor, muscles coiled ready for any threat.

"East side. Third window from the right," Nick's voice crackled through. "You've got a 15-second window on the guard rotation."

"Copy that," Martin murmured, timing his approach.

He moved with the stealth of a panther, dark clothing rendering him nearly invisible against the backdrop of the night. Reaching the predetermined entry point, he withdrew a slim titanium lockpick set from an inner pocket of his jacket. Within seconds, the lock gave way, and Martin slipped inside like a whisper.

The senator's penthouse loomed above, its opulence unseen from the street but known to them by reputation—a fortress of luxury built upon deceit. They slipped past the initial layers of security with the ease of phantoms, exploiting blind spots and bypassing electronic locks with devices that whispered in code.

Inside, the apartment was a testament to vanity. Priceless art adorned the walls, each piece carefully curated to project power and taste. A Picasso, bold strokes capturing the tumult of the soul, hid the safe that held their quarry. Martin approached it with reverence masked by intent, deploying a sleek device that interfaced silently with the lock mechanism.

"Vault ahead," Nick directed. "Biometric lock. You'll need to use the override I sent you."

Martin retrieved the small device, attaching it to the panel beside the vault door. Lights flickered, and with a soft click, the door swung open. to reveal its contents: the counterfeit microchip, the one stolen from Nick's home by Zaprinski, and a hypersonic computer that hummed with latent potential. Their hands moved with practiced efficiency, securing each item even as their ears remained alert to the sounds beyond the richly paneled walls. All the incursion was filmed to keep record of the incredible discovery.

"Got it," Martin confirmed, tucking the computer into a protective briefcase. The weight of the evidence felt monumental, the potential to shift the tides of power resting between sheets of paper and ink.

"Extraction point in three minutes," Nick instructed. "Martin and Michael en route."

"Understood," Martin responded, retracing his steps with the briefcase in hand, the future of their nation now hinging on what lay within its confines. As he emerged back into the cloak of night, a sense of profound responsibility settled over him. This was bigger than any one man; this was about the very pillars of democracy.

"Let's bring the truth to light," Martin vowed silently, disappearing into the darkness, ready to confront the storm that awaited them. In the fact Two of Hargrave's private security breached the room, weapons drawn, eyes wide with surprise at the sight of the intruders. Michael that was protecting Martin responded with lethal precision, his actions a grim dance he wished never to perform but could not hesitate to execute.

"Time to go," Martin uttered, urgently lacing his voice as he pocketed the important microchip. Adrenaline surged as they retraced their steps, knowing that the net was closing fast. Sirens wailed in the distance, the cavalry racing to protect the senator's secrets.

They emerged into the chaos of flashing lights and confusion, splitting apart to evade capture. Nick and Martin, astride two black Ducatis that roared to life beneath them, became specters of speed that vanished down narrow alleys. Michael, blending into the crowd with the casual air of a tourist, disappeared in another direction, his steps measured and calm against the rising clamor.

The rendezvous point was a nondescript hotel, a haven of anonymity amidst the city's heartbeat. In a room clouded with tension, the team regathered. Sergey welcomed them with a nod that conveyed relief and expectation.

"We got it," Nick announced, holding up the microchip as if it were Excalibur itself. "The key to 'The Castle'."

Michael, his face a mask of resolve, connected the hypersonic computer to his laptop, fingers dancing across the keyboard. Ron, the young prodigy from MIT, was their digital guardian angel, guiding them through the cyberspace maze in real time.

"Here we go," Ron's voice crackled over the speakerphone, the excitement of youth mingling with the gravity of their mission. "You're looking at the heart of the conspiracy."

Payments, communications, contacts—it was all there. A network sprawling like a sinister web across the globe, ensnaring politicians, criminals, and kingpins in its threads. The screen flickered with damning evidence, including a recorded conversation that laid bare the treachery of the world's most powerful.

"Got the Italian Minister and the German Senator on record," Michael read aloud, his voice steady despite the weight of the revelation. "They're all in it together."

"Good work, everyone," Nick commended, his eyes reflecting the flames of justice that burned within him. "This is more than just proof. It's a declaration that the truth cannot be buried, that the corrupt will be held accountable."

Their gazes met, each man's face etched with the resolve to see this fight to its end, whatever the cost. They were united, not by coincidence, but by the unyielding belief that freedom and integrity were worth any battle.

"Let's make sure the world knows," Martin said, the conviction in his voice echoing through the room. "The age of 'The Castle' ends tonight."

CHAPTER 96

The room buzzed with a silent intensity as Nick Taylor, his square jaw set in grim determination, hunched over the stolen hypersonic computer. The soft glow of the screen reflected off his weathered face, a testament to his years spent in the shadows of espionage. Martin De Simone, his broad shoulders tensed like coiled springs, watched closely, his dark eyes scanning for any signs of intrusion.

"Are we ready?" Nick's voice broke the silence, a calm yet steely timbre that carried the weight of their monumental task.

"Ron's patching through now," Michael Freeman replied, his fingers flying across the keyboard as he established encrypted connections with media outlets. "We're going live."

Nick gave a nod, and Ron's youthful, eager voice piped in from the speakerphone. "CNN is on board. Al Jazeera just confirmed receipt. It's happening, guys."

"Good," Martin muttered. "Let's blow the lid off this thing."

As Michael initiated the data transfer, each file siphoned off into the cyberspace ether felt like another step towards justice. The tension in the room was palpable, thick enough to slice through as they awaited the world's reaction.

"Freedom of information," Nick said solemnly, glancing at each of his comrades. His gaze lingered momentarily on Martin. "That's the cornerstone of democracy. We're holding it up."

"Here goes nothing," murmured Michael, hitting the final 'send' button. A symphony of pings and acknowledgments from the receiving news agencies filled the room, a chorus heralding the dawn of exposure.

Suddenly, the hotel room seemed to shrink, the walls pressing in as the reality of their actions set in. Martin paced, his usually stoic demeanor betrayed by the slightest quiver of apprehension. Michael clenched his fists, the muscle under his tanned skin rippling with ready energy.

"Some very powerful people are about to have a very bad day," Nick commented, a wry smile touching his lips despite the severity of the moment. They all knew what was at stake, yet there was an unspoken understanding—they would see this through, come hell or high water.

Without warning, the steady hum of the city outside was shattered by the wail of sirens. Blue and red lights flashed through the gauzy curtains, casting an eerie dance of shadows across the luxurious interior of their temporary stronghold.

"Damn, they didn't waste any time," Michael swore under his breath, peering out between the heavy drapes. Below, the street teemed with FBI agents and Washington police, pouring out of black SUVs like ants from a kicked nest.

"Looks like the siege is on," Martin growled, his hand instinctively reaching for the sidearm concealed beneath his tailored jacket.

"Stay focused," Nick commanded, his voice a beacon of clarity amidst the chaos. "They can't stop the truth now."

Sergey glanced at the television, where anchors were already scrambling to report on the breaking story. The room fell silent as they watched the beginnings of their handiwork unfold in real time.

"Look," Michael pointed at the screen, where the scrolling ticker tape announced the sudden plummet of stock markets worldwide. "It's starting."

"Let them come," Martin said, his voice laced with defiance. "We've done our part. Now it's up to the world to see it through."

And as the special forces began their tactical approach, surrounding the hotel with an ironclad grip, the team stood shoulder to shoulder, united by a bond forged in the crucible of truth. They were ready for whatever came next, be it the wrath of the elite or the vindication of the masses.

CHAPTER 97

Nick scanned the horizon from the hotel suite's panoramic window, his eyes tracing the perimeter of law enforcement that now encircled the building. The JTTF agents were a sea of tactical gear and grim determination, their movements precise and coordinated as they set up barricades and directed traffic away from the zone.

"Over two hundred of them," Martin reported, squinting down through binoculars. "They're not skimping on firepower. We've got SWAT rolling in with full combat loadouts."

"Snipers on the rooftops," Nick added, noting the subtle glints of sunlight reflecting off scopes. He watched as two Black Hawk helicopters punctuated the skyline, their rotors cutting through the tension like buzzsaws. They hovered ominously, casting shadows over the hotel that felt like premonitions of doom.

"Let's keep our heads," he muttered, the graying at his temples betraying the years of service that had honed his instinct for survival. "We need an exit strategy. We need this very fast or they will kill us"

"Window's closing fast," Martin acknowledged, checking the chamber of his sidearm. His athletic frame was coiled, ready to spring into action, every muscle a testament to a life spent in the field.

"Rooftop extraction," Sergey announced suddenly, his thin fingers tapping a message back to his contacts at the Russian Embassy. His chess player's mind was already plotting moves ahead, considering angles and outcomes with the dispassionate calculation of a grandmaster.

"Any minute now," Sergey confirmed, his sharp gaze never leaving the scene below. "We stick to the plan."

Amidst the clinical sterility of the hotel room, the evidence they had compiled lay scattered across the coffee table – a stark contrast against the polished wood. It was a mosaic of conspiracy and corruption, each piece a damning indictment of power gone rogue.

"Remember why we're doing this," Nick said, breaking the silence. His voice was a beacon, rallying his comrades in the face of overwhelming odds.

"Justice and democracy," Martin affirmed. "Whatever it takes."

"Exactly," Nick replied. There was no room for doubt, only the unwavering resolve that had brought them to this precipice.

The team shared a look, a silent pact between warriors who had chosen to stand against the tide. Outside, the setting sun cast an orange glow over Washington DC, the fading light symbolic of the old order that was about to be challenged.

"Time to move," Sergey said as his encrypted phone lit up with confirmation. "Extraction Now."

Together, they gathered their scant belongings, the tools of espionage that had served them well. With one last glance at the screens displaying chaos unfolding across global markets, they stepped towards destiny.

"Let's end this," Nick declared, leading the charge to the rooftop where salvation—or perhaps a new battle—awaited.

Nick's muscles tensed as he heard the distant thumping of helicopter blades slicing through the air, an ominous harbinger of the chaos that was about to unfold. He stood on the rooftop, flanked by Martin, Michael and Sergey, his eyes scanning the horizon. The crisp evening breeze brushed against his weathered face, carrying with it the electric charge of imminent peril.

Below them, the streets teemed with activity as more than two hundred JTTF operatives swarmed the hotel perimeter. Dressed in tactical gear that melded with the encroaching darkness, they moved with lethal precision, their weapons – a bristling array of pistols, assault rifles, and shotguns – at the ready.

"Here we go," Martin murmured, his jaw set, mirroring Nick's own determination. Together, they had faced down countless threats, but none so dire as this.

The sky above the hotel became a battleground as six Sikorsky S-70 helicopters sporting Russian diplomatic flags entered the airspace. Their rotors beat a rhythm of defiance against the backdrop of the encroaching night. Two FBI tactical helicopters loomed nearby, the tension between them palpable even from this distance.

"Helicopters incoming!" Nick warned, his voice barely audible over the din.

"Colonel Vassiliev is not one to play by the rules," Sergey quipped with a wry grin, recognizing the audacious piloting style of the lead Sikorsky's pilot.

Indeed, Colonel Nikita Vassiliev executed a daring maneuver known amongst the Russian aviators as 'the flying cat.' With finesse that belied the size of the aircraft, he banked sharply, guiding his Sikorsky towards the hotel roof in a breathtaking display of aerial agility.

"Talk about making an entrance," Michael remarked dryly, watching as the Sikorsky touched down with a precision that spoke of years of experience.

Twelve heavily armed FSB operatives disembarked swiftly from the landed Sikorsky. They were clad in dark tactical gear, faces obscured by balaclavas, eyes scanning for threats as they moved with purpose. Every movement was calculated, silent save for the soft clink of gear.

"Stay close," one operative commanded in heavily accented English, gesturing for the group to follow. As they did, Nick noted the glint of intelligence in the man's eyes, the sureness in his stride. These were men familiar with the dance of danger.

The extraction was further complicated by the sudden entry of SWAT teams storming into the hotel, their heavy boots echoing through the corridors as they began their systematic search. Time was slipping away like sand through fingers.

CHAPTER 98

In the White House War Room, the President watched the unfolding events with a mixture of anger and fear. His hand hovered over the red phone as he gave a terse order to Captain Williams. "Shoot down the Sikorsky's."

"Sir, the collateral damage..." Captain Williams hesitated, his voice strained over the comm link.

"Dammit, just do it!" the President snapped, his finger jabbing towards the screen displaying the live feed.

"Negative, sir. We can't risk it," Williams pushed back, aware of the innocent lives below.

Defeated and sensing the shift in tides, the President ordered his secret evacuation, the weight of his impending doom settling upon him like a shroud.

"Checkmate," Sergey whispered, a smirk playing on his lips as the six Sikorsky lifted off in unison, leaving the frustrated FBI helicopters behind. There was no pursuit; the gambit had paid off.

"Kasparov's best move ever," Sergey said, invoking the name of the legendary chess grandmaster. The comparison wasn't lost on any of them; they had just outmaneuvered one of the most powerful nations on Earth. "Finally, the Castle is down" added Nick with energy.

As the helicopters raced towards the safety of the Russian Embassy, the world below erupted into pandemonium. Financial markets plunged into freefall, with Wall Street losing fifteen percent of its value in mere moments before trading was suspended. Across the Atlantic, European exchanges followed suit, closing down trading in a ripple effect of uncertainty. This day was a black swan day!

"Let's hope our next moves are as good as this one," Nick mused, watching the city shrink away. In the distance, the lights of the Russian Embassy beckoned, a temporary haven in a world gone mad.

The frenetic pace of the newsroom was tangible, palpable in the electric air as anchors and journalists scrambled to keep up with the flood of information bombarding the screens. At the epicenter of it all was an animated news anchor, his tailored suit a sharp contrast against the backdrop of digital chaos on the screen behind him. With every word, the gravity of the situation settled deeper into the bones of the viewers worldwide.

"Good evening," he began, voice steady despite the pandemonium, "we are interrupting our regular programming to bring you a story that will undoubtedly reshape the global political landscape."

The camera zoomed in on his face, every line and crease etched by years of breaking hard truths to the public. His silver hair, usually immaculate, was a touch disheveled – testament to the rush against time. Behind horn-rimmed glasses, his eyes were intent, focused, conveying the seriousness of the revelations about to unfold.

"Tonight, we stand at the precipice of a truth so profound, it has the potential to unravel a conspiracy that has ensnared the highest echelons of power across the G20 nations." He paused for effect, letting the words sink in.

"Documents, recordings, and irrefutable evidence have surfaced detailing a nefarious plot orchestrated by none other than the President of the United States..." The anchor let the accusation hang in the air, a moment of silence for its weight to be felt.

"Allegedly dubbed 'The Castle,' this conspiracy has controlled the flow of narcotics from South America to Asia, with Europe caught in its web. Leaders of these nations implicated in a scheme generating over one hundred billion dollars annually."

The screen flitted between images of classified documents, grainy surveillance footage, and intercepted communications—each piece more damning than the last. The anchor's delivery was unrelenting, each sentence another nail in the coffin of the international cabal.

"Let's listen to a segment from a recorded conversation that implicates not only the President but also key figures in global politics." His finger hovered over a tablet, and the audio clip played out for the world to hear—the voices of those in power, bartering and scheming for their share of the illicit treasure.

"Think of the repercussions," the anchor continued, turning back to the audience. "From the streets of Medellin to the corridors of the Downing Street and Elisee to the skyscrapers of New York to the bustling markets of Shanghai, no place remains untouched by the fallout of these actions."

The anchor stood, leading the camera through the studio, the bustle of the newsroom a stark juxtaposition to the darkened skyline of the city beyond the panoramic windows. The offices were a hive of activity; screens lit up with graphs showing plummeting stock markets and frantic traders.

"Governments around the world are now faced with the task of untangling this web of deceit. The implicated leaders must be held accountable, justice must prevail," he proclaimed, coming to a stop beside a large, antique globe—a symbol of the world they were now tasked with protecting.

"Make no mistake," he concluded, gaze fixed directly into the lens, "this is a defining moment in our history. How we respond will shape the future of international relations and the very concept of governance."

"Stay tuned as we continue coverage of this unprecedented exposure. For now, this is" —his name flashed briefly onscreen— "reporting from" —the network logo emblazoned below— "where the truth is always our top story."

As the broadcast cut to a montage of global reactions, Nick Taylor watched from the sanctum of the Russian Embassy, a grim satisfaction on his weathered face. He, along with Martin and the rest of their team, had risked everything to bring this conspiracy to light. The world now knew the disgraceful truth; the gears of justice could finally turn.

"May the fallout bring a new dawn," Nick murmured, a man no longer bound by shadows, standing tall amidst the winds of change.

CHAPTER 99

Nick Taylor reclined comfortably on a handcrafted wooden lounge chair, the kind that spoke of traditional Swiss craftsmanship, as he observed the serene vista before him. The lakeside cabin, nestled amid Switzerland's verdant embrace, was an idyllic retreat far from the espionage and shadow games that had defined much of his life. The water lapped softly at the shore, a rhythmic sound that harmonized with the wind rustling through the leaves.

Beside him, Martin De Simone, whose muscular frame seemed almost out of place in such a tranquil setting, leaned back, the light glinting off his dark hair. They shared the contentment of warriors who had found a temporary respite from battle. Sergey Komutov, the ex-KGB mathematician whose thinning hair did nothing to diminish the sharpness of his mind, lounged nearby, absorbed in a book of complex theories. Dr. Emma Stein, her long brown hair cascading over her shoulders, sat cross-legged on the deck, her piercing blue eyes reflecting the peacefulness of the scene.

Inside the chalet, luxury and rustic charm intertwined seamlessly. Antiques that whispered tales of old Europe adorned the rooms, each piece meticulously chosen to complement the rich wooden interior. The atmosphere thrummed with quiet celebration, the air still resonant with their recent victory—a tangible feeling that lived within the walls, woven into the very fabric of the space.

At the heart of the main room, a chessboard lay between Nick and Martin, squares of black and white creating a battlefield for the mind. Nick moved his knight with precision, a smile playing on his lips as Martin watched, contemplating his next move. The game unfolded like a dance, each piece advancing and retreating in a silent rhythm known only to those who saw the world through the lens of strategy and foresight.

"Your queen's looking a little exposed, Nick," Martin quipped, fingers tapping a bishop thoughtfully. The camaraderie between the two men was palpable, years of trust and shared experiences lending weight to their every interaction.

"Ah, but sometimes, it's the exposed pieces that hold all the power," Nick countered, his green eyes twinkling with the reflection of the setting sun filtering through the expansive windows.

Martin chuckled, acknowledging the truth in the metaphor. These were men accustomed to lives where vulnerability often proved to be a guise for strength. Their moves on the board mirrored their approach to life—calculated, bold, and always with an undercurrent of mutual respect.

"Checkmate," Nick declared moments later, his voice carrying no hint of triumph, only the satisfaction of a challenge well met.

"Bravo," Sergey said, closing his book with a soft thud and joining them. "Chess is the perfect exercise for the mind. It teaches us to think ahead and anticipate the consequences of our actions."

"True," Emma added, standing up and stretching gracefully. "But sometimes, the best part is simply playing the game with good friends." She smiled warmly at the group, her gaze lingering on Nick.

As the sun dipped below the horizon, its dying light cast long shadows across the chalet's interior, turning the luxurious space into a haven of golden hues and soft warmth. The laughter and conversation of four allies filled the room, a symphony of human connection born from the most unlikely of circumstances.

In this moment of peace, surrounded by nature's majesty and the opulence of their hideaway, they allowed themselves to forget, if only briefly, the dangerous world that awaited outside their sanctuary. Here, they were not spies or doctors, not agents of governments or pawns in a greater game. They were simply friends, united by bonds forged in the fires of adversity, celebrating the simple joy of living.

CHAPTER 100

Nick stood on the wooden deck of the chalet, his hands clasped behind his back as he gazed out over the tranquil lake. The water's surface mirrored the twilight sky, a canvas of deepening blues and purples that calmed the soul. Alpine trees whispered secrets in the gentle breeze, their leaves rustling like soft applause for the day's end. It was a moment ripe for reflection, and Nick Taylor, a man whose life had been spent unraveling hidden truths, found himself introspective.

His eyes, sharp as ever despite the creeping touch of time, took in the scene with a blend of gratitude and contemplation. He'd walked through shadows to stand in this light, navigated labyrinths of deception to find this simple truth: peace. And yet, even as he breathed the crisp air, his instincts hummed beneath the surface—a silent sentinel never fully at rest.

"Quite a view, isn't it?" Martin De Simone's voice cut through the stillness as he joined Nick on the deck. His frame, though not as towering as Nick's, carried an undeniable presence—a testament to countless hours of rigorous training and a life of discipline.

"Reminds us what we're fighting for," Nick replied, his voice low but clear in the quiet evening.

"True," Martin agreed, leaning against the railing. His dark hair was cropped short, a stark contrast to the silver threads that had begun to claim Nick's temples. In Martin's eyes, a spark of admiration shone alongside the weariness of battles fought and won.

"Never thought we'd see the day," Nick mused, thinking back on the convoluted path they had taken, the incredible manipulation of the highest political power of the Western World—a plot so intricate that only the most daring could have hoped to unravel it.

"Nor did I," Martin chuckled. "And let's not forget Mr. Romanov's part. Discreet, yet decisive—the way true power often moves."

"Indeed." Nick allowed himself a small smile, remembering the enigmatic Russian who had tipped the scales in their favor. Sergey and Emma, engrossed in conversation within the chalet, seemed distant now, their laughter a backdrop to the gravity of their own dialogue.

"Shall we make that call to Michael" Martin suggested, pulling out his phone—a sleek, modern device that belied the encrypted labyrinth within. "He deserves our thanks, and more."

"Let's do it." Nick nodded, the action firm, filled with purpose. Together, they dialed the number, waiting for the secure line to connect. Michael's voice soon filled the air, warm and steady—a reminder of the good forces working in the shadows, protecting America, the CIA, and the DEA.

"Michael, it's Nick Taylor and Martin De Simone," Nick began, his tone respectful, aware of the weight his words carried. "We wanted to extend our gratitude for your decisive help during White Swan Down."

"Your connections were invaluable," Martin added, his sincerity resonating through the speaker. "Without you, the outcome might have been very different."

"Thank you," Michael responded, his voice tinged with relief and pride. "It's an honor to work with agents of your caliber. Remember, we're all part of the same fight."

"Indeed," Nick echoed, cutting the call short as both men knew the risks of lingering on the line too long. They exchanged a glance, unspoken words passing between them—a shared understanding of the delicate dance they performed, a waltz of shadows and light.

As they turned back to the comforts of the chalet, the opulent interior welcomed them with its promise of brief respite. Antiques dotted the space, each piece telling a story of history and craftsmanship—a fitting setting for those who shaped history in their own way.

"Back to the game?" Martin suggested, nodding toward the chessboard where pawns and kings awaited their next command.

"After you," Nick replied, his stride confident as they returned to the warmth of friendship and the sweet illusion of victory, if only for the night.

Nick wandered away from the chessboard and found Emma in the kitchen, her hands artfully arranging a platter of artisan cheeses and fresh fruits. The soft glow of the setting sun caught in her chestnut hair, turning it to burnished gold. She looked up at him, her piercing blue eyes alight with the reflection of the lake outside.

"Need a hand?" Nick asked, his voice warm.

"Only if you can promise not to eat all the grapes before our guests do," Emma teased, her smile reaching her eyes.

He chuckled, stepping closer to wrap an arm around her slender waist. "I make no such promises, Dr. Stein."

She leaned into his embrace, her head resting against his broad chest. The tension that had braced her shoulders for months seemed to melt away in his hold.

"Can you believe it's over?" she murmured. "After everything..."

Nick kissed the top of her head, breathing in the scent of her shampoo—a crisp, floral fragrance that always reminded him of their first meeting. "Thanks to you, Emma. Your brilliance saw us through."

"Me?" Her laugh, light and genuine, filled the room. "You're the hero, Nick Taylor. I just follow where you lead."

"Heroes are only as good as their allies," he replied, his gaze sincere as he met hers. "And I've never had a better one." The words hung between them, a testament to their bond forged in adversity and trust.

"Let's not keep everyone waiting," Emma said, her voice softer now, a whisper of shared secrets and nights spent planning their next move.

"Right behind you," Nick assured, releasing her reluctantly to carry the platter out to the grand dining room.

The dining table was a masterpiece of craftsmanship, its surface gleaming beneath the crystal chandelier overhead. Martin was already there, pouring wine into long-stemmed glasses, as Sergey gathered, their laughter mingling with the clink of fine China. Each face bore the marks of the mission—lines of worry now smoothed by relief, shadows under eyes brightened by the light of victory.

"Here's to White Swan Down," Martin declared, raising his glass high. His dark eyes were alight with triumph, the muscle in his jaw working with unspoken emotion.

"To new beginnings," Emma added, her voice carrying the weight of their collective hope.

"And to alliances that withstand the test of time," Nick concluded, his glass joining the chorus of crystal that sang in the quiet mountain air.

The toast marked more than the end of a mission; it was an acknowledgment of the peace they had carved out, a rare moment of tranquility in a life otherwise spent in shadows. As they drank, the golden liquid seemed to seal their camaraderie, casting a spell of contentment over the group.

"Peace like this is hard-earned," Sergey commented, his Russian accent coloring the words with gravitas.

"Indeed," Nick agreed, feeling the truth of it deep in his bones. "But tonight, we celebrate."

The cabin, nestled in the embrace of the Swiss Alps, sheltered them from the world's chaos. It was a sanctuary of old-world luxury, where polished wood and plush fabrics whispered tales of refuge and rest. For a night, they could pretend they were just friends enjoying the harvest of the earth, rather than players in a game much larger than themselves.

A fire crackled in the hearth, the flames dancing merrily as if to celebrate with them. Outside, the stars began their nightly vigil, watching over the chalet and its occupants with a timeless, unwavering gaze.

"May every mission end like this," Martin said, lifting his glass once more, the flickering firelight reflecting in his determined eyes.

"May it be so," Nick whispered, allowing himself to bask in the warmth of friendship and the sweet illusion of lasting peace.

CHAPTER 101

Nick leaned back in the leather chair, the soft glow of the laptop screen illuminating his stoic face. Across from him sat the cartel boss, a broad-shouldered man with a neatly trimmed beard and a suit that whispered of power and danger. His dark eyes held a glint of respect as he regarded Nick.

"Your assistance was critical," Nick said, his voice steady and sincere. "Without it, it would have been another story."

The boss nodded; his hands clasped together on the mahogany table that bore witness to their unlikely alliance. "We have mutual interests, Nick. And respect is the currency that binds us."

"Agreed," Nick replied. "The next move needs to be calculated with precision."

"Always," the boss affirmed, his deep voice resonant in the cabin's luxurious confines.

The distant chime of an incoming message pulled Nick's attention away. He glanced at the laptop, where an encrypted message flickered onscreen. "Thanks Phoenix! stay sharp! Romanoff" it read. A tight smile formed on Nick's lips as he closed the lid, the words searing into his mind like a clandestine mantra.

"Problems?" Martin inquired; one eyebrow arched inquisitively.

"Never." Nick's reply was curt but carried the weight of shared understanding.

The tension of the moment dissipated as laughter erupted from the other room. Martin's jovial voice rose above the rest, recounting an absurd anecdote from their mission that had Sergey doubled over in laughter. Emma's melodic giggle harmonized with the deeper tones, the very sound a balm to Nick's ever-vigilant heart.

CHAPTER 102

Nick Taylor slipped out of the chalet's side door just as dawn's delicate fingers caressed the Swiss sky, painting it with hues of pink and gold. The morning air was crisp, a gentle reminder of the Alpine altitude, as he made his way down to the water's edge. There, the lake lay still, mirroring the awakening heavens with such clarity that Nick found himself pausing, his breath visible in the cool air.

He walked slowly along the shoreline, his hands tucked into the pockets of his fleece jacket. His athletic frame moved with an ease that belied his years, each step a testament to a life spent mastering both body and mind. As he ambled, Nick's gaze swept across the calm waters to the rugged mountains beyond, their peaks like sentinels guarding the serenity of this hidden retreat.

The tranquility of the scene allowed Nick's thoughts to wander to his apartment in New York—his sanctuary amidst the urban clamor. The thought of returning there brought a twinge of longing; its walls, once cracked and peeling from an unfortunate incident, were now hopefully being restored to their former glory. It would be good to be home again, surrounded by the familiar.

"Beautiful morning, isn't it?" Martin's voice cut through the stillness as he joined Nick by the water. His short, dark hair was slightly tousled from sleep, but his eyes were alert and focused.

"Never thought I'd find peace like this after all we've been through," Nick replied, a small smile playing on his lips as he turned to face his friend. Martin nodded, his muscular physique relaxed yet poised, much like his demeanor.

"Let's walk," Martin suggested, gesturing towards a path that wound its way around the lake. As they set off together, the two men fell into an easy silence, each lost in their own reflections until they came upon a weathered wooden bench overlooking the water.

They sat, the wood creaking slightly under their weight, and Martin turned to Nick, his expression serious. "We've come a long way, Nick. 'White Swan Down'... it pushed us to our limits."

"It did," Nick agreed, his sharp gaze softening with introspection. "But we learned a lot. Adaptability, resilience—we're not just operatives, Martin. We're survivors. And more than that, we're protectors. Maybe we save the World from the biggest political scam ever."

"Protectors with quite the diverse skill set," Martin added with a wry grin. "I mean, who else can say they've outmaneuvered political puppeteers, joined forces with unlikely allies, and played chess with life and death?"

"Speaking of chess," Nick chuckled, a glint of mischief in his eyes, "I think you owe me a rematch."

"Only if you're ready to lose again," Martin shot back playfully.

"Never," Nick smirked, rising from the bench. The sun had fully risen now, bathing the landscape in a warm glow. The promise of another day loomed before them—one without covert operations or encrypted messages. For now, at least.

"Let's head back," Martin said, clapping Nick on the shoulder. "Emma and Sergey will be up soon, and I smell coffee."

"Lead the way," Nick responded, taking one last look at the picturesque view before following his friend back to the cabin. Their footsteps left twin trails in the dew-soaked grass, marking the start of a new chapter—one penned not by espionage, but by the enduring bond of friendship and the quiet strength born from trials overcome.

CHAPTER 103

Nick's fingers worked methodically, folding the delicate rice paper into a perfect cylinder. The lantern's frame took shape under his practiced hands, a symbol of light amidst the encroaching dusk. Around him, Emma and Sergey were similarly engaged, their movements almost meditative as they constructed their own beacons of hope.

"Remember," Nick said, his voice low but clear, "write something on it. Something you're leaving behind, or something you're looking forward to."

Emma's pen danced across the paper in elegant script, while Sergey scrawled with a soldier's brusqueness. Nick hesitated, then wrote a single word: 'Freedom.' It was as much a release from his past shadows as it was an embrace of the uncertainty and promise that lay ahead.

They stood at the water's edge, the Swiss chalet's silhouette a comforting presence behind them. Its luxury interior, a haven of rare antiques and modern design, now felt like part of a world they had all transcended. The lake before them, reflecting the first stars, was a canvas waiting for their stories.

With a collective breath that mingled in the crisp air, they lit the lanterns. The flickering flames kissed the paper, casting a soft glow upon their faces. One by one, they released their burdens into the night sky, each lantern soaring upward like a gentle prayer.

"May our paths be bright," Emma whispered, her eyes tracking the ascent of her lantern.

"May our burdens be light," Sergey added, a rare smile breaking through his stoic facade.

"May we always find our way back to each other," Nick concluded, his heart swelling as he watched the specks of light climb higher until they joined the constellations above—diamonds sparkling against the velvet curtain of night.

The moment lingered, a silent vow etched into the heavens before they turned back to the warmth of the cabin and the company of friends.

A bonfire crackled merrily in the stone pit, illuminating the circle of faces with its golden radiance. They settled around the fire, the logs popping and sending sparks up to chase the lanterns they had just freed. Nick found himself unwinding in a way he hadn't in years, the tension of his previous life dissipating like smoke in the wind.

For now, the world's machinations could wait. Tonight was about them—their resilience, their unity, their indomitable spirit. Tomorrow would bring new challenges, but they would face them together, armed with the knowledge that even in the darkest times, there was light to be found, and freedom to be had.

Nick leaned back, feeling the heat of the bonfire on his face. He closed his eyes, letting the symphony of crackling wood and distant night sounds wash over him. In this tranquil cocoon, surrounded by his comrades-in-arms, he allowed himself to believe that peace, however fleeting, was possible.

THE END

Printed in Great Britain
by Amazon

51298848R00247